ONE NIGHT WITH
Tulip

CHAPTER 1

London, England
August 1827

"MISS FARTHINGALE, WHAT is the matter?" Alexander Havers, the new Duke of Davenport, had not expected to run into Tulip Farthingale when he stepped into Lady Fullerton's garden on this hot summer evening, hoping to get away from the crush of revelers in the ballroom at one of her famous routs.

The night was steamy, threatening rain, if the heavy scent of grass and damp leaves was any indication, although not a drop had fallen yet. But a light haze had settled over the trees and lush shrubbery, dimming the rows of lanterns gaily strung along measured intervals and giving the impression of a fairy garden hidden in mist.

A church clock *bonged* in the distance to mark the midnight hour.

This also marked his last night in London before Alex returned to Somerset and the Davenport estate his predecessors to the title had left in shambles. He thought he had been alone out here until the lovely Tulip had run straight into him and bounced off his chest, for she had been moving very fast.

She had a tendency to do this, having run into him in this same manner the first time they had met, and he had been thinking of her ever since.

He caught her in his arms to steady her, the softness of her lithe body familiar as he wrapped her securely in his embrace.

Wispy tendrils of haze encircled them.

Blessed saints.

She felt remarkably good in his arms.

"Oh, dear!" She looked up at him, her big blue eyes reflecting the firelight from one of the garden lanterns. "I've done a dreadful thing, Your Grace."

"You have?" He struggled not to grin at the earnest expression on the face of this charming bluestocking he would have liked to know better. "What have you done? You know I am no longer working for the London magistrate, an impossibility now that I have inherited a dukedom, so I will not report you to the authorities. Your secret is quite safe with me."

Until a few months ago, he had been simply Mr. Alexander Havers, and had yet to get used to being addressed with the deference accorded his new title. While he had not changed who he was in essence, most around him had suddenly turned into fawning toadies because he had inherited a dukedom. Those who ignored him in the past now fussed over him, pretending they had always admired and adored him.

Young ladies went to great lengths to throw themselves at him now that he had become London's most sought after bachelor.

Not Tulip, however.

She avoided him as much as she could because she was wary of the Davenport reputation. Only recently had she started to thaw toward him, hopefully understanding he was nothing like the dishonorable Davenport dukes who had come before him.

He kept hold of her, rather liking the feel of her body against his palms.

She was draped in pale blue silk, a hue that matched the color of her striking eyes, and he thought her the prettiest thing he had seen in an age.

"Lord Finley Caruthers took me for a stroll in the garden," she said, clearing her throat as though it pained her to make the announcement.

"That is a serious crime," he intoned, taking care not to laugh.

"Please do not tease me about it. He wanted to kiss me and–"

"You let him?" He frowned, knowing exactly what a dishonorable hound like Caruthers meant to do once alone with

Tulip, and it was not restricted to a single kiss.

"No!" Her eyes rounded in horror, then her expression turned sheepish. "But I almost let him do it."

"Almost?"

She nodded. "You see, I wanted to be kissed."

Dear heaven.

Alex would have obliged her, and been a far safer partner than that lout, Caruthers.

"But then I realized that I did not wish *him* to be the one to kiss me. Especially not for my first time."

"Your first?" His heart lurched, and then suddenly began to pound erratically.

Why was his heart pounding?

This was his last night in London. One night. Only one night and he would be off to Somerset for as long as it took him to get his dukedom back in order.

You fool, just let this evening pass quietly.

But he ignored the warning.

He ignored the simple and effective rules that had kept him out of compromising situations all summer long. Do not engage a girl in conversation, especially not this girl and not while you are holding her in your arms. Do not look at a girl's lips, especially not this girl's lips that he had ached to kiss since their first meeting.

She was now giving her fleshy lower lip a soft nibble.

He could go on with more rules that he was obviously abandoning because this was Tulip Farthingale and he did not understand why he could not get enough of her.

To his chagrin, she seemed quite comfortably nestled in his arms and was making no attempt to move away when she could have done so with ease.

She should have done so.

He would never be so boorish as to prevent her.

"Yes, my very first kiss." She nodded again, the dark curls surrounding her lovely face bobbing delightfully. "Because I have never been kissed before."

"That is usually what a *first* indicates," he said, then quietly chided himself for his snide response. He blamed it on the heat coursing through him. "So, never?"

"Not once in all my life," she continued, giving him a slight frown for his impertinence. "And I thought it was time to take the leap. But as his lips drew closer to mine…"

"What happened?"

The expression on her face turned to one of distaste. "I panicked and ran off. How could I kiss anyone who did not have my heart? Should it not be splendid and meaningful, a kiss to cherish all the days of my life?"

Oh, gad.

This is why he stayed away from innocents.

They were so…innocent.

"All right, I'll keep an eye on you as you head back into the ballroom. Just promise me you will stay close to your family for the rest of the evening."

Tears now formed in her eyes as she solemnly promised. "I feel so ashamed."

"Why? It was just a harmless kiss that never took place, although it might have led to something far more compromising."

"I know. I think this is what scared me into running away from him. He was not looking at me in any nice way."

Alex glanced around the garden, wondering where Caruthers had got to. Should he not have caught up to Tulip by now? "Um, did you by any chance hit him before you ran off? With a heavy object, perhaps?"

"No," she said with a sniffle. "I simply ran off when he attempted to stick his face close to mine. And then he stuck his tongue out from between his pudgy lips and…*ew*. But, oh. I see. He should have walked right past us to return to the ballroom, but he hasn't yet. I promise you, I did not touch him. And the garden paths are sufficiently lit so that he should not have lost his way or tripped over a tree root."

Alex let out a breath as he repeated his earlier instruction. "Go back inside the ballroom. I'll stay out here and watch you walk in."

"Then you'll go in search of Lord Caruthers? Should I not go with you?"

"That entirely defeats the purpose of getting you safely away from him."

"But I am with you, so he would never dare anything. Besides, I know exactly where I left him and you do not."

He ignored the stubborn look on her face. "This is not a large garden, Miss Farthingale. Just point me in the general direction and I will find him. *Without* your assistance. I do not want you within reach of him again."

"All right, I–"

Several lanterns close by began to sway and pebbles crunched as Caruthers trod heavily toward them, looking ferociously angry. "There you are, you little… Ack!"

Alex did not wait for the curse to come out before he tossed Tulip behind him and in the same motion grabbed the angry lord by his throat to prevent him from uttering a crass word or worse, pouncing on her. "The lady refused. It is over, Caruthers. Do not make more of it than it is."

"She's a shameless tease," he growled when Alex released him a moment later, for he was not trying to strangle the lout but merely startle him into stopping.

"She is young and innocent, and you ought to have known better than to lure her away from the ballroom."

"You mustn't blame him, Your Grace," Tulip said, but had the good sense to remain behind him as she spoke. "I am the one who suggested it. I give you my sincere apology, Lord Caruthers. It was wrong of me, quite foolish and wrongheaded. I beg your forgiveness for any embarrassment it may have caused you."

"Your turn now, Caruthers," Alex prompted when the oafish lord said nothing in response. "Accept her apology and move on."

"I'll show you acceptance," he muttered, appearing ready to take a swing at Alex, then remembered he was now a duke, and thought better of challenging him. Not to mention Alex was bigger and stronger, and a more ruthless fighter.

"You'll regret this, Davenport! And so will your pretty pigeon!"

"Not as much as you will if you dare trouble her again," he

said while making certain Tulip remained safely behind him.

Obviously frustrated by the impenetrable barrier Alex presented, Caruthers repeated his curses and threats, and then stormed off toward the ballroom.

Tulip watched with trepidation as her spurned suitor stomped up the terrace steps. "What do you think he means to do?"

Alex did not know, but he doubted the man was going to stay quiet.

He glanced up at the sky that was covered in a layer of clouds, as though the heavens had slammed their door against him, refusing to listen to his silent plea for this little altercation to resolve without further problem.

But he knew it would not.

An entitled lord like Caruthers was not going to take rejection lightly.

Sighing, he placed Tulip's hand in the crook of his arm. "Come back inside with me."

Tulip held him back a moment. "But is it safe for you? I mean, people might think I went into the garden to kiss *you*. Is it not better for me to walk in alone as you first suggested?"

"No. That was before Caruthers leveled his threat." He was not going to risk that angry lord deciding to stake a claim on her and alleging he had compromised her.

If any false accusations were to be leveled, better they be leveled against *him* because he would always protect Tulip.

She held him back again. "But it is certain to cause you more trouble if we walk in together."

He arched an eyebrow. "Why are you so concerned about me, Tulip?"

"Should I not be? Haven't I caused you enough of a headache for one night?"

"Aren't you Farthingales notorious for this very thing?" he teased. "Do not alarm yourself. This is nothing I cannot handle."

But Alex knew trouble was afoot when he saw Caruthers march out of the ballroom with John Farthingale in tow not a moment later. John was the Farthingale family patriarch entrusted with Tulip's care, and Caruthers was obviously giving him an earful of lies. On their heels came a small army of ladies and gentlemen, several of whom he recognized as indiscriminate gossips.

The snake had wasted no time in spewing his venom.

"There! I told you! There's your precious ward, Farthingale. See how cozy she looks beside Davenport? Did I not tell you he had ruined her?"

Tulip gasped and curled her hands into fists. "How dare you spout those abominable falsehoods! And to think, I–"

Alex held her back. "Be quiet, Tulip."

"But he is a lout," she said in a whisper, knowing they had to get their stories straight. "I apologized to him and he took it with utter lack of grace. Well, I'll show him."

"No, you'll be quiet and let me handle the matter," he said with quiet authority.

She was only going to dig herself into a deeper hole than she had already dug for herself if she told the onlookers it was Caruthers she had lured into the garden. Did she not realize she might be forced to marry the wretch?

Alex would never allow this to happen. "Tulip, close your eyes."

She widened them. "What? Why?"

"Because I am going to kiss you. Do you or do you not want a first kiss? Would you mind terribly if it was with me?"

"Why would *you* ever want to kiss *me*? And why now when everyone is watching?" She gasped, suddenly realizing the implications.

"Quickly now, yes or no. They are marching down the stairs toward us."

"Are you mad? It will ruin you."

"To be precise, it will ruin *you*. It has already ruined you."

"And you are determined to save me?"

He nodded. "It is me or Caruthers. Do you mind becoming my duchess?"

"Yours? But–"

"*Choose*, Tulip."

"You."

He drew her into his arms and kissed her with all the heartfelt sincerity he could muster, which was surprisingly a lot because he actually liked her.

In addition to her obvious physical charms, she had shown moral rectitude. What other young lady would have apologized to him and Caruthers? What other young lady would have felt any remorse for her mistake and not blamed anyone but herself for her lapse in judgment?

What other young lady would have sought to protect *him*?

But was it not up to Alex to protect her?

"Wise choice," he murmured, pressing his lips deeper onto her slightly open mouth that was open because she was still trying to talk sense into him, but he was beyond listening. Nor would anyone else among the approaching throng ever listen to what she had to say in her own defense.

They had seen her standing beside him in the shadows of Lady Fullerton's garden and were already poisoned by Caruthers' lies into believing the worst had taken place.

That beast was determined to destroy the sweet innocent forever.

Alex counted to three before removing his mouth from hers, already regretting the end of their kiss because she had the prettiest lips, soft and plump, and they tasted of mint and champagne.

He stared down at her.

She appeared distraught as she returned his gaze. "Why did you do this? Don't you realize what this means?"

He nodded. "You've just received your first kiss...and your first marriage proposal."

CHAPTER 2

TULIP'S STOMACH BEGAN to twist in knots as she watched the family patriarch, John Farthingale, stride down the steps of Lady Fullerton's terrace in an obvious rage. "Tulip, what in the name of heaven?"

"Oh, dear," she whispered, watching his approach with trepidation.

"I have you," Alexander Havers, this new Duke of Davenport, responded with surprising calm.

She had to admire him for his cool resolve as he slid a proprietary arm around her waist, all the while knowing what was about to happen.

"Ah, Mr. Farthingale. Perfect timing. I was just coming to look for you."

John arched an eyebrow. "And for what reason might that be?"

"Has Caruthers not told you? Well, he might be a little sore because he has lost this courtship battle. I just proposed to your ward," he said, glancing at Tulip, "and she has accepted to marry me."

A collective gasp arose from the throng of curious onlookers who had followed John out of Lady Fullerton's house, one that ended in disappointment because there was no scandal in a couple kissing upon a marriage proposal. Not only was there no scandal, but murmurs of frustration could be heard from several marriage-minded mamas and their daughters who now realized that the Duke of Davenport had just been taken off the marriage mart.

Lord Julius Thorne, who was Davenport's best friend, made his way through the crowd. "Davenport! Well done! May I be the first to extend my hearty congratulations? Gory," he said, referring to his wife, the former Lady Gregoria Easton, "will be thrilled when she learns of this."

"Thank you, Thorne," he said with a gracious nod, offering no hint that his life had just been upended by a wayward Farthingale.

Oh, Tulip felt so bad about this.

How were they to fix this mess?

The slight tightening of Davenport's arm around her waist was his way of warning her *not* to confess anything, and certainly not the truth.

She fully intended to follow his lead because she was quite out of her depth at this moment.

Julius's brother, Ambrose, Duke of Huntsford, offered the same warm cheers. "Adela and I shall happily second my brother's good wishes."

Adela, his wife who was standing beside him, nodded enthusiastically. "Oh, yes. We offer our hearty congratulations. Davenport, you've chosen wisely. Tulip shall make you an excellent wife."

"I know," he said with surprising conviction, smiling as he glanced at Tulip.

Oh, dear heaven.

The Thorne brothers and their wives had to be aware this was all a ruse.

While Davenport had become good friends with the Thorne brothers, she had become best friends with their wives. They all knew she had spent the last few months running *away* from Davenport and not encouraging their acquaintance.

Having issued his congratulations, Julius had to now be silently trying to figure out what had really just happened. Tulip noticed him staring at Davenport and gesturing with raised eyebrows, as though trying to communicate in a secret code.

Well, they would all learn the truth soon enough.

But for now, they would go along with this sham of a marriage proposal because this is what friends did.

Supported each other.

Davenport had saved Julius's wife, Gory, last year after she had been involved in the mystery surrounding her uncle's death, so Julius was going to stand by his friend no matter what later transpired.

Davenport, not then a duke and merely known as Alexander Havers, top investigator for the London magistrate, had been assigned to solve this difficult crime that everyone was still talking about because Gory's uncle, the Earl of Easton, had been murdered.

Worse, suspicion had fallen on Gory.

It was Davenport's keen mind and sharp observation abilities that probably saved Gory's life, for not only was she innocent, but the killer intended her to be the next victim. Of course, Julius had been by Gory's side at every step, intent on protecting her and doing a very able job of it. But it was Davenport who had figured out how the crime had been committed and who had done it.

He was brilliant.

All of London knew this.

Tulip smiled up at this man whose kiss still lingered pleasantly on her lips. "Davenport is quite excellent himself. A better man than I ever realized. I was surprised, but most grateful for his offer of marriage."

"I'm not," Julius said with a satisfied nod. "Well, I am only going by what Gory told me. She saw the spark between the two of you immediately and hoped for this happy outcome."

Tulip suspected this was a complete exaggeration.

Gory was engrossed in bones and medical dissections, and now caught up in preparing to give birth to their first child, for she was about eight months along.

This explained why Julius had come alone to Lady Fullerton's rout. His wife was the size of a small whale right now.

Tulip smiled sweetly as Adela added to their ruse. "I saw it, too. The sparks between you two could light up the night sky."

"Ah, you are so very clever," Davenport said smoothly. "We thought it might be impossible to fool our good friends."

John's wife, Sophie, now made her way through the crowd.

She was the matriarch of the Farthingale clan and the one to be credited for holding their large family together.

"Oh, my word," Sophie said with a groan. "Am I hearing right? Is there to be another wedding?"

What she really meant, as she cast Tulip a look of exasperation, was that not a single Farthingale female had ever managed a proper courtship, and now Tulip was about to be added to that growing list.

Tulip cast her a wincing smile. "Yes, Aunt Sophie. Isn't it wonderful?"

Sophie sighed.

The last dozen Farthingale weddings had been chaotically patched together affairs. Poor Sophie had been the one charged with organizing a wedding breakfast within a matter of days each time.

Tulip hoped her count was a little off and she wasn't number thirteen.

Not that she was superstitious, but why tempt fate?

Having this number of rushed weddings within the family did not speak well for the Farthingale brides involved, she supposed.

"Hooray! Another wedding!" Tulip's cousin, Marigold, cried as she pushed her way forward through the crowd. Marigold had been the last Farthingale to wed in haste and was now happily married to Leonides Poole, the Marquess of Muir. Having been caught kissing Leo in similar circumstances, she had to know this announcement was utter fakery. But ever softhearted, Marigold would never give them away.

Of course, her cousin was going to ask a hundred questions afterward.

Davenport turned to John. "I would appreciate discussing this matter with you privately, Mr. Farthingale."

Tulip coughed to stifle her laughter.

Had Davenport just asked for a private meeting?

Did he not realize with whom he was dealing? The Farthingales had raised meddling to an art form.

The word *private* did not exist within the family's vocabulary.

The elders were already starting to gather around John. Those included John's two brothers, George and Rupert. George was a revered doctor, London's finest, and among the smartest men she had ever met. Nothing ever got past him, although the same could be said of Davenport who still had his arm protectively around her waist and did not appear inclined to remove it anytime soon.

Both of John's brothers were going to insist on participating in the betrothal discussion.

Listening in through the peephole of John's study door would be herself and a handful of her female cousins, likely to include several of John and Sophie's five daughters, and Marigold for certain. Probably her cousin, Violet, too, since she lived next door to John and Sophie on Chipping Way with her husband, Captain Romulus Brayden.

Marigold and her husband also lived on Chipping Way.

Lord Caruthers, having suddenly reassessed the situation, was livid as he approached her and Davenport. "It is lies! All lies! She was in the garden with *me*. I am the one she must marry!"

Lady Fullerton strode forward, no doubt seeking to regain control of her party. "Lord Caruthers, it is well known you are in the desperate hunt of a fortune to save your estates from your own reckless actions. I must say, this is a new low even for you. The hour is late, and it is time for you to leave."

To make certain the lout gave her no difficulty, Lady Fullerton motioned for two of her burliest footmen to escort him out.

Tulip was worried Caruthers might try something else, although not at this party but at a later time. He had lost out and this should have been the end of it, but the venomous gleam in his eyes warned there was more to come.

Perhaps she was better off marrying Davenport and gaining his protection instead of looking for ways to wriggle out of this coil.

Well, they would discuss this shortly upon returning to John and Sophie's residence.

If Davenport was willing to marry her, why should she resist? The prior Davenport dukes had awful reputations, which was of deep concern to her. But he did not appear to be like them at all. He was a nice looking man, big and muscled, and that was a heady combination when matched with his intelligence. Least in importance was his title, but Tulip could not deny the protection gained in becoming his duchess.

If there was fault to be found with Davenport, it was that he kept too much to himself. Yet, he had come to her aid without hesitation. She loved the way he still held her close, quietly positioning himself to keep her safe.

This spoke well of his character, did it not?

"Thank you, Lady Fullerton," he said, his voice a deep and authoritative rumble, as Caruthers was shown the door. "My sincere apologies for disrupting your party."

Lady Fullerton was all smiles. "Nonsense, Your Grace. My party shall be the talk of London tomorrow and every hostess will be green with envy that I snared this coup. You and Miss Farthingale, secretly in love, and now you are to marry! And to declare it at my rout! It is wonderful, simply wonderful."

She called for her butler to bring champagne for everyone. "I shall offer a toast to your good fortune and many, many years of happiness."

They both thanked her sincerely.

Tulip hoped they might get a *day* of happiness out of this fiasco.

After the toast, the orchestra resumed playing.

It happened to be a waltz.

"Would you care to dance with me, Miss Farthingale?" Davenport asked. "I believe it is expected of us."

She stared up at him, dismayed because he was incredibly handsome. Perhaps it was the splendid way he looked in his formal evening attire, the impeccably tailored jacket that molded to his muscles and made his shoulders look so broad. Perhaps it was the heat she noticed in his piercing, dark eyes that had her melting a little as he stared at her while awaiting her answer.

All of that magnificence was capped by glorious waves of dark hair.

She smiled at him in gratitude, but also felt some hesitation because she was worried about what would happen once their betrothal announcement was shown to be a hoax.

But for tonight, they were a young couple in love. "Yes, it would be my honor."

He led her onto the dance floor and took her in his arms with the confidence of a man who knew how to hold a woman and make her melt.

Oh, she was so out of her depth.

The butterflies in her stomach were in a mad flutter and her legs were in danger of turning to sand and crumbling beneath her.

She understood why a young lady could fall in love with this man.

But whatever had possessed him to make this sacrifice for her?

"Thank you for everything," she said with heartfelt sincerity as the music started because there was no denying he had defended her reputation tonight.

"No need to thank me, Miss Farthingale. I did you no favor."

"Please call me Tulip, for we are now betrothed and a certain familiarity ought to be acceptable. But...how can you deny your good deed? You saved me from Caruthers and from my own foolishness. It was quite valorous on your part."

"You think so? Well, no matter. We'll continue the conversation at your uncle's home." He said no more as he guided her with obvious proficiency around the floor.

This man had all the skills and made everything look easy.

She followed his lead and remained silent as they danced, for she was trying to make sense of him. He now looked severe and authoritative, yet had shown himself to be wonderfully valiant and protective.

He sighed upon noticing her dismayed expression. "You think I am angry with you."

She nodded. "Aren't you? And do you not have every right to be?"

"No, I knew the risks involved in coming to your rescue. But I also knew this might work out well for us."

"How?" She did not see any advantage to him in taking her on as his wife.

Well, perhaps there was one. He would no longer be considered eligible and hunted down by every debutante wishing to snare him. It could be more accurately said that they were hunting the title and not the man himself.

Another advantage was that as a duke, he had the power to set whatever terms he wished for in their marriage.

Who would dare contradict him or deny his demands?

Was that it? Did he want a wife in name only and thought he had settled on someone biddable? Namely, herself.

This might make sense if he had a reputation as a rake, but he did not. If anything, he was the quiet sort who spent most evenings on his own, working or reading.

And if he thought he had just proposed to someone docile and easily managed, someone who would not interfere with his style of living, then he was about to receive a rude awakening.

She was not docile.

Although she understood why he might mistakenly think she was. Having been raised in the countryside, she had not yet gained confidence going about in a big city such as London. After months of living here, she was only now beginning to learn her way around the bustling streets.

What also confounded her were these rules of Society that seemed so arbitrary.

She was still grappling with them, particularly when they felt so hypocritical. Why make a fuss about a young lady's virtue when so many of the married ladies had affairs after marriage?

Some of these ladies were not even discreet in their liaisons.

Neither were their husbands, for that matter.

"Do you doubt our marriage could be advantageous to both of us?" Davenport asked, responding to her question with one of his own. "You could be useful to me. The seat of the Davenport dukes is in Somerset, and this is where you were born and raised."

"Yes, I grew up in the village of Burnham which is not far from Thornwycke Hall," she said, referring to the impressive estate that was his ducal seat. "But I did not realize you were aware of this. Then again, it is no secret and must have come up a time or two in conversation."

"Yes, it did."

But those conversations were never with her because she had

spent much of their acquaintance avoiding him.

No doubt, Marigold had told him all about her.

Her cousin was sweet and delightful, but could also chatter like a magpie.

"I am still not sure how my Somerset background helps you," she said. "I was not raised among the titled elite and can tell you little about the prior Davenport dukes or their families beyond what I noticed from a distance or what I heard going around our village as common gossip."

"That is far more than I know about them. I've had no dealings with them since I was a little boy. By purposeful design, but now I wish I had kept a closer eye on what was going on over these past few years."

She regarded him thoughtfully. "Because a string of Davenport dukes have died in quick succession? Yes, the local magistrate could have used your skills to investigate those untimely deaths. You do not need to marry me to find out all the lurid gossip I've heard about that. I will gladly tell you."

He arched an eyebrow. "They were ruled accidental deaths by the local coroner in each instance. Have you heard anything to the contrary?"

"No," she admitted. "Although to lose so many family members within a short period of time seems quite unnatural, don't you think?"

"Not unnatural. People die, and this is the *natural* way of things. My predecessors did not have sterling reputations. Who knows what damage they did to themselves with their profligate ways?"

Tulip merely nodded, choosing not to argue the matter. But four Davenport dukes had died within a span of five years. Was this not significant enough to raise doubts about how innocent those deaths were?

She had lost both her parents in a tragic accident years ago.

One accident that had led to both deaths.

But this is not what had happened with these Davenport dukes.

Four had died in quick succession, although the first had died quite innocently of old age. But the others? Each had met his abrupt end in a different way.

Two had died after falling off their horses.

One had drowned.

"Tulip, I did question how I came to be the next duke. Until a couple of years ago, I was too far down the Davenport line to ever consider that I might inherit the title. But you have to understand my family."

"Oh, I know your family's reputation quite well."

He cast her a wry smile. "Yes, which explains why you so diligently avoided me all these months. The Davenport men are hedonistic wastrels. Name any vice, and I'll give you a Davenport duke who indulged in it to the extreme."

She nodded. "We all saw how they lived their lives of excess and indulgence. They cared only for themselves and gave no consideration to the harm they caused others. Is this why you believe their deaths in short succession plausible?"

"Yes, although I did have my doubts. Ultimately, I could draw no other conclusion. I've read the coroner's reports and they were quite thorough. He ruled the deaths accidental. No hint of foul measures."

"Oh? When did you read them?"

He cast her a wry smile. "Shortly after I inherited the title. I thought it prudent to do a little investigation, just to be certain nothing more was going on. I was not keen to become the next duke about to meet a quick and untimely end. Must we discuss this now?"

"No, I suppose not." But she was relieved he had looked into those deaths and was satisfied there was nothing sinister going on.

She had enough concerns about marrying him.

A murderer on the loose should not be one of them.

Her greatest worry was in regard to the terms of their marriage.

What was he offering?

Having come from a large and loving family, this was important to her.

She did not care about becoming his duchess. A title in itself was not going to secure her happiness. What she wanted was a true and loving friendship between them. The hope of children in their future.

She had grown up surrounded by caring family, for both her father's Farthingale relations and her mother's Hester family had taken active roles in raising her. Every cousin, whether related by first, second, or third degree of consanguinity, treated her as one of their own.

John Farthingale was actually her father's cousin, but she referred to him as Uncle John because it felt odd to call him cousin.

The same for George and Rupert, since they were the older and wiser family members and it felt right to address them as uncles, too.

Perhaps this was why she appealed to Davenport, a man denied the warmth and protection of his blood kin.

By marrying her, he would acquire a ready-made, closely knit family.

Was not his desire to be a family man among a good family like hers another point in his favor?

Tulip was still trying to make sense of him when he regained her attention. "What are you thinking now, Tulip?"

"That you are an excellent dancer," she said lightly as he continued to twirl her around the crowded dance floor with effortless grace.

"Is that all?"

"Truthfully, I am thinking of us and trying to figure out what I should hope for in our marriage. And also learn what you are hoping for in this union, should it come to pass."

"Still reluctant to believe this is real? It is, Tulip. At least, for my part. But yes, it is something important that we must discuss."

She nodded. "This is what I am trying to organize in my mind. Why did you choose me? Merely because of my connection to Somerset? I know it quite well, but so do many other people. It seems you have just saddled yourself with a convenient tour guide. You could have paid anyone to tell you more about the area and your family than I could."

"Why are you dismissing your importance to me?" He frowned while continuing to lead her through the steps of the waltz that would soon come to an end.

"Because we are not equal in any respect. Not in height or strength. Not in bloodlines. You are a duke. My father was not even gentry. You are experienced in worldly matters and I have been sheltered in the countryside for most of my life." She took a deep breath and let it out slowly. "After months of balls and routs and musicales, I still feel awkward and uncertain. But you...you are one of those annoying people who do everything well and make it appear easy."

He laughed at her last remark, a deep, mirthful rumble that felt quite nice as it wrapped around her heart. "Is this what you think of me?"

His gaze was piercing as he stared at her.

He had a disconcerting way of appearing aloof and icy on the surface, but there was a smoldering heat that simmered just below that expressionless exterior.

That heat now surfaced as he asked, "Tulip, you have now told me what you think of me and what you think of yourself. But you haven't asked the most important question yet."

She had no idea what he was talking about. "What question is that?"

"Do you have any idea what I think of you?"

CHAPTER 3

DO YOU HAVE any idea what I think of you?

This is what Davenport had just asked her, and Tulip did not know the answer to his question. Until tonight, she had not realized he thought of her at all. And frankly, she was afraid to ask him and find out.

How could he possibly think her special in any way when she had never done anything noteworthy or admirable?

How could she ever come close to matching his accomplishments?

Davenport had made quite a name for himself as the London magistrate's top investigator.

He had earned his good standing in Society.

"Care to give me a hint?" Tulip replied in jest. "I have done nothing of significance in all my life, yet you have solved hundreds of crimes and saved so many lives before ever reaching your thirtieth birthday. I am not counting your proposing to me as a noteworthy feat on my part because it was a matter of entrapment rather than anything to be considered a triumph."

"I was the one who stepped forward," he said with some impatience. "You did not make me do it. How old are you, Tulip?"

She laughed. "Twenty."

"Then you have eight years to catch up to me. You are just coming into your own, and there is no telling what good you will do once you become my duchess."

She almost stumbled while staring up at him. "You've said it again. Are you truly serious about our betrothal?"

He nodded. "Serious. Determined. Implacable."

"Quite remarkable," she muttered. "Why?"

Why choose her out of all the young ladies available to him in London?

The reason could not be something as simple as she was from Somerset.

She had a decent dowry, which was why Caruthers wanted her. But it was not an outrageously generous one and could only go so far in restoring the Davenport properties to their former grandeur.

If the general gossip was to be believed, generations of dissipated Davenport dukes had severely ruined many good assets, including Thornwycke Hall, the residence of every Davenport duke for the last five centuries or longer.

The manor house had originally been built as a fortress overlooking the Bristol Channel. It was attacked, partially destroyed, and rebuilt over the years. However, due to the neglect of too many dukes over this past century, Thornwycke Hall was once again in danger of falling into ruin.

Or so it was rumored.

She had never visited the place and did not know its exact condition. A good friend of the family worked there and said it was no place suitable for a young lady, but that was because the dukes were libertines and held wild parties there. She hoped it was habitable, merely needing fresh paint and polish to restore the manor house, since she and Davenport would likely take up residence there.

She continued to ponder the question…why marry her?

He was not seeking a union in order to improve his bloodlines, either. No one in her family held a noble title, and he was fully aware of this.

Not even the hint of blue blood could be found in the Farthingale ancestry.

Only in her generation had some of her cousins married well and gained noble titles through those marriages.

She found it hilarious that Marigold was now a marchioness and that Dillie, the youngest of John and Sophie's daughters, was a duchess. Several cousins were now countesses, another a viscountess, and yet another a baroness.

"Still confused about why I might want you for my wife?"

She nodded.

"Here's a clue. Look within yourself."

"Haven't I been doing that? Tell me more."

But the waltz ended, and with it their conversation.

Davenport escorted her back to her aunt and uncle.

She spent the remainder of the rout staying close to her Aunt Sophie.

When Lady Fullerton's affair ended, Davenport followed Tulip and her family home.

Since coming to London she had resided with John and Sophie, for they were the ones sponsoring her for the Season that had now drawn to its end. They lived on Chipping Way, a charming garden oasis within London.

There were only six homes on this tree-lined street and Farthingales resided in three of them. Lady Dayne, grandmother of Gabriel Dayne, the earl who had married John and Sophie's daughter, Daisy, owned the fourth home.

John led Davenport into his study the moment they arrived home.

John's brothers and Sophie followed him in.

Tulip thought Davenport might need an ally and attempted to follow after them, but Rupert held her back. "Be patient, Tulip. We will call you in shortly."

She wound up standing in the entry hall with Pruitt, the faithful family butler. "Ah, what a surprise," he remarked in his light, Scottish brogue as some of Tulip's cousins made their way up the walk despite the lateness of the hour.

She sighed and greeted them at the front door. "Hello, Marigold. Violet. Holly. Dahlia." Then some of John's daughters marched in. "How nice to see you, Dillie. Daisy. Rose."

Several had brought their husbands along.

Dillie was happily married to the Duke of Edgeware. Although her name was Daffodil, everyone knew her as Dillie. Perhaps it was because she had an identical twin called Lily, and those names rhymed.

Lily and Dillie.

Two peas in a pod.

"I see you have followed in the proud family tradition of making an utter wreck of your Season and necessitating a hasty marriage," Dillie remarked with a trill of laughter and gave her a quick hug. "Well done."

Tulip groaned. "Oh, we should not find this amusing at all. Poor Davenport. We hardly exchanged two words in all these months, and now he is forced to marry me."

Marigold shook her head. "That man cannot be forced to do anything he does not wish to do."

"That is what he told me, too," Tulip admitted.

Marigold greeted Pruitt before turning her attention back to Tulip. "I am not surprised. I thought my Leo was tough as old boots, but Davenport is just like him. Wild horses could not have dragged them to doing something they did not wish to do. You must stop worrying about him. Perhaps he has held a secret torch for you all the while."

"Him? Desiring me?" She shook her head and laughed at the hilarity of it. "Not possible."

"Stop belittling yourself, Tulip," Rose insisted. "You are exceptionally pretty, so how could he resist?"

"No prettier than dozens of other young ladies who made their debut this year."

Rose shrugged off her remark. "He might have seen you at some of the British Museum lectures or noticed you touring the Huntsford Academy exhibits and realized you had a brain. He might have overheard you talking to others at a dinner party and liked your cleverness and wit. Obviously, he has seen something worthy in you."

She thought it was ironic that Rose, now a viscountess who was also a brilliant artist and ran a successful pottery and glassworks business, should be complimenting her.

"Hush," Daisy said, bending down and putting her ear to the

door. "I cannot hear a word of what they are saying. But Davenport sounds awfully calm."

"And what about Papa?" Rose asked. "Mama must be numb by now, for she's the one who has to do all the work to put these weddings together. We'll help her out, of course. You needn't worry about that, Tulip."

Daisy glanced up, but kept her ear to the door. "Papa's awfully calm, too. I think he has stopped being surprised by us. But how are any of us at fault when trouble seems to follow us around?"

"And always with a handsome bachelor ready to leap in to rescue us," Holly said with a grin. "Perhaps there is something to this Chipping Way curse after all. Didn't you knock down Davenport right here on Chipping Way when you first met him, Tulip?"

"Oh, that? I was across the street at Marigold's house when Mallow, her imp of a dog, slipped through the gate and darted onto the street. I had to chase after him. I didn't actually knock Davenport down. I ran into him, and then bounced off him because that man is built like a wall of granite. He caught me before I fell. There was nothing more to it."

Her cousins laughed heartily.

"The Chipping Way curse," Dillie insisted.

Perhaps, but how odd that this very thing should have happened again tonight. She refused to believe there was any significance to it at all.

The study door suddenly opened and Daisy toppled in.

John sighed and helped his daughter up, then frowned at the rest of them who had also been hovering by the door. "Tulip, come in. The rest of you, go home."

Of course, no one was going home until they got all the scandalous details.

John shut the door to keep the rest of the family out.

Tulip took a seat beside her aunt.

However, she spoke up immediately because she wanted to get a word in before the elders started hurling questions. "I think what needs to be answered is, how do we quietly end this betrothal with the least harm done to me and Davenport?"

"Are you still going on about that?" Davenport was standing by her uncle's desk and now folded his arms across his chest so that he looked quite big and massive, like a warrior guarding an impenetrable gate. "There is no going back from this without irreparable harm to you, Tulip. The right question is, how soon do we marry?"

"Why are you still going on about *that*? Weren't you supposed to leave for Somerset tomorrow? Well, since it is past midnight, you should be leaving this very morning. We can settle things when you return."

He shook his head. "No, I have no idea when I will be returning and this needs to be addressed now. I cannot leave you here while Caruthers is still angry and bent on getting his revenge. You are at risk so long as you remain unmarried."

He had a point, but were they not making too much of that lord's animosity. "Surely, he will calm down in a day or two."

Davenport arched an eyebrow. "Oh, you think so?"

She gulped. "Well, one can never be certain. I have no experience in such matters."

"But I do," he insisted. "I will postpone my departure for a few days. Mrs. Farthingale, does this give you enough time to assemble a wedding breakfast? I shall undertake all the costs, of course."

"No, that is my responsibility," John intoned. "You just let my wife know who you would like us to invite."

"In truth, no one but the Thornes. I have no close family."

John nodded. "They'll have to be verbal invitations followed by a confirming note since there's no time for formal invitations to be printed. I'll leave the responsibility of a Somerset wedding celebration up to you."

"I'll take care of that," Tulip assured, then realized she may have spoken out of turn. "I am very close to my mother's family, Your Grace. It does not have to be anything lavish, just a simple dinner party will do to introduce you to the Hesters and perhaps a few friends of mine. Would that be all right? They'll be so sad to have missed my wedding, but there's no time for them to join us here."

Her uncle, William Hester, and his wife, Perty, had taken primary responsibility for raising her after her parents had died.

"Of course," Davenport said with surprising gentleness.

"That takes care of the wedding plans." John gave a nod of satisfaction. "Tulip, I'll let you and Sophie get to work on those details right away. His Grace and I shall next discuss the betrothal terms."

Sophie rose, but Tulip hesitated. "Should I not be involved in that discussion?"

"No," John and his brothers said in unison.

Rupert smiled at her. "You are best served by having us act as we deem best without your presence."

A polite way of saying they did not want her interfering and botching their negotiations.

"I am merely a doctor," George added, "but my brothers are quite good at this sort of thing. Let them do what they must to protect you."

She frowned. "The duke has already shown he has valor and will do whatever he must to keep me safe. Should we not trust him to do what is right? Has he not already shown he has an excellent moral character?"

"And this is why we do not want you in here," John said, taking her by the shoulders and nudging her toward the door. "You are naively softhearted, Tulip."

Davenport smiled. "And an excellent negotiator on my behalf."

"Because I know you are a man of honor," Tulip said, talking over her shoulder as her uncle steered her out. "I apologize for taking so long to realize it."

John rolled his eyes.

George laughed.

"Where is Hortensia when we need her?" Rupert muttered.

"Oh, yes," Tulip warned. "You had better come to an agreement before Hortensia sticks her nose in our business, Davenport."

"Who is Hortensia?" Davenport asked.

"The family dragon," they all happened to respond in unison.

John chuckled as he sought to explain about the eldest of the family elders. "She can be a bit difficult."

"But she'll make for a wonderful ally if she likes you," Tulip assured him as John gave her a final, gentle nudge.

"Thank you for the warning," Davenport called out as John shut the door behind her.

Everyone considered their elderly, maiden aunt a total dragon who did not believe in compromise and struck fear in the hearts of all mere mortals. In truth, Tulip was surprised Hortensia hadn't swooped down from her bedchamber and set forth her edicts about what was to be done. No negotiation. Her terms only. Scorched earth and no mercy shown. If Tulip or Davenport had any objections, too bad.

Hortensia was not the sort to listen patiently while others spoke.

Perhaps the hour was too late for Hortensia to join them.

She would be in fine fettle come morning, and Davenport had better hope the betrothal terms were agreed upon and the matter concluded before she awoke.

Tulip was now left to stand in the hall with her cousins, none of whom had yet to leave.

The gentlemen ended their discussion not long afterward.

Davenport walked out of the study, his features expressionless.

Tulip could not tell if he was pleased or angry.

She followed him to the door. "Well? How did it go? Were they too demanding?"

He tucked a finger under her chin. "All is agreed upon."

"That easily? What were the terms? The discussion did not take more than fifteen minutes. How is this adequate?"

"Come to my solicitor's office tomorrow with your uncle and you will find out."

She tugged lightly on his arm. "Can you not tell me tonight?"

He shook his head. "It is late, and I need to revise my travel arrangements before I retire."

"Yes, of course. I do feel awful about this."

He tilted her gaze upward to meet the dark glint of his eyes. "It is done and we will make the best of it."

He glanced at the other family members who were still

gathered in the hall, the elders now being peppered by questions from her cousins. But he kept his attention on Tulip. "I would kiss you," he said softly, "but I do not like to have an audience when undertaking such matters."

"Do you often kiss ladies?"

He cast her a surprisingly affectionate smile. "There's only been one, lately."

She cast him a look of confusion, for she had not seen him escorting any young lady around London or heard his name connected to anyone else. "Do you mean me? Am I the one lady?"

"Yes, Tulip. Who else? See you tomorrow," he said and walked out.

Did he mean it?

No one but her?

Was this not remarkable?

CHAPTER 4

TULIP KISSED JOHN and Sophie before retiring to bed. "Thank you for all you are doing for me."

Sophie hugged her. "I will admit these hasty weddings overwhelmed me, at first. But I can prepare them in my sleep now. What matters is that you are betrothed to a good man who will be a caring and attentive husband."

"We'll take a shotgun to him if he isn't," John muttered.

Sophie gasped. "John!"

He shook his head. "Just letting Tulip know she can always come to us if she is unhappy. She needs to know we will always protect her."

"Thank you, Uncle John." Tulip went to bed thinking about all that had happened tonight.

Her dreams ought to have been happy ones, of weddings and new beginnings.

After all, she had snared a handsome duke.

Unfortunately, he happened to be a Davenport duke.

For this reason, her dreams were of dark skies and crashing waves, of roiling seas and dangerous turmoil. In her dreams, she saw a rundown manor house isolated atop a hill. Thornwycke Hall, no doubt. She had only ever seen it from a distance, and hoped not to find an ominous house with secret rooms, ghostly hauntings, and a housekeeper with shifty eyes.

Davenport was also in her dreams, handsome and brooding.

Full of his own secrets.

She could not shake off this malevolent aura and it caused her to wake up abruptly several times during the night.

"I have to stop reading those scandalous novels," she whispered each time and fell back into a fitful sleep.

She awoke grudgingly when Sophie's maid drew aside the drapes to allow in the bright sunshine. "Good morning, Miss Tulip. It's to be a lovely day. Congratulations on your betrothal, and to such a man as Mr. Havers. Well, he's His Grace now, isn't he? And you're to be his duchess. You must be so thrilled."

"Thank you, Annie. Yes, he is quite something." Despite not feeling her best, she did not hesitate to get out of bed and ready herself for the day.

She did not want to miss the very important meeting with Davenport's solicitor.

John was waiting for her as she came downstairs. "Are you ready?"

She nodded eagerly and took his arm as they strode to their waiting carriage.

Sunlight sparkled upon the Thames waters as Tulip and her uncle rode to the Inns of Chancery where Davenport's solicitor had his office. The morning light fell soft and gentle upon the waves, and she found it a welcome distraction from her worries.

Sir Deverel Whitby, the senior solicitor and head of the firm of Whitby & Whitby, hurried out to greet them as soon as they walked in. "Welcome, Mr. Farthingale. Miss Farthingale. May I offer my felicitations?"

He escorted them into his spacious office that contained rows of bookshelves laden with what appeared to be legal texts, a massive desk piled with papers, and an elegant table where he obviously sat when meeting with his clients.

Sir Deverel was an imposing man despite being of average height and little brawn. Perhaps it was his snow-white beard and thick, white eyebrows that gave his countenance that aura of *gravitas*.

Davenport was already in the solicitor's office, seated at the table with several official looking papers before him.

He rose as Tulip and her uncle were escorted in. "Good

morning."

Tulip smiled as he drew out the chair beside his and motioned for her to take the seat. Their shoulders grazed as she sat, sending tingles shooting through her. "I hope we did not keep you waiting."

"Not at all, you are right on time," he assured. "I came early to set out the betrothal terms for Sir Deverel and his clerks to put in writing."

She nodded. "How quickly can a betrothal agreement be prepared?"

"Oh, not before the end of the week at the earliest," Sir Deverel replied, taking a seat at the head of the table.

"What your uncle and I will sign today," Davenport explained, "is merely a letter of intent setting forth the terms of our agreement. I know Sir Deverel would prefer the agreement itself entered into before our wedding, but there simply isn't time."

"Why insist on this rush? I know you are worried about what Caruthers might be planning," she said, "but I will remain on my guard now that I know the sort of man he is. Our wedding can wait."

Davenport frowned. "Tulip, do you not wish to marry me?"

The question surprised her, and the tone of it, too. He seemed saddened by the thought she might not want him.

She silently chided herself for failing to give proper consideration to his feelings.

Was it possible he really wanted to marry her?

It felt so implausible.

But this doubt sprang from within her and had led to those awful dreams she'd had last night. If she were honest about it, his behavior had always been polite and considerate toward her.

In truth, above reproach.

She was the one who always found an excuse to run away from him, unfairly branding him as a man to be avoided at all costs because the prior Davenport dukes had such bad reputations.

But he was nothing like them.

Or was he? And just hiding it very well.

There would be no avoiding him once they were married.

For this reason, she had a very important question that needed answering before they proceeded any further. "Your Grace, do you think you could ever find it in your heart to love me?"

His eyes widened. "If you are asking whether I want our marriage to be something real, to be one of friendship and commitment to each other, the answer is yes. This was the first question your uncle asked me."

"Oh." She turned to her uncle. "Why did you not tell me?"

"I thought you understood we would never agree to your marrying any suitor unless there was the possibility of love," John said.

"I see. Thank you." She returned her attention to Davenport. "Then you think there might someday be love between us?"

"It is what I hope for, Tulip. Is it not wisest to enter into this marriage wishing for it and working to make it a good and happy union?"

"Yes, for certain. It is exactly what I want for us."

The answer seemed to please him. "Then shall we move ahead with these wedding arrangements?"

She let out a breath and nodded. "Yes."

Sir Deverel began to read out the terms negotiated, a short list that was far simpler than Tulip expected. "Am I hearing right? Are you leaving all the assets that are not a part of the Davenport entailment to me?"

Davenport nodded. "I could tell you that your uncles drove a hard bargain, but the truth is that I would not trust my surviving relatives with any of it. There was never a question it should all go to you and our children, assuming we have any. Of course, if we had a son then he would be the next Davenport duke and have the usufruct of the entailment, as I do now."

"Usufruct means the right to the use and advantages of the assets tied to the dukedom," Sir Deverel hurried to explain. "It means His Grace does not own them outright but has exclusive claim to all the income and other benefits, and may reside or otherwise enjoy all the ducal properties within the entailment as he wishes, short of destroying them."

Tulip smiled to acknowledge the solicitor's explanation, although she hadn't needed it. She was aware of what that term meant. "What about setting aside bequests for any members of your family?" she asked Davenport.

"No," he said with finality.

"All right, if that is your wish. However, if you decide afterward that your relatives ought to get something from you, then that is fine, too."

He shook his head. "There won't be any changes. Whatever you choose to do with those assets will be far worthier than anything any Davenport will ever do with them."

She said no more since his mind seemed firmly made up.

He meant to give his family not a shilling.

Truly, this was so contrary to her own upbringing.

Well, he had never made a secret of loathing his relatives.

She was sorry for it.

But something troubled her and it had nothing to do with financial matters. In truth, Davenport was being quite generous with her. "May I ask you another question, Your Grace?"

He arched an eyebrow. "Of course. Go ahead."

"Who raised you?" Because someone had done a proper job of keeping him from ruining his life as his predecessors had done.

"My mother did." He leaned forward, casting her a severe look. "What you are really asking is how I avoided becoming as loathsome and debauched as the other Davenport dukes. As for that, I can only say that my mother did her best to keep me away from their influence. She taught me what things in life mattered most. Whether she succeeded or not has yet to be determined, I suppose. Unfortunately, she died many years ago, long before I became an investigator for the London magistrate."

"I am sincerely sorry. I know she would have been very proud of you."

He leaned back and nodded. "Any other questions?"

She shook her head. "No, not at the moment."

In truth, she had plenty more.

But those were best left for later.

Sir Deverel and her uncle were growing impatient to have the terms finalized and set in writing.

Once the letter of intent was signed, they could move on to securing the marriage license. Since she was still several months away from her twenty-first birthday, her presence was not required for any of these official arrangements.

However, she wanted to be there for all of it.

She was relieved when their next stop after leaving Sir Deverel's office was to obtain the license. This brought them back to Mayfair where their church was located on its outskirts. She sat in a pew at St. Mary's, a lovely house of worship built of stone and draped in ivy, while the prelate discussed the wedding procedures with all of them. Then Davenport and her uncle went into the prelate's office and signed whatever documents were necessary.

"May I invite you to tea at the Denby Arms?" Davenport asked upon their conclusion of this second piece of business.

Her uncle declined. "Please forgive me, but Rupert and I have important customers coming into town today and I cannot be late for our meeting. I still must return Tulip home and then dash back to the Farthingale offices which are close to the Inns of Chancery."

Tulip was disappointed, for the Denby Arms was one of the most elegant hotels in London and everyone raved about their afternoon tea.

She was eager to try this popular place.

Her desire must have been obvious to Davenport.

He cast her a smile and then turned to her uncle. "Now that Tulip and I are officially betrothed, would you mind if she joined me? I will escort her home immediately afterward."

Her eyes lit up. "Yes, please. That is an excellent idea. Isn't it, Uncle John?"

He nodded. "All right. Davenport, I want your word on this. Tea at the Denby Arms, and then you take Tulip straight back to my house."

"Upon my honor, Mr. Farthingale."

She and Davenport watched her uncle climb into his carriage and ride off.

"The Denby Arms is not a long walk from here," Davenport

said. "Or would you rather ride there in my carriage?"

"I'd love a walk. I think this is one of the things I have missed most since coming to London, those morning strolls I used to take along a country lane in the fresh air."

"Well, there'll be plenty of that once we are in Somerset. Not much fresh air around here, however."

He ordered his driver to go on to the hotel without them. "Meet us there, Trent."

"Aye, Your Grace," the man said and flicked the reins to start the team of matched bays forward.

Davenport held out his arm to her. "It is obvious you have a lot more to ask me, Tulip."

She nodded as she placed her arm in his. "I do. But it is my fault for not trying to get to know you better. I've spent these past months avoiding you when I should have kept an open mind and engaged you in conversation."

"Well, you have your chance now."

She studied him as they strolled along the busy street, liking the way he quietly drew her closer whenever he thought someone was about to knock into her.

In truth, she liked *him*.

But none of this made any sense to her.

Why should a duke commit to marrying a commoner over a simple kiss? Was there something she was not seeing?

"Go ahead and ask your question, Tulip. Why are you looking so perplexed?"

She sighed. "Your Grace, are we about to make a terrible mistake?"

CHAPTER 5

ALEX FROWNED AT the question Tulip had just posed.

He had not considered his proposing to her to be a mistake at all. In fact, he felt quite comfortable with the inevitability that she would become his wife. He wasn't certain of the reasons why he felt this way, only that his every instinct told him that she was the right one for him. "Why are you worried we are making a mistake?"

"I cannot get over the feeling we are a mismatch."

She had mentioned this before, her belief that he was perfect and she found it not only daunting but quite irritating.

"Ah, yes. That." He laughed softly, for she would soon find out he was not the paragon she imagined. "You'll see that our roles will be reversed once we reach Somerset. I know London like the back of my hand. I understand the poetry of it and the musicality of its rhythms, the beauty and the blight. I know its seedy back streets and alleyways, and I am all too familiar with the scent of the Thames and the choking smoke of hearth fires in winter. I know the dockside taverns where the lowest scoundrels sit in wait for an easy mark and also know the elite ballrooms where the privileged amuse themselves in splendor."

She looked up at him as he spoke, her lovely eyes glistening like pale blue crystals beneath her long, dark lashes. "You will adapt fairly quickly to Somerset, Your Grace. We work at a slower pace than London, but we are not completely provincial. Your estate is not far from Bath which is quite popular in the summers with Londoners. You'll feel quite at home there. There's also Taunton that may not be as elegant as Bath, but it is a financial and business center, as well as the center of our local government."

"Yes, I am aware. Those are not the things that concern me."

"Then what does?"

"I am a crack investigator. What do I know about running a farm or a mill? There are several farms within the Davenport demesne. I understand there is also a cider press on the property and an abandoned cheese works. How am I to fix them up when I do not even know how to milk a cow, till soil, or use a butter churn?"

She laughed. "And you think I do?"

He raised his eyebrows and cast her a knowing smile. "Don't you?"

"Yes, but only because my uncle and his wife kept a vegetable garden and raised a few cows and chickens on their property. Some of the Hester relatives happen to be farmers, too. I've been to their grain mill once or twice. But you have an estate manager to oversee the farms and dairy, and any other Davenport operations. Your Mr. Carver is solid and reliable. I have known him forever. I'm sure he will instruct you in all you need to know."

His smile broadened. "Perhaps, but he won't be as pretty as you."

She laughed again. "I should hope not. Mr. Carver is a sturdy, barrel-chested fellow, and one of the most capable men you will ever meet."

"See, you knew this and I did not. How do you know him?"

"He grew up in Burnham and went to school with my mother and her brother, William Hester. Uncle William and Mr. Carver stayed quite friendly over the years. He's a good soul. You only need ask him a question and he will answer truthfully."

"That eases my mind greatly. See, you are already proving yourself to be invaluable to me."

She smiled and shook her head. "Mr. Carver is the one to be appreciated. You could not ask for a better man. I think this is one of the first things you ought to do, have him walk you around the properties and inspect what is going on. He will be happy to do it. And if you wish to sit on a milking stool and milk a cow, or take a basket into the chicken coop and collect eggs, he won't stop you," she teased.

"But I do want to learn these things," Alex said in earnest.

"And I would love to watch you make your first attempts," she said with a soft trill of laughter. "Well, that is up to you. But if you were to ask me, I think you should concentrate on reviving the Davenport cheese works first."

"Why that?"

The sidewalks were heating up as the day grew warmer, but Tulip did not seem to mind walking beside him.

In truth, she seemed to be enjoying their walk immensely.

Perhaps it was that they were finally having an extensive conversation, something she had avoided doing with him for months.

It felt nice to have a pleasant chat with her and not experience the disappointment of watching her run away from him as though he were an ogre.

The Davenport ogre.

"Have you never heard of the Davenport cheeses?" she asked.

"No." He had made it a point to stay away from his family and not stick his nose in anything remotely connected to them.

"Your estate was once known for its excellent cheddars. That cheese-making process originated in the nearby town of Cheddar itself. The Davenport dukes had extensive holdings there, too. So, you also adopted the name of the town for your cheeses."

He grunted in surprise.

"But the Davenports stopped making their cheeses about twenty years ago. I was but a newborn at the time, so I do not know what happened. I've only been told that they abruptly stopped production. Mr. Carver will know, for certain. I heard it was a profitable operation at one time. Your great grandfather was the Davenport duke just before your grandfather inherited and it is said he had some business acumen. Unfortunately, he also happened to be a big gambler."

"So was my grandfather."

She nodded. "Yes, your grandfather was certainly an eccentric character. Mr. Carver claims he was also a very smart man, but something happened around that time and it changed him."

"What was it?"

"Mr. Carver didn't know. All he ever said was that your grandfather began to live life heedlessly and spent whatever came in rather than amassing his fortune or protecting it for future generations."

"There's a surprise," Alex muttered sarcastically.

Tulip grimaced and continued. "The dukes that followed were no better. Your grandfather, despite his dissolute ways, tried to keep the farms and dairy going. But there was never enough money to properly maintain them, or so Mr. Carver would complain to us. Many of those assets are still going, but I don't know for how long. The cheese production has stopped completely, as I mentioned. It was the first to go under. Other businesses run by the Davenports have had to close down since then. Not that any of the subsequent dukes cared. I think one of the first things you must do is take a close look at each asset and determine what is needed to revive it."

"Tulip, do you realize that your eyes shine when you speak of Somerset and the Davenport estate?"

"No, I hadn't. But I do love Somerset and I have missed it." She looked up at him again. "I cannot believe I will be returning there as your duchess. My friends will have quite the laugh. Are you going to demand they refer to me as Your Grace?"

Alex shook his head. "No, let them call you whatever you wish. You carry yourself with the grace of a duchess. They'll know you are one whether you toss the title at them or not. You look very pretty, by the way."

She blushed and glanced down at her gown. "The color of this muslin is incredibly beautiful, isn't it? The dye is Venetian blue and comes from the indigo plant. The intensity of the color is enhanced by mixing the indigo with other sources of blue, such as minerals like lapis lazuli, and did you know that snails also emit a blue dye?"

He laughed. "Seriously?"

"Yes. The ancient Egyptians cultivated this snail. The Romans also had snails, but theirs exuded a purple dye, one that was quite rare and expensive. Which is how the European monarchs chose purple as the color for their royal robes. It became a symbol of wealth and power. Commoners could be killed for wearing that color. Even wearing a small square of it could be viewed as a treasonous threat to a ruling monarchy."

"Fascinating," he said and actually meant it.

She smiled. "Isn't it? I love to hear my uncles speak about the science and history of their fabrics. I think this is why their Farthingale cloths stand apart from the rest and are so popular. They seek out the unusual, the best weaves and the rarest dyes. They will not accept just anything. Uncle Rupert picked up these vibrant muslins along with some exquisite silks and velvets on his last trip to Italy."

"Ah, yes. I've heard a little about those silks, in particular. They do not actually come from Italy, do they?"

Tulip nodded. "Some do, but most are brought along the Silk Road from China and make their way to the Continent. Several centuries ago, the European traders discovered the secret of making silk and smuggled silkworms out of China in the hope of creating the fabric here. But there must have been more to the process because the Europeans still have not figured out how to create the same luminous shine to the fabric."

Alex grinned. "I'm surprised your uncles do not take you on their buying trips. You seem to know as much as they do about their merchandise."

"Oh, I've only learned this recently. It is one thing London has to offer that is unmatched anywhere else in England. The wealth of scholarly information available just about any day of the week and only a short carriage ride away. I attended so many interesting lectures at the Royal Society, the British Museum, and the Huntsford Academy. I particularly loved the Huntsford lectures and their exhibit hall, especially the Hall of Dragons. I got a special after-hours tour because I was friendly with Adela, Syd, and Gory," she said, referring to the wives of the Thorne brothers.

Alex knew the Thornes had built the Huntsford Academy to honor their father who was a noted naturalist and admirer of all the sciences. It was a family undertaking and their bluestocking wives were heavily involved. "I enjoyed the lectures, too. Unfortunately, I was too busy solving crimes to attend many that I would have loved to hear," he admitted.

"Uncle Rupert used to travel the world and has so many exciting stories to tell. But he confines his trips mostly to Italy and Greece now. Uncle George's son, William, is the one who takes the more adventurous journeys along the ancient trading routes through Samarkand, the Himalayas, and on to China."

"Is William as clever as his father?"

"Oh, yes. The men in my family are all very smart."

"The ladies, too," he said. "I clearly saw that, especially in you."

Tulip appeared surprised. "You did?"

"Oh, yes. It was obvious in the liveliness of your eyes. You have no idea how excruciating it can be when trying to make conversation with someone who looks back at you with vapid eyes. If I try to broach any topic that is remotely intellectual, they look at me as though I am talking gibberish."

"Oh, that is awful."

He winced. "Excruciating, as I said. But do go on, you were telling me about the Farthingale fabrics."

She laughed. "And you find this topic fascinating?"

He nodded. "Yes, I do."

Mostly, he enjoyed hearing Tulip speak.

She had an inquisitive mind and was smarter than she gave herself credit for. But this was most likely because going about in Society was difficult for her. The false facades, schemes, and manipulations were not suited to her temperament.

They weren't suited to his, either.

Nor did he have any patience for gentlemen like Lord Caruthers who took pride in never doing anything worthwhile, and yet, felt themselves worthy above all others.

"My uncles used to send me bolts of their prettiest cloths and I would sew gowns for myself and my aunt. The Italian velvets are my favorite, I think. The colors are so striking, the deep reds and dark greens. The exquisite blacks and these magnificent blues. And they are so soft and warm. Of course, once I arrived here, none of my gowns would do."

"Why not?"

She grinned. "You are no London dandy, are you? My gowns were stylish enough for Somerset but never the height of fashion. They would never pass muster here in London."

"I doubt any man would care or notice the difference," he said with a snort. "We look at the girl, not at what she is wearing. Forgive me if I sound crude, but let this come as a warning to you. A man's object is to get the girl *out* of the gown, not just stand around and admire her in it."

She blushed. "I assume this is what Caruthers meant to do."

"Yes," he said, suppressing his irritation with that oaf.

"And you?"

He arched an eyebrow. "Oh, yes. But it is not something I would ever act upon outside the bonds of marriage. You will always be safe with me and I will always respect you. There's the difference between me and Caruthers."

They were now approaching the Denby Arms and he was looking forward to sharing a pleasant meal in Tulip's company.

An elegantly garbed steward came forward to greet them.

Tulip ought to have been used to lavish luncheons and teas by now, but it did not dampen her delight upon entering the hotel's dining room and viewing the sumptuous displays of sweets and savory treats.

There was a refreshing liveliness about her as she took it all in.

This was one of the many things Alex liked about her.

He was a cynical clot.

But Tulip grabbed life with innocent enthusiasm.

Her eyes were wide as the steward escorted them past the abundant displays.

"Will this do, Your Grace?" the man asked, leading them toward a table by the window.

Alex glanced at Tulip who smiled brightly as she gave her approval.

Yes, she was a sunny thing.

This is why he thought they would make a good match.

She would balance his tendency to be dour.

"It is perfect," Alex said, for the table was slightly apart from the rest of the dining room and would afford them a measure of privacy as they continued their conversation.

They filled up on tea, buttered breads, and lemon tarts as they spoke of the travel plans he had made for them after the wedding.

He also encouraged her to tell him about her mother's family, the Hesters, who had raised her in Burnham after the death of her parents.

Conversation with Tulip was easy, but he had known it would be.

He was never a talkative man.

However, there were many topics that interested him.

Tulip was a bluestocking at heart and could match him in intellect and curiosity.

Even if she was not familiar with a particular topic, she still knew how to ask interesting questions and was always eager to learn more.

"That is odd," she said, her tone suddenly turning serious as she was about to put her teacup to her lips, "do you know that man?"

Alex turned around and followed her gaze to a gentleman staring at them from the street corner.

"No." The fellow was dressed like a gentleman, but Alex had an excellent memory for faces and knew he had never seen him before. "How about you, Tulip? Recognize him?"

"No." She set down her teacup and frowned. "He's been staring at you these past five minutes."

"At me? And not you?" After all, Tulip was beautiful, even though she did not seem to realize it.

"He's been studying *you*. I am certain of it."

"Excuse me, I'll be right back." Tulip was not a trained investigator and might be wrong about this, but he would find out soon enough when he confronted the man.

Why was he standing there spying on him?

Alex set aside his table linen and rose.

Tulip gasped. "What are you going to do to him?"

"Just have a friendly conversation," Alex assured her, his thoughts no longer on their wedding plans but on finding out this gentleman's purpose.

The fellow had darted out of sight by the time Alex walked out of the hotel to confront him.

He glanced up and down the street, then halted at one of the hotel windows and peered inside the tea room where Tulip was seated. She gestured that the man had run across the street and disappeared into the park.

Alex nodded and walked back inside.

The steward bustled over to him as he resumed his seat. "Your Grace, is there a problem?"

"No, just thought I saw someone I knew." He settled his account and escorted Tulip to his waiting carriage.

"Tulip, are you certain he was not looking at you?" he asked, assisting her into his conveyance.

"Quite certain." She leaned back against the soft leather squabs. "I could have sworn he was looking straight at you, as though he knew you. Was he a Davenport relation, perhaps? At first glance, there appeared to be a slight resemblance."

Alex grunted, and then took a moment to question his driver. "Trent, did you notice anyone peering into the tea room from the street?"

"No, Your Grace. My apologies, but I was instructed to drive the carriage to the mews and wait until summoned by one of the hotel stewards."

"Yes, of course." He climbed in and settled in the seat opposite Tulip. "So, you think the man was a relation of mine?"

"There was definitely a resemblance between the two of you, although he was not nearly as tall or handsome as you."

He laughed. "If he is one of my Havers cousins, I'm sure he'll come around soon to beg money out of me."

"He had better make it quick, for we'll be off to Somerset within a matter of days. Your Grace, there is something important we have yet to discuss."

"Go ahead," he said with a nod as the carriage got underway. But he knew what it was, for her expression gave her away.

The bedchamber.

Their sleeping arrangements.

In truth, he hadn't known quite how to raise the topic with her.

It did not seem proper to chat about such a thing over tea and biscuits in a public tea room.

Since she was now determined to raise it, he listened.

Her face turned crimson and she cleared her throat. "Are we to…well, the sleeping…you see?"

"Are you trying to ask me if we are to share a bed?" He certainly wanted to, but that was a lot to demand of Tulip considering how their betrothal had come about. "The choice is entirely up to you."

"It is?" Her eyes widened, obviously not expecting his answer.

"Yes."

It would not take them long to arrive on Chipping Way, so he was not going to delay in resolving the matter. "I hope that we will. I understand that it is not common for dukes and duchesses to share quarters. Also, a two-day betrothal and then rushing into marriage is not ideal circumstances, is it?"

"No, not ideal," she said with a wince. "Poor Aunt Sophie."

"I am less worried about her than I am of you. She is merely throwing us a party, something she has done for your family fairly often over the years, I expect." He leaned forward and took her hands in his. "Marriage is new to both of us, and has created an immediate upheaval to our lives. We will soon settle as newlyweds in Somerset. I'll give you all the time you need, Tulip. Just know that I would like us to share a bed once you are ready."

"I hadn't thought to ask, but are we to share quarters while traveling to Somerset?"

"Yes, but that is for your protection. I do not think it is safe for you to be in a room by yourself in any of those coaching inns. It will be one room for us, but I will set a pallet for myself on the floor, if you are reluctant to share the bed."

"I see."

He released her hands and leaned back against the squabs.

"Something more for you to contemplate. No answer needed yet."

"All right." She looked out the window as his carriage turned onto Chipping Way. Her cousins, Violet and Marigold, were on the street conversing with each other. "I'm going to miss them."

"Your family has very strong bonds."

She nodded. "I liked being able to walk next door or just across the street to chat with my cousins. We'll be rather isolated at Thornwycke Hall."

"It might not be so bad. We'll be forced to rely on each other, and this could strengthen our bonds of marriage," he pointed out.

"Yes." She nibbled her lip. "But it is also a reason to take it slow and not leap into something we might regret as we get to know one another better. Don't you think?"

Actually, he thought the opposite.

Their isolation was enough reason to go all in, leap straight into that fire. Trust each other, and hope for the best. Sometimes, closing one's eyes and jumping in was the most sensible thing to do.

But Alex knew Tulip had been burned by her impulsive decision to ask Caruthers for a first kiss and was not looking to repeat that mistake.

He groaned inwardly.

Being close to Tulip and not touching her was going to be agony for him.

He wasn't certain why he felt this strong desire for her.

He'd never felt this way about anyone before.

These amorous feelings had taken him quite by surprise and he was still trying to understand them.

What made Tulip stand apart from the other young ladies he had met?

He observed that Violet, Marigold, and Tulip could have been triplets, they looked so much alike. And yet, his heart did not beat faster when looking at Violet or Marigold, two obviously pretty ladies.

The three of them had the same shade of dark hair that curled in the same way. They had big eyes framed by sooty, black lashes, although Violet's were a pale lavender while Marigold and Tulip had striking blue eyes.

Yet, one glance at Tulip's dazzling eyes and hesitant smile had been all it took to capture his heart.

And then months of frustration because Tulip ran from him whenever she saw him approaching.

There would be no running from him now, he hoped.

After seeing her to the door, and greeting her cousins as they scurried over to Tulip, he returned to the carriage and instructed his driver to take him past the Davenport townhouse in Belgravia before heading to his apartment in Bloomsbury where he still resided. "Aye, Your Grace."

His carriage rolled away from Chipping Way.

He had chosen not to move out of his Bloomsbury apartment and take up residence in Belgravia for several reasons.

First, his apartment was large and comfortable, and more than met his needs.

Second, Bloomsbury itself was a lively, student area where taverns stayed open late and he could always find a meal at odd hours.

His investigative work often kept him out scouring the streets of London into the wee hours, so it was much simpler to sit in a quiet corner of the tavern and eat whatever was on the day's menu rather than attempt to make anything for himself.

Of course, he had a housekeeper.

But the poor woman had no way of knowing his schedule when he did not know it himself.

Having her come in for a few hours daily to clean his apartment, restock the basics needed for a proper home, and tend to his dirty clothes and linens was enough for him.

He stared out the window as he rode along the park toward Belgravia and wondered what he should do with the once elegant Davenport townhouse that was becoming an eyesore for his neighbors. Another reason he hadn't bothered to move in was because it was rather shabby and would require considerable refurbishing before it rose to the standards worthy of a duke.

He had inherited a small staff along with the townhouse and chose to keep them on for now because an empty house would attract thieves. Also, he was a working man and could not see himself dismissing others who probably needed their jobs to support their families.

He had not spoken of this to Tulip, but knew she would approve.

As for the townhouse itself, the structural bones were good.

The servants quarters and kitchen areas were also in far better condition than the rest of the house because no one trespassed in those areas except for the servants who had a respect for property.

Everything else within the house that had been touched by a Davenport was a wreck. There was a grand staircase that was not so grand at the moment. Doors were scratched. Floors were gouged. The walls were chipped of paint, and there were rips and stains in the wallpaper.

It was as though animals had resided in the main part of the house.

Not much of a surprise.

The Davenport dukes were mostly animals.

In truth, this troubled him very much.

His mother had done her best to keep him away from the Davenport influence, but it could not be denied that he closely resembled that side in looks.

Indeed, the family resemblance was surprisingly strong among the male line.

The man Tulip had noticed staring at him through the window at the Denby Arms could very well have been a relation of his.

Drat.

He needed to learn more about his family.

And he knew just where to get reliable information on them in the shortest amount of time.

No one was a better source than the tiny terror who struck fear among the *ton* elite, Lady Phoebe Withnall. The lady was not merely well connected, but had a better web of spies and informants than the Home Office itself.

He knew of several constables who relied on her assistance whenever they were puzzled by a particular crime, especially one that involved the Upper Crust.

He had spoken to her on one or two occasions.

No secrets were safe from her.

After checking on the Davenport townhouse, talking to the servants to see if anything was needed urgently and being assured all was in order, he strode back to his carriage. They seemed to be a good staff, and had walked him through the rooms of the house with a sense of pride and obvious care.

Even though the townhouse itself was a bit of a rambling wreck, the staff was organized, efficient, and presented him with a workable budget for the coming months.

The monthly allowance he had already authorized for them would do the trick.

One less thing to worry about.

"Back to Bloomsbury?" his driver asked as Alex approached the carriage and got ready to climb in.

"No, Trent. A change in plans."

"Aye, Your Grace. Where to next?"

CHAPTER 6

ALEX KNEW IT was not polite to drop in on Lady Withnall unannounced, but there wasn't time for niceties.

Her elderly butler's knees creaked louder than the front door when he opened it to allow Alex in. The ancient man then showed Alex into the well-appointed parlor, walking at such a slow pace that Alex wanted to lift him up and carry him forward because anything would be faster than this inching crawl.

"I shall let Lady Withnall know you are here to see her, Your Grace."

Alex stifled a groan as the man shuffled out again with all the speed of a sluggish turtle.

Dear heaven.

It would be dark by the time she was notified.

Of course, that was a complete exaggeration because Alex had more to do today and this made him particularly impatient.

After several minutes of pacing, he heard the familiar *thuck, thuck, thuck* of Lady Withnall's cane as she approached the parlor at a sprightly clip. Preceding her arrival was the scent of a lavender perfume she must have applied too thickly.

He coughed to dispel the overpowering scent.

"Blasted perfume bottle broke as I was dabbing some on this morning," she muttered, motioning for him to take a seat on her yellow silk settee. "I'll hit you with my cane if you cough again, Davenport. Is it still that strong?"

He laughed and chose not to answer, for denying it would

prove him a liar and telling her it smelled like a perfume workshop in here would earn him a wallop in the shins with her cane. "Thank you for agreeing to see me."

She took a seat in one of a pair of elegantly embroidered chairs beside the settee. "Go on then, tell me what information you are seeking this time."

"It's about the Davenports."

She arched an eyebrow. "Your own family?"

He nodded as he settled his large frame on the delicate settee. "I have ignored them all my life."

"With good reason," she said with a *harrumph*.

"But I need to be better prepared now that I have more than myself to think about."

She smiled. "Ah, yes. Congratulations, dear boy. I heard about the stir you and Tulip Farthingale caused last night. What a naughty thing you did, kissing her in front of everyone. But I suppose you saw the opportunity and seized it. I just received a note from Sophie Farthingale inviting me to your wedding. You don't waste time, do you?"

He grinned. "Not when I know what I want."

"What happened to bring this about?"

He told her about Caruthers, and how he saw no alternative but to step in.

"Quite chivalrous of you. But then, you were always hoping for a chance with Tulip, weren't you?"

He grunted. "Yes. How did you know? I did not think I was that obvious."

"You weren't, but it wasn't hard for me to tell. Anyone with excellent observational skills could have discerned it. Of course, no one is as skilled as I am. I knew it the instant I spotted the two of you together."

"From that first moment?" He shook his head and grunted. "What gave me away?"

"Well, as I said, I am never fooled. It was in the way you glanced at her, each glance lingering just a moment too long."

This was true.

Whenever he saw her, it was as though the entire room lit up.

His pulses raced and his heart beat faster.

He could not get enough of her.

But no one should have realized it, for he thought he had perfected the ability to hide his feelings. As an investigator for the magistrate, he needed to keep his face expressionless while suspect after suspect lied to him and thought they had gotten away with their crimes.

He never wanted anyone to know what he was thinking or feeling.

"She likes you, too. But the Davenport reputation worries her."

He nodded. "She avoided me for months because of it."

Lady Withnall cast him a look of sympathy. "Yes, sadly. But now you are betrothed and she can no longer ignore you."

"I think we will be all right," he said, leaning forward. "I'll do my best to put her mind at ease about me. But I am worried about my relatives. Tulip and I were having tea at the Denby Arms a short while ago and there was a man watching us from the street. She thought he might have been a relation of mine because the man resembled me."

"Describe him further. I want more details."

Alex told Lady Withnall everything that Tulip had mentioned as well as the glimpse he'd got of the man before he disappeared into the park.

"That has to be your cousin, Harold Havers. He's the eldest son of your father's younger brother. Before you break your head trying to work down the family tree, just be aware he is the next in line should something happen to you before you have sons of your own."

"What do you know of him?"

"Very little." She then proceeded to give Alex a detailed history of his medieval ancestors, moved on to an account of those who had recently died, and brought him up to date on the currently living Davenport heirs.

Her *very little* was far more than he ever knew and proved he had made the right decision in coming to her for a quick study on his family.

"Harold has two younger brothers, Neddy and Barton," she

said, finishing up her account of his ancestry and the offshoots of his family tree. "They are all wastrels, just as their father, your father, and your mutual grandfather were before them. Your father also had two older brothers, one of whom died years ago. But the other one died recently as did his two sons."

"Yes, those are the suspicious deaths that occurred within quick succession and were reported to be accidental."

"It seems they were just that," she confirmed. "I would tell you if I had heard anything to the contrary. I think we were all assuming there must have been foul play because of the timing of these deaths. How can one not be concerned when your grandfather, uncle, and two cousins all passed within such a short period of time?"

He nodded. "Four deaths within five years."

"Like dominoes falling in a row. They were all tragic, of course. No one rejoices upon the untimely passing of another. But these men were up to their eyeballs in vices that only grew worse once they inherited the dukedom, for there was no one to stop their outrageous behavior once they held all the power."

"That is true," Alex remarked.

"So, I suppose it should not shock anyone that each met an early death through his own reckless depravity and carelessness."

"What were their specific vices?"

"I do not think that is relevant. As most good-for-nothing gentlemen, they were all sots, gamblers, and lecherous devils. But many of our government ministers exhibit those same deplorable traits and England miraculously manages to function," she said with a disdainful snort.

"And what about Harold, Neddy, and Barton's vices? Anything in particular that stands out?"

"They are just as bad as the other males in your family lineage. As I said, wastrels. Name the vice and they have it. I'm so sorry, Davenport. I wish I could point to one ancestor in recent history who was not greedy, lazy, or self-indulgent. There's no one other than you who has risen above the fray and become a decent person. Perhaps there is hope for future generations of Davenports now that you are duke and your offspring shall be next in line to inherit."

He hoped there would be offspring, but that meant Tulip had to trust him enough to allow him into her bed.

He had husbandly rights, of course.

But he had no intention of forcing her into doing anything she did not wish to do.

If they were to have a happy marriage, there first needed to be a strong foundation of trust established between them.

Mutual respect.

Lady Withnall smiled as though reading his thoughts.

This irked him, but he was not surprised she could see into his mind. After all, she was a master at this game. "There's a reason these Farthingale girls marry well, you know."

"What is the reason?" he asked, genuinely curious because it was quite a feat for a commoner to marry a man of rank. Yet, so many of these Farthingale females had accomplished this very thing.

Not only married well, but these were love matches that had grown into happy marriages over the years.

"Take Tulip, for example," Lady Withnall said. "What do you see when you look at her?"

Alex was not one to talk about his personal feelings, but he did not hold back with Lady Withnall. She probably knew all the answers already and was asking for his benefit and not hers. "I see a beautiful young lady who is also intelligent, honest, and compassionate," he said after giving it a moment's thought.

"Go on."

Did he have to say more?

He sighed and continued. "She values character over an impressive title. If she ever tells me that she loves me, I will know it is the truth because she is no liar. She is perhaps a little too honest. For this reason, she feels her mistakes deeply, especially if she believes she might have hurt someone because of her actions."

"Are we speaking of Caruthers now?"

"Yes, she places too much blame on herself for leading him on. She is kind to everyone, even that oaf who did not deserve it. She sincerely cares about others and wants to be good to them. I know she will be warm and loving to our children, should we have any. In time, I hope she will grow to love me, too."

Lady Withnall now cast him a doting smile. "I knew you were an admirable fellow. After all, you are descended from a once noble family. The Davenport dukes were among the most valiant warriors who defended our medieval kings. That valor was lost for several generations, until you."

He shook his head in dismissal. "I don't know about that. How does one retrieve a nobility that was lost probably over a century ago?"

"It is in you, Davenport. But you are worried that being drawn back into the Davenport fold will somehow corrupt you and bring out your vices." Lady Withnall had read his mind again and now wagged a finger at him. "No, you are nothing like them. Your mother was very brave in pulling you away from your father and grandfather's influence, and this has saved you."

He hoped so, for Tulip's sake.

"Since you have come to me not only for knowledge but for advice, let me give you a piece of it now. You will need to take care of Harold, Neddy, and Barton in order to protect yourself."

"How do you mean?" She wasn't suggesting more 'accidental' deaths, was she?

"Those three will destroy whatever is left of the Davenport dukedom if they ever get their hands on it. But you are the current title holder and must hold onto it fiercely."

"Easily done, so long as I remain alive," he muttered.

"Well, you must try your best to stay that way. Think about Tulip and your offspring. Your cousins are lazy and slothful, probably too lazy to devise a scheme to be rid of you. But even they can be pushed to desperation."

"And become murderers?"

"Anyone can be pushed too far. They might be tempted to contrive an accident for you because they have no source of income other than the allowance the last several dukes in the line gave them. That stream of revenue stopped when the last Davenport duke died a few months ago and you inherited the dukedom."

"Are you suggesting I continue to support those lazy louts?"

Of course, this is what Lady Withnall meant when she suggested he 'take care' of them. Not kill them. Just give them enough of a monthly allowance to keep them from getting off their lazy arses and plotting something sinister against him.

"Yes. As infuriating as it may be, you need to keep them under control. They will happily be bribed to remain as they are." The snowy-white curls on either side of her head bobbed as she shook her head to emphasize her point. "Your grandfather survived his long reign by paying off his four sons and all of his grandsons except for you. His surviving sons did the same. Although, I'm not sure whether your two cousins who inherited the title just before you kept up that practice. I expect they did. You ought to look into that as you study the Davenport ledgers."

"I also intend to read the coroner reports again to make certain I have overlooked nothing," Alex muttered. "Ordering them sent to me was one of the first things I did upon becoming duke."

"You are ever sensible," Lady Withnall said with a nod of approval. "Do you think there is something in them that you are missing? I will admit, I was also skeptical about those deaths, but I have heard nothing to contradict those reports."

"Nor have I. As soon as I received them, I pored over every detail but saw nothing that stood out as suspicious. Still, it sticks in my craw. Perhaps it is merely my investigative instincts that leave me unsettled. I have no proof of wrongdoing, but I will look deeper into the matter once I get my hands on the Thornwycke ledgers and see which family members were given an allowance and how much. I'll also look for anyone outside of the family receiving payments."

"Yes, it is always a good idea to follow the money," Lady Withnall observed with the arch of an eyebrow. "Perhaps those last three deaths would not have been ruled accidental had you been the one investigating. All the more reason to have a care and not rile those Havers cousins to action just yet."

Alex frowned, for Harold was only one death away – Alex's death – from inheriting the dukedom and that could be an overwhelming temptation. "So be it, at least for now. I'll hold my nose and maintain their allowance because nothing matters more to me than keeping Tulip safe."

"She will be. This is the right course, as distasteful as it is. You cannot have them plotting against you, especially while you are still new to the title and vulnerable. Do not underestimate your enemy."

"You just described them as lazy and slothful."

"Which is what they are. I do not think Harold, Neddy, or Barton had the brains to devise plots intricate enough to do away with each heir down the line and have no one suspect a thing. No, dear boy. You are dealing with idiots here. But that does not mean you can dismiss them. After all, they only need to hire someone clever enough to do the job they cannot do for themselves. So, give them an allowance, but just enough to meet their needs and no more. It would be the height of irony if they used *your* funds to hire someone to do *you* in."

"All right. I'll see what our grandfather was providing them by way of monthly allowance and match it."

"You are a sharp-eyed fellow. I have no doubt you'll be able to spot trouble before it arises and do all in your power to avert it."

"Perhaps, but can Tulip? I won't be with her at all times. She'll want to visit her friends and family in Burnham, and I have no intention of denying her that pleasure."

"Stay close to her as much as you can, at least for now."

He laughed with little mirth. "If she can stand to be around me."

"She will. Trust me when I say she likes you. She would not have agreed to marry you if she did not believe in her heart that love could flourish between you."

On that encouraging note, Alex left Lady Withnall and returned to his apartment in Bloomsbury.

He was surprised to see his friend, Julius Thorne, waiting at his door.

They exchanged friendly greetings.

"What brings you here, Julius?"

"My brothers and I received Sophie Farthingale's note inviting us to your wedding. Adela," he said, referring to Ambrose's wife, "and Gory immediately got on me to make certain you are properly outfitted for your wedding day."

He groaned. "I'm sure I have something suitable to wear."

"No, you do not. So you must come with me to Savile Row because there is not a moment to waste."

"Bollocks. Is this a jest?"

"Afraid not," Julius replied, his expression one of determination. "The wives have said you require proper garb and I have been tasked with enforcing their wishes. By the way, this is a lesson I am certain you will learn soon enough. When your wife insists on something, just go with it. You will be happier in the long run."

Alex had his doubts. "You let your wife set the rules?"

"No, we agree on them together. But Gory rarely asks anything special of me. So when she does, I know it is important to her and have no problem accepting to do whatever she needs of me. See? This is how a good marriage works."

"I'll take your word for it." He shook his head and laughed in disbelief.

"Seriously, Davenport. Just think about it and you will see that I am right."

Well, his friend was no fool.

Nor was Julius the sort to be led about by the nose.

"Very, well. I appreciate the advice. Tulip and I obviously have a lot to work out, and I would hate to start off on the wrong foot with her. I have been on my own for too long and have no idea how a proper marriage works."

"Tulip comes from one of the best families. She'll teach you, and will appreciate your honesty in requesting her help. Just don't be a stubborn arse and resist what she is telling you. She isn't the sort to turn you into a puppet to appease her whims. If anything, she will go out of her way to sacrifice for you."

Alex merely nodded, preferring to say nothing.

This would be something new for him, for he had turned very much into a lone wolf in all aspects of his life, both personal and professional.

Having Tulip as a partner in marriage might take serious adjustment.

And here was his first test, acquiring wedding attire befitting a duke.

Spending the remainder of the afternoon being measured and pinned by one of London's finest tailors was not what Alex had planned, but there was little else he needed to do today now that the important matters, the letter of intent and the marriage license, were out of the way.

He listened as Julius argued with the tailor who was insisting he could not possibly have his wedding outfit ready by tomorrow afternoon. "My brother," Julius said, referring to the Duke of Huntsford, "has authorized me to double your fee. You seem to think we are negotiating this arrangement, Mr. Chesney. There is no negotiation. Take the offer or we walk out and find another tailor who will do this for us."

Since the Thorne brothers had been good customers of Chesney & Sons for many years, Alex expected the tailor would grumble some more and then agree because he did not want to lose their business.

"All right, double fee," Chesney said, proving Alex's expectation correct. "Come back tomorrow afternoon, but not before three o'clock."

Julius smiled. "Done."

"What if I have a meeting at that time?" Alex asked, just to be contrary as they finished with the tailor and walked out of the shop.

Julius shook his head. "I don't care if you are scheduled to meet with Lord Liverpool or a member of the royal family. Beg out. This is more important."

Alex groaned. "Gory really has you hopping to do her bidding."

"No, she does not. Although, I will admit that I am getting you properly attired out of love for her and my friendship for you. And here's another bit of advice…"

Alex stopped him before Julius could offer it. "Do you hear yourself? You are talking like an old married man. Yet, you and Gory are still newlyweds."

"What can I say? I'm a fast learner. Plus Octavian," he said, also referring to the middle Thorne brother who was of highest rank within the Admiralty, "taught me well. He happens to be married to Syd, a very strong-willed woman."

"All the Thorne wives are strong-willed, especially yours," Alex muttered, for he had dealt with Gory during his investigative work, and she was just as dogged as he was when on the trail of criminals.

"Well, yes. None of them will shirk from a confrontation. For this reason, my brothers and I thought there were oftentimes when marriage might be a battle. But what actually happened is that we rarely fight with our spouses. Loving one's wife, as I love Gory, means that there is nothing worth fighting over that matters more than her. If she is asking for something important to her, then I'll agree to it. But the same applies for her. She will agree to my wishes if they are important to me. It is never worth fighting or holding resentment over the little things. Never go to bed angry with each other."

Alex took in the advice, but knew he and Tulip were not even close to achieving that level of commitment to each other.

"We've been fortunate, I suppose," Julius continued as they climbed into Alex's carriage to return to Bloomsbury where Julius had left his driver and carriage, "that we haven't yet encountered anything big to tear us apart. I don't think we ever will."

"I'm glad you and Gory have such a strong marriage. It is too soon to know what will happen between me and Tulip. That Davenport dark cloud of doom is going to hang over our heads for a while, I fear."

"I suppose it is her fear, too. This is why she avoided you all these months."

Alex arched an eyebrow. "Ah, you noticed her constantly running away from me?"

"Hard to overlook. But fate stepped in and you are now betrothed to her. Heed my advice. Do not ruin your chances for a good marriage because you are too prideful to give in."

When they returned to Bloomsbury, Alex noticed the same man who had been watching him at the Denby Arms was now seated at a pub across the street from his residence. "Bollocks."

"What's wrong?" Julius followed his gaze. "Who are you looking at?"

"That fellow in the green jacket has been following me around for much of the day. He was at the Denby Arms earlier. I thought he was eyeing Tulip but she seemed certain he was interested in me and not her."

"Guess she was right," Julius said as their carriage drew to a halt. "What are you going to do about him?"

"Buy him an ale and chat, I suppose," Alex said. "I think he is a cousin of mine, Harold Havers."

"What do you think he wants from you?"

Alex gave a mirthless laugh. "Money, of course. Our grandfather gave him and his brothers an allowance. The subsequent dukes did the same, I believe. That stopped when I inherited. I expect he wants me to restore it."

"Will you?"

"Yes, Lady Withnall suggests that I do."

Julius regarded him with some surprise. "That little termagant? How is it any of her business?"

"I stopped by to see her earlier today because I wanted to learn more about my family history. Who better than Lady Withnall to ask? Is there any secret or scandal she does not know about?"

Julius laughed. "She's scary the way she noses out trouble, like a wild boar on the scent for truffles. She'll dig through that dirt and find the secret no matter how deeply it is hidden. Are you sure you want to approach your cousin now?"

"Yes, may as well get it out of the way."

"I'll come with you," Julius said as they now stepped down from the carriage.

But Alex held him back. "Wait here. Keep a lookout and shout a warning if you see anyone else approaching me and Harold. He has two brothers, both of them worthless."

"Botheration, are you going to pay them, too?"

"Yes, I think it is prudent to follow Lady Withnall's advice for now." He scanned the crowd seated at the pub's outdoor tables for men who resembled Harold or himself but no one caught his eye. He then peered up and down the street, paying particular attention to partially shadowed doorways for anyone standing in them who looked suspicious.

It seemed safe enough, so he approached the man in the green jacket. "Mind if I join you?"

He did not await a reply before pulling out a chair and settling in it.

The man cast him a wry smile. "Sure, sit down."

"Care to introduce yourself?"

"As I am sure you suspect, I am your cousin. Harold Havers at your service."

Alex nodded. "Why are you following me around?"

"Hoping for the chance to speak to you."

Alex glanced around once more. "Where are your brothers?"

"Unfortunately, Neddy and Barton are indisposed at the moment."

Probably drank too much last night and were still sleeping it off, he surmised. "Are you here for yourself or speaking on their behalf?"

"Speaking for all of us."

Alex folded his arms across his chest and nodded. "What is it you want?"

"Our allowance restored. You cannot expect us to survive on thin air," he said with an aura of haughty indignation that rankled Alex.

But he expected no less from his cousin who had been taught he deserved everything despite having contributed nothing. "You could find work for yourselves."

Harold's eyes rounded and he drew back as if slapped. "We are gentlemen. How are we to hold our heads up high if we are *employed*?"

"As I was for all these years?"

"And we mocked you for it," his cousin said with disdain.

Gad, did he really have to give them anything?

But Lady Withnall had advised him to do so, at least until he had solidified his position as duke, consolidated his power, and put trusted people in place to alert him to whatever his cousins might be doing. Of course, he also needed trusted people to assist in the restoration of the Davenport holdings. "Best to keep them quiet and concentrate on important matters," she had warned.

He placed Tulip and their marriage at the top of his list in importance.

What would all his work be worth if his family interfered and he could not gain her love?

It pained him to admit he agreed with Lady Withnall. "I'll have your allowances restored on one condition…"

"And what is that?" Harold asked, sounding indignant once again.

"When I am in London, you and your brothers are to be elsewhere."

The lout slammed his fist on the table. "That is outrageous! Where are we supposed to be?"

Alex arched an eyebrow. "I don't care, just not in Town when I am here. But take heart, I do not intend to spend much time in London. Parliamentary duties and an occasional visit to see good friends. That's all."

"Fine, we'll go to Somerset whenever you are here."

And sponge off him at Thornwycke Hall?

He meant to reside there with Tulip.

No way in bloody blazes would he allow his wretched cousins anywhere near her. "No, you are to stay out of Somerset. That is the other part of my condition. If you want your allowance to continue, then you are *never* to step foot there."

"Never?" Harold slammed his fist on the table again. "Are you mad? You are marking off the entire shire? What if we wish to follow our friends to Bath?"

"Then write to me and ask for permission. Those are my terms. Do you want your allowance or not?"

"What a bastard you are," he muttered. "Does this mean we must leave London now?"

"No, I'll be leaving shortly. There's nothing you or your brothers need to do for the moment. What's it to be?"

"Pig," Harold said, kicking his chair back as he rose so that it tipped over and knocked into the man seated at the table next to theirs.

The poor fellow had been minding his own business and enjoying an ale, but now turned angrily toward them.

Alex apologized on his cousin's behalf.

Thankfully, this mollified the man.

Not that his cousin cared.

The lout was incensed Alex had tacked on conditions to his allowance. "We'll take the deal," he grumbled and stormed off.

Alex watched him bull his way through the tables of patrons, angrily elbowing all in his path aside. He was heedless of who he bumped into or the ale that was spilled.

"Ah, family," Julius said, righting the chair Harold had overturned and taking his seat. "I heard what he called you. Those fellows deserve nothing."

"I know, but I don't need to be fighting them while I am also trying to restore the Davenport holdings to profitability. However, it is more for Tulip's sake. I don't want them around us while we are also trying to make a go of our marriage."

"Sensible." Julius glanced at his watch. "Speaking of marriage, I had better get home to Gory. I'll meet you at the tailor's tomorrow at three. Any plans for tonight?"

"No. Tulip and the Farthingales have been invited to dine with their neighbor, Lady Eloise Dayne."

"Do not be surprised to find an invitation waiting for you at home. It's probably sitting on your entry hall table as we speak," he said, motioning across the street to his apartment.

Alex had been looking forward to a quiet night, an ale in hand and a good book to read. But that was not likely to happen now. "I'll see you tomorrow, Julius."

He watched his friend ride off in the Thorne carriage.

Only then did he march into his apartment.

Just as Julius had predicted, there was the invitation waiting for him on the small table in his modest entry hall.

It sat there on a silver tray.

He was about to reach for it when the little hairs on the back of his neck began to prickle.

Something felt off.

"Mrs. Gayle?" he called to his housekeeper.

When he received no response, he called out to her again.

Still nothing.

His heart beat a little faster.

Had something happened to her?

He was about to go in search of her when he heard someone humming a tune just outside the front door.

He let out a breath of relief, for Mrs. Gayle was coming up the walk with a shopping bag in hand.

"Your Grace, is anything wrong?" she asked, marching into the hall and immediately noticing his frown.

"I don't know." He took her gently by the elbow and escorted her back outside. "Wait here. I think someone might be in the apartment. Let me investigate first."

She put a hand to her throat. "Oh, Your Grace. Do be careful."

After years working for the London magistrate, he had been trained to always be on his guard.

He knew how to handle himself in a fight.

"Don't worry about me. Chances are, if there was an intruder, he fled when he heard me open the door."

Alex's residence had two bedrooms upstairs, one of which had an ample dressing room attached to it. The other, he used as a study. The main floor contained a spacious parlor, a kitchen with a large pantry, and a dining room that could accommodate a party of up to twenty. Having a dining room of that size was quite ironic since he mostly kept to himself and never had anyone over to dine with him.

He made a quick search of the downstairs rooms, needing no more than a cursory inspection of the parlor, dining room, kitchen, and pantry to know there was no one lurking in them. There weren't really any places a man could hide in those rooms.

Nor was there anything of notable value worth stealing.

He quietly made his way upstairs and opened the door to his study with care.

"Bollocks," he muttered, immediately noticing the disaster made of it.

Papers that had been neatly stacked on his desk were strewn all over the floor.

Desk drawers had been yanked out and were also lying on the floor overturned.

Was this what Harold meant when he had said his brothers were indisposed?

"Of course," he muttered, raking a hand through his hair, furious and frustrated that those louts had gotten the better of him.

While their eldest brother was talking to him, the younger ones had broken into his apartment to search for money or any valuables that could easily be stuffed into their pockets and later sold.

Or was it only documents they wanted?

It did not appear so, because they had merely shuffled through the papers on his desk and those tucked in his drawers before tossing them aside.

They were not going to find any sensitive documents in here, for he kept those in a hidden compartment under his bedroom floorboards.

Thankfully, his account books were left untouched and no bank drafts had been removed from his ledger. This confirmed they were looking for things that could easily be sold.

He released a breath, relieved the letter of intent he'd signed this morning concerning his betrothal had remained in his solicitor's office for safeguarding.

He now patted the breast pocket of his jacket to make certain his marriage license was still there.

Yes, it was.

Staring at the mess, he decided it was safest to carry the license with him at all times for these next two days until the wedding.

He'd kept one hundred pounds in a decorative jar on the fireplace mantel. The jar was shattered and the money missing.

No surprise there.

Was this all his cousins were looking for?

Another thought struck him.

Would they next attempt to break into the Davenport townhouse in Belgravia? Well, that would be harder to do because he kept a small staff there, so there would always be someone present.

He had stopped by that residence a few hours ago and found all to be in order. His staff was already on the alert for thieves, but it would not hurt to send them a warning about his cousins.

He went downstairs and walked back outside. "Come in, Mrs. Gayle."

He led her upstairs and showed her the mess made of his study. "Oh, dear me! This is such a nice neighborhood. What fiends could have done this?"

His cousins, of course.

Well, he would deduct one hundred pounds from their next allowance.

Let them yelp, he didn't give a rat's arse.

Mrs. Gayle set aside her shopping bag and assisted him in cleaning up the mess they had made of his paperwork. "Shall I look for a constable and report this crime, Your Grace?"

"No, it's all right. I know who did this." After all, he had worked in the magistrate's office for years as their top investigator and easily spotted the clues. "They won't be troubling us again."

Because a stern warning from him that he would terminate their allowance if so much as a button went missing from his home or any of the Davenport residences ought to do the trick.

"What is this world coming to?" Mrs. Gayle muttered while scooping up his papers. "Brazen thievery in broad daylight. Well, I never." She was still mumbling to herself as she walked down to the kitchen to put away the shopping items.

Alex debated whether to attend Lady Dayne's party.

It was a hastily sent invitation and he could always plead that he hadn't opened it until too late.

The ransacking of his study was a plausible excuse.

Yet, to not attend could be considered rude and might give Tulip reason to doubt him.

He washed up and readied himself, resolving to attend Lady Dayne's dinner party. However, he was going to stop first on Bow Street and call on Homer Barrow, the experienced runner he had worked with on several investigations, the most noteworthy being the murder of Gory's uncle.

His primary concern was to have the Belgravia residence

belonging to the Davenport dukes guarded.

Even though Alex would send a messenger over there to put the servants on alert, he also wanted the place watched by a professional investigator. Homer Barrow and his runners would know how to handle his idiot cousins should they decide to break in during the wee hours of the night and ransack the place.

Was there a doubt they would attempt it?

After getting away with no more than a hundred pounds from his Bloomsbury residence, they would want more.

Any Davenport silver or artwork of value would be found at the Belgravia townhouse instead of here in his apartment. Of course, this assumed his predecessors had not already sold off the real valuables and replaced them with fakes.

Which was quite likely, for their vices were expensive.

However, another concern loomed in his mind, and that was Tulip. Should he engage Homer Barrow to protect her for these next few days until they left London?

He did not want Caruthers bothering her or thinking to abduct her.

Was she at risk from his cousins, too?

CHAPTER 7

AFTER MEETING WITH Homer Barrow, Alex headed to Lady Eloise Dayne's dinner party. He arrived late and gave no reason, but was nonetheless welcomed graciously by the dowager and her guests. This party was more of a casual family gathering since most of those in attendance were Farthingale family members.

This was a new experience for Alex, and one he found himself enjoying despite his initial reluctance.

Lady Dayne introduced him to several Farthingales he had never met before.

They all greeted him cheerfully, although he wasn't certain why they should be so quick to accept him.

Perhaps Tulip had spoken kindly about him.

He hoped so.

Lady Dayne's grandson, Gabriel, took him aside as soon as introductions all around were completed. He was married to John and Sophie's daughter, Daisy. "My wife was the one spying through the keyhole who toppled into John's study when he yanked open the door after your betrothal discussions were concluded."

Alex grinned.

So did Gabriel. "She's a snoopy bit of goods."

"It seems to be a Farthingale trait," Alex remarked.

Gabriel nodded. "She and the other cousins were worried about Tulip and just wanted to protect her. I hope you can forgive them."

"I cannot be angry with any of them for caring about Tulip."

"Glad you are so understanding," he said, giving Alex a friendly pat on the back. "And do not mind John or his brothers if they frown at you. In truth, they like you but are not ready to show it yet. John wanted to spear hot pokers through me when I was first courting Daisy. They all thought I was the vilest, most loathsome creature."

"Were you?" Alex asked.

He nodded. "But it was only a cover. I was on a dangerous assignment for the Crown. Daisy saw me clearly for who I was and caught hell from everyone for believing in me. That's a strength in these Farthingale females. They have excellent instincts."

Which was why Tulip had spent months avoiding him, Alex knew.

But he must have done something right because she had started to thaw toward him over the course of these summer months and now agreed to marry him.

She would have chosen to endure the scandal rather than enter into an unwanted marriage if she still held doubts about him.

"The family came around once the truth was revealed and I was awarded an earldom," Gabriel continued. "So, you are way ahead of the game in comparison."

Alex laughed. "That's comforting."

As it turned out, titles were not used to address each other throughout the evening.

Despite being an earl, Eloise's grandson was merely referred to as Gabriel.

Dillie's husband, the Duke of Edgeware, was merely Ian.

In truth, Alex felt far more comfortable being addressed in this casual manner.

He liked it very much when Tulip called him by his given name, something he should have asked her to do before this evening.

After all, they had shared a kiss and were now betrothed.

Since this dinner party was far more informal than most *ton* gatherings, he also had the chance to converse with Tulip at length because they were seated beside each other at the dinner table.

"You look nice, Tulip."

She blushed and glanced down at her gown, a vibrant yellow silk that somehow brought out the lovely blue of her eyes. "Thank you, Alex. So do you."

He grinned. "Thank you."

Her hair was styled in an elegant chignon that followed the natural wave of her hair. The style was simple and quite becoming on her.

He debated whether to tell her about his encounter with Harold or the ransacking of his residence.

Ultimately, he decided that she needed to know.

It would not be fair to let her think there were no risks involved in marrying him. Well, she knew very well there were risks because she was more familiar with his relatives than he was.

He had gotten a dose of what worthless hounds these Davenports were just today.

Yes, he needed to be honest with her.

It would crush him to lose her, but she needed to be given the choice to back out of their wedding if this proved to be too much for her.

He waited until they had finished the soup course, a delicate onion broth designed to stimulate the palate, before he brought up the topic.

"Tulip, there's something I need to tell you," he said quietly as they watched the main courses being served. Those consisted of fish in a butter and white wine sauce, goose in a plum sauce, and honeyed ham. Roasted potatoes, peas in garlic and lemon, and glazed carrots were the accompaniments.

"Alex, you are frowning. What is wrong?"

He quickly told her all of it, his afternoon encounter with Harold Havers at the tavern across the street from his Bloomsbury apartment and the ransacking of his study.

She appeared genuinely distressed. "Do you think giving them their allowance will keep your cousins quiet?"

"I have no idea. But I do know that without it, they are more likely to turn to desperate measures."

"Beyond ransacking your study and stealing that one hundred pounds from you?" she remarked with indignation.

"Yes, because actually having to work for their livelihood is out of the question for them. They are *gentlemen*," he said, placing derogatory emphasis on the term.

He also told her about his visit with Lady Withnall. "She was the one who urged me to keep them on an allowance."

Tulip nodded. "It makes sense, I suppose. Do you think they will honor the conditions you imposed on them to stay out of Somerset?"

He winced. "No idea about that either."

"It was a good idea to include that restriction. Worth a try," she said with a nod of approval.

He waited for her to say something more, perhaps bring up the matter of their betrothal. He would not blame her if she suggested they put off the wedding or part ways altogether.

To his surprise, she made no mention of either possibility.

He took a deep breath and told her the last of it. "I hired Homer Barrow to keep watch on the Belgravia townhouse and on you, as well."

Her eyes widened as she stared at him.

She had the softest eyes.

Lovely eyes.

"Do you think I am in danger from your loutish cousins?"

"I don't know, but I am not about to take any chances. I did not rescue you from Caruthers just to toss you into greater danger."

"Have you spoken to my uncles about this?"

"No, I wanted to discuss it with you first."

Her expression softened and she smiled at him. "Alex, thank you. To be honest, you've surprised me."

"How so?"

"I thought it would take a while before you considered sharing your concerns with me. I know how private you are."

He shook his head and cast her a wry smile. "Julius gave me some advice this afternoon, a lecture on the rules of marriage he thought I sorely needed because I am used to being so much on my own. It isn't very hard, is it? Confiding in each other.

Discussing these problems."

"Being honest and keeping no secrets from each other? It is rather nice. I hope we do it often." However, she frowned.

"What is it, Tulip? Are you thinking we ought to end our betrothal?"

She glanced up at him in surprise, if the widening of her eyes was any indication. "No. The more I learn about you, the more I am grateful for your offer of marriage. Do *you* wish to end it? I seem to be an added burden you do not need at this time."

"No," he insisted. "You ease my burden, not add to it. I am happy with my choice of bride and would like to marry you. But John and the Farthingale elders might not feel the same. What will they think once they hear what happened?"

"Must you tell them?"

He sighed. "I think so. They'll be livid if they learn of it from others…and they will learn of it. Gossip spreads fast around London."

"That is true."

He placed a hand over hers. "John's own daughters gave him fits when making their debuts. Gabriel told me as much."

Tulip laughed softly. "Oh, yes. I shall tell you all the stories while we ride to Somerset. Poor John and Sophie. I don't know how they endured all the upheaval and excitement. There seemed to be danger at every turn."

"Danger? Seriously?"

She nodded. "We'll have hours to talk within the privacy of your carriage. I'm surprised Lady Withnall did not spill all the stories."

"She mentioned a few," he admitted. "She told me about Rose abducting her husband and Laurel almost trampling her husband with her horse."

"All true," Tulip said. "I suppose Lady Withnall wanted to provide you with ammunition should the family elders decide this betrothal was a mistake."

"She seems to think of everything."

"Because she likes you and has faith in you." Tulip cast him a determined look. "I will stand by you when you tell them. It is best if we present a united front."

"Then you are all right with marrying me?"

She nodded.

His heart felt lighter.

It was a ridiculously contented feeling, one he had not experienced before. This ran deeper than the satisfaction he felt when solving a crime.

This realization of no longer being alone in the world scared him and also elated him.

He was going to like having Tulip beside him.

In truth, he was eager to confide in her because she was always going to give him an honest and intelligent opinion.

He thought once more of Julius's words of advice.

Yes, he fully intended to follow them.

The Davenport aura was a dark one and even his mother, despite loving his father, had felt the need to run away.

He would take it very hard if he ever lost Tulip's love and support.

Having told Tulip of his concerns, they spent the rest of the meal discussing lighter topics.

After the dessert course, the ladies retreated to Lady Dayne's parlor for tea and sherry while the men remained at the dinner table enjoying their port and discussing important issues of the day.

He listened with half an ear, for his thoughts remained on Tulip.

"Come outdoors with me a moment," he said, approaching her as soon as the men had rejoined the ladies.

He felt the need to be alone with her before the party ended, for he intended to talk to John and his brothers about today's incidents once it did.

Things could get heated between him and her guardians.

If they were going to rescind their consent to the marriage, he wanted a taste of Tulip before they were forced to part.

Not that he meant to forget about marrying her.

He would simply wait the few months until she turned one and twenty, at which time she could decide for herself.

He took her by the hand and led her into Lady Dayne's garden.

"Oh, no," Tulip teased. "Another garden at midnight."

Alex chuckled. "You are quite safe with me."

"Safe? I hope not." Her eyes captured the silvery glow of moonlight and sparkled with mirth. "I would much rather be in danger of being kissed by you."

He laughed and gave her cheek a light caress.

The evening was warm and humid.

A light mist surrounded them as he drew her into the shadows of the lilac trees in Lady Dayne's garden and placed his arms around her.

The scent of grass and late summer blooms filled the air.

Alex bent toward her, inhaling the lavender scent of her skin that he found irresistible. He brought his lips to her neck and kissed her lightly there.

She tasted so sweet.

"Tulip," he whispered and brought his mouth down on her soft, plump lips with the desperate urgency of a famished soul.

She seemed to understand his turmoil.

And seemed to hold magic in her response, for she calmed him and at the same time excited him.

Was this real?

Could this last?

Or would their marriage prove cursed and destroy them both?

CHAPTER 8

"TULIP, YOU LOOK beautiful," her cousin Violet said, stepping back after helping her into her gown on the morning of her wedding.

"Davenport's tongue will roll to the floor," Marigold added, smiling in approval as she looked on. "Are you ready to marry that gorgeous man?"

Tulip merely shook her head because words failed her.

She stared at her reflection in the mirror, hoping her cousins were right and she might steal Alex's heart when he set eyes on her. They were to be married within the hour at St. Mary's Church, followed by the wedding breakfast to be held here, at John and Sophie's house on Chipping Way.

The household was astir with activity.

Everyone had been up before dawn, including Violet and Marigold who showed up shortly after sunrise determined to serve as her handmaidens.

The butterflies in Tulip's stomach were in a mad flutter and not only because this was her wedding day. This would also be her wedding *night* and she was completely unprepared for it despite having received advice from all her married cousins. Well, it hadn't been instructions so much as general statements to trust her husband and follow his lead, then an inordinate amount of giggles.

Just where was he supposed to lead her?

Someplace nice, she supposed.

The second kiss Alex had given her two days ago still lingered on her lips and in her heart. He'd kissed her with devastating effect, for it felt as though he'd held nothing back. His kiss had scorched her, leaving her marked as his, even though he had demanded nothing from her.

In fact, he had been the one to give all of his heart.

It was his willingness to openly put his own heart at risk that had won her over.

How could she do anything other than surrender?

That kiss had made her feel as though he loved her.

Or was he merely adept at kissing any lady as though he did love her?

Probably the latter because it was too soon for either of them to be certain of their feelings for each other.

But she hoped his kiss was real.

She was already on the way to falling in love with him.

Loving a Davenport was always going to be dangerous, but Alex was different.

He *had* to be different.

And now he was going to be her husband within the hour.

Their dowager aunt, Hortensia, marched into her bedchamber as her cousins were putting the last touches to her hair. No one knew just how old Hortensia was exactly, but she seemed to be as immortal as dragons and resembled one.

"You haven't touched your breakfast," she noted, instantly dominating the room by her mere presence.

Tulip put a hand to her stomach. "I dared not eat. I don't think I can hold anything down this morning."

Hortensia *harrumphed*. "I could have married a prince, you know. But the man was a complete idiot. Davenport appears to have some brain matter between his ears."

"He's handsome, too," Marigold said. "Almost as handsome as my Leo."

"And Romulus," Violet added, not wanting her handsome husband neglected.

"Silly girls," Hortensia remarked. "I don't know why I am so proud of you when you are little more than giggling geese."

They all hugged her because this was Hortensia's grumpy way of telling them all that she loved them.

"Enough of this nonsense," she said after giving them each a kiss on the cheek. "Stop dawdling and get into the waiting carriages."

Before Tulip knew it, they were on their way to the church.

She rode with John and Sophie who had taken on the role of parents and done a fine job of it, if anyone asked for her opinion.

She told them that she loved them and mentioned how much she appreciated all they had done for her.

John had tears in his eyes, for he was obviously quite sentimental about his family. It struck Tulip that Sophie was the perfect match for him because the real work of holding the family together fell to her. She did it remarkably well and usually without complaint, although Tulip knew there had been some fretful and even argumentative moments when their daughters had taken their turns on the marriage mart and unleashed havoc.

Getting caught kissing a man in a garden was nothing compared to the trouble John and Sophie's daughters had gotten themselves into.

Alex was already at St. Mary's, impatiently pacing by the massive front doors of the church.

He smiled as their carriage arrived.

She smiled and waved at him.

"Tulip," he said in a whisper as he helped her down, "how are you holding up?"

She laughed softly and let out a breath. "I am shaking all over."

"You look beautiful."

"So do you...I mean, you look incredibly handsome."

He grinned and helped her smooth out her gown as she fussed with it when a sudden gust of wind threatened to blow everything out of order.

The gown was a beautiful cream silk and lace creation that she had meant to wear to one of the grand balls at the start of the Season but it had not been ready in time. Wearing it now for her wedding was a much better use for this stunning gown. "It is hitting me now that we are about to be bound to each other for the rest of our lives."

"Yes, I know. I'm looking forward to it." He held out his hand to show there was not a single tremor. "See, no qualms about marrying you. Once you are my duchess, you will never lack for anything. I will always take care of you."

"And I'll do the same for you," she replied in earnest.

He cast her an affectionate smile. "I don't think it's supposed to work that way. I'm the one who will be pledging to protect you and keep you safe from harm."

"Should I not do the same for you?"

"Not if it places you in danger."

"But aren't we supposed to support each other through the good and the bad?"

"Yes, lend support. But you are not to die for me. You are not signing on to military duty," he remarked, his voice holding a trace of irritation that was not really aimed at her, although he obviously did not want her risking her life for him.

He released a lengthy breath. "You Farthingales are an odd breed. Certainly different from the *ton* elite."

"Because we wish to honor our vows?"

After a moment, he leaned forward and gave her a light kiss on the cheek. "If you wish to look after me and fuss over me, then who am I to complain? I'm sorry if I came across as tense and inconsiderate just now. I've never had the tender ministrations of a woman before."

"And it unsettles you?" Since he was a very private person, she did not think he would care for too much fussing.

"I'm just not used to it."

"I won't be too overbearing." She was not the sort to spend her waking hours doing nothing but thinking of him or waiting upon him since she had her own dreams and desires to fulfill.

She wanted his support and approval.

But she was hardly going to ignore his needs.

However, he was the sort of man who preferred mostly being left to his own thoughts. "I'm sure your mother took good care of you."

"In truth, she did not." He shook his head. "She meant to, but she could not. Her health failed soon after removing me from the Davenport influence. She did not survive very long afterward. I've made my own way ever since."

"I'm so sorry, Alex," she said, her heart tightening because she understood how difficult it must have been for him, merely a boy at the time, to see her succumbing to ill health. Then to be left alone in the world, the only one who loved him and fought to protect him, gone.

Losing her own parents had been painful for her, but she had immediately gained the Farthingale clan and the Hester clan as her protectors and had never once felt unloved. Quite the opposite, she was doted upon and cared for by both families. "Well, you will have me to look after you now," she assured him.

He nodded. "That sounds nice, but you must promise never to put yourself in harm's way for me. This is not how I ever want you to care for me."

She frowned. "Do you really think there will be danger? From your cousins?"

"Harold Havers and his brothers? No. That threat has been addressed for now. They have been drinking themselves into a stupor these past two days, ever since I restored their allowances." He placed his hand over hers as it rested on his forearm. "Do not mind me. I seem to find reasons to needlessly fret. The hour is growing late. Care to marry me?"

"Yes," she said with a gleam of amusement in her eyes. "Now that I have stopped running away from you, I have come to realize you are quite nice."

He also looked impossibly handsome in his elegantly tailored coattails.

All chatter quieted when the vicar stepped up to the altar and motioned for them to join him.

Tulip had not expected the abundance of feelings that suddenly overwhelmed her as John walked her down the aisle and gave her over to Alex. As she stood beside her handsome betrothed, she felt the permanence of these vows they were about to exchange.

With her family looking on, she promised to love, honor and

obey him.

He quirked an eyebrow at the 'obey' part and grinned.

He promised to love and protect her.

If not for the warmth of his hand as he clasped hers, she would have thought this was a dream.

The vicar's voice resounded through the church as he pronounced them husband and wife.

Alex surprised her by giving her a tender kiss on the lips. "How does it feel to be the new Duchess of Davenport?" he whispered as he ended their kiss.

Duchess Tulip was not a very elegant name, she thought.

If he did not mind it, then neither would she.

"It will take a little getting used to," she admitted in all honesty.

"You'll be wonderful." He gave her hand a light squeeze before releasing it to accept the handshakes and congratulatory pats on the back from family and friends.

Her cousins and the several friends she had made during her time in London now surrounded her, hugging her and squealing with excitement. Even Gory was present, waddling about while eight months along and scaring every male present because she really looked about to pop out the next little Thorne at any moment.

Well, *little* was a misnomer because these Thorne men were big.

So was Alex.

Tulip's heart did not stop racing, not during the ceremony or the entirety of the wedding breakfast, for her path was now irrevocably set.

She was a Davenport, for better or for worse.

Alex, true to his reputation, remained calm throughout.

She found herself becoming quite sentimental and burst into tears when John gave his speech. Her cousins did the same, for John had been like a father to them all.

They burst into more tears for the silliest reasons and often for no reason, but these were happy tears, she hurried to explain to Alex so that he would not worry.

Tulip found herself crying again when other family elders took turns speaking about her and all the incredible things they knew she would accomplish.

"You are a fortunate man, Your Grace," George said, raising his champagne glass in toast. "Treat her well."

"I will," Alex replied, turning toward her. "Always."

She smiled at him through more tears.

Gad, why was she such a watering pot today?

She noticed the loving way Sophie looked upon her husband as he sat beside her. John, it turned out, had already dampened two handkerchiefs with his joyful weeping.

All right, then she was not so bad.

Perhaps brides and their families were permitted to behave this way.

In truth, Tulip adored this love Sophie and John shared.

She hoped this is what she and Alex would look like thirty years from now.

They had yet to get through a single day.

Alex understood what she was thinking. "This will be us, Tulip. Never give up on me."

Give up on him?

Did he believe she would leave him as his mother had left his father?

She could not see herself doing such a thing.

Perhaps his mother had felt the same about his father, going into their marriage with all the hope of love and then seeing it fade.

The Davenport reputation was a foul one, indeed.

This was why she had avoided Alex all these months, but he had won her heart anyway. Would their marriage turn out to be a big mistake?

No.

She could not think this way.

The wedding breakfast went well into the evening because no one wanted to leave. Tulip was also fretting about embarking on this next phase of her life and did not mind delaying its start.

She supposed their marriage would be like the phases of the

moon, at times glowing and bright, at times waxing and other times waning, and sometimes dark when the moon fell in shadow.

The hour was approaching nine o'clock by the time they departed Chipping Way and made their way to Alex's apartment in Bloomsbury.

They traveled in the twilight hour, the fading sun extremely bright as it settled over the Thames.

The moon was already out, hardly more than an inconsequential white ball against a pale blue sky.

"We're here," he said.

She peered out of the carriage window as the team of horses drew to a halt in front of his residence. This would be her home now, although only for tonight because they were leaving tomorrow morning for Somerset and the Davenport estate.

Her trunks had been brought over earlier in the day, but nothing was to be unpacked since they would not return to London for months, and possibly not until next year.

Alex introduced her to Mrs. Gayle, his housekeeper, who had waited for them to return before going home. She was a pleasant, older woman who had a bountiful smile and a kind expression in her eyes. "Welcome home, Your Graces." She then turned to Alex. "It is a pleasure to meet the young lady who has captured your heart."

Tulip did not think she had managed that feat yet, but was hopeful he would come to love her in time. "Thank you for taking such good care of him, Mrs. Gayle."

"It has been my honor, for he is an excellent man. Works too much and thinks too hard."

Tulip laughed. "Yes, I suppose that is him in a nutshell."

She noticed that her trunks were stacked in a corner of the parlor along with his own, as well as some special pieces of furniture and furnishings that probably held sentimental value for him and were to be brought along to Thornwycke Hall. "We'll never fit all of these into your carriage."

Alex nodded. "We'll have two conveyances. A carriage to haul us and a cart for all of our belongings."

"Mostly mine," she realized, for she had three trunks to his one.

"Gowns take up more space. The luggage cart will follow us, but it will be more heavily laden and likely move at a slower pace. Do you have enough clothes for the next two weeks? We'll load those onto our carriage. That ought to get you through until the rest of our belongings arrive."

"I'll be back first thing in the morning to help you," Mrs. Gayle assured Tulip. "His Grace has thoughtfully arranged for Trent to see me home tonight and pick me up early tomorrow."

Once Mrs. Gayle left, Alex gave Tulip a tour of his apartment.

"I don't expect we'll reside here," he said. "It wouldn't do for a duke and his duchess to live like students. I would have us move into the Davenport townhouse, but it needs quite a bit of fixing. I'm thinking of selling it and purchasing a better property, perhaps in Mayfair where you'll be closer to your family."

She nodded. "That sounds nice. But can you sell it?"

"Yes, full power. It is not part of the Davenport entailment." He rubbed a hand across the back of his neck. "In truth, I'll be glad to rid myself of that Davenport stench."

He'd spoken with such unaccustomed venom, it surprised her.

And that dark look as he'd uttered the words.

It was just a flicker of darkness and then it was gone, but it revealed the depth of his animosity toward his family.

She had not realized quite how much bitterness Alex held inside.

He always appeared so calm and unaffected, almost indifferent most of the time. But she understood now that his resentment ran strong.

"Let me show you to our bedchamber," he said, his manner once more polite and controlled while he led her upstairs. "I thought it would be more practical to sleep here instead of taking rooms at a hotel since we'll be leaving early in the morning and all our trunks are here."

"I don't mind."

He cast her a wry smile. "But I do. It feels kind of shabby to me now. And I did not even think to ask if you would prefer a fancier accommodation. I'm sorry, Tulip. I'll make it up to you."

"No need. These past few months have been a whirlwind of

lavish balls and elegant parties. I think I have had my fill of excess and ostentation. A quiet wedding night will do just fine."

He chuckled. "Well, I don't know how quiet it will be."

"Oh, do you have noisy neighbors?"

He started to say something, then choked on his laughter. "No," he said, grinning, "that wasn't…never mind. You'll see. Hard to explain."

She shrugged and followed him into his quarters. "Ooh, this is nice."

"Yes, it is a comfortable room," Alex said.

It was more than merely comfortable, for it had beautiful damask drapes, a large bed that would easily accommodate both of them, elegant furniture, and an obviously well-crafted carpet of oriental design. She noted several books piled beside a plump, cushioned chair and ottoman beside the hearth where she imagined he spent his quiet hours reading. There was also an adjoining dressing room for privacy while grooming.

"Surprised?"

She nodded. "I don't know why I thought you would be sleeping on a cot in a sparsely furnished room and a bed sheet used as a makeshift curtain hanging over your windows."

"I came into a little money when my mother died. This is why I managed to stay independent after she passed away. I was still young, not yet of age, but old enough to manage without the supervision of adults. Most of those childhood years were spent in boarding schools, anyway. My mother's family did not want me around, either."

"Because you were a Davenport?"

He nodded. "They never forgave the Davenports for my mother's death."

"But you were a child and she tried to save you. How could they assign any blame to you?"

He shrugged. "I suppose it was easier to despise me than bother to get to know me. They were angry and wanted to lash out. I was the closest Davenport at hand, so they took their sorrow and frustration out on me."

She placed a hand on his arm and felt the ripples of tension within him. "Alex, I am so sorry. Did they come around afterward and apologize to you? Do you ever keep in touch with them?"

"No. They're mostly gone now, only a few elderly aunts remain and they won't ever accept to see me. As I said, easier to cast blame somewhere."

"Except upon themselves," Tulip muttered.

He shrugged. "It could have been worse. I wasn't left penniless."

"But you were left completely on your own."

"Yes, thank goodness. My greatest fear was that I would be dragged back into the Davenport life from which my mother had tried so hard to shield me. Perhaps my father thought it was for the best, too. He did not attend her funeral. Nor did he ever try to contact me after she died. Then he was gone shortly afterward."

Tulip's heart was breaking as he spoke. "It won't be the same for us."

He said nothing, merely smiled.

He had a beautiful smile, but this one held a little heartbreak.

Alex returned downstairs to properly close up the house.

Tulip followed him, peering out the window onto the street and the taverns that lined it. They were coming alive now that students had finished their studies for the evening and were meeting up with friends. "Alex, why does Mrs. Gayle not live in? Isn't this usually expected of a housekeeper."

"I had no need of someone attending me full time. But she'll be staying on and coming by every day to check on the apartment."

Tulip was glad, for it was obvious Alex had needed someone kind to look after him, and Mrs. Gayle had taken on that role. "How long is your lease term?"

He chuckled. "As long as I wish it to be."

"I see. The landlord must be happy to keep you on, especially now that you are a duke. It adds a certain *cachet* to this place. Do you think he will raise your rent?"

"He won't ever."

She glanced at him in confusion. "Why wouldn't he?"

"Because I am the landlord and own this townhouse. It was already broken up into four student apartments when I bought it, so I combined two for myself and kept the others to let in order to provide a small income on the side."

Tulip's eyes rounded in surprise. "This place is yours?"

This explained why he was in no hurry to move out of here. It also explained why this apartment had been decorated with such permanence. "Oh, Alex. We could live here whenever we are in London. This seems like a fun place to be."

"It is, but I think it must be Mayfair for us…or Belgravia if we decide to keep the Davenport townhouse. As for this place, we might get away with living here for a few months. But eyebrows will be raised if we settle here permanently. It was fine for a bachelor, and I was hardly ever here while my services for the magistrate were in dire need. Investigations took up all of my time. People will expect me to provide something finer for you."

She listened while continuing to follow him as he checked the windows and doors.

"I would like to keep Mrs. Gayle on as my London housekeeper, if you have no objection," he said, giving the kitchen door a solid shake to make certain it was securely latched.

"No objection," Tulip assured him.

"But I do not mean for us to remain in this place. I would like to bring her with us wherever we settle in London."

"Yes, I suppose it must be a grander home for us." Tulip sighed, for she would have been quite happy right here. "But this also means Mrs. Gayle may need some training to run a fully staffed residence. As a married duke, you will now be expected to do quite a bit of entertaining."

"Would you be able to properly train her, Tulip?"

"Yes, with the help of my cousins. Dillie will happily instruct us. She is a duchess herself and her home is impeccably run. But do you think Mrs. Gayle wants this added responsibility? It is not the same as caring for a single man who mostly takes his meals outside of the home and never entertains company."

He arched an eyebrow.

What did that mean?

Was he in the habit of bringing home friends?

Lady friends?

In the next moment, she blushed and began to stammer. "That is, I assume you did not bring anyone here. Never mind. It is not my business to know who you invited over before we were betrothed."

"I did not bring ladies here, if this is what concerns you." He wrapped an arm casually about her waist as he led her to the parlor. "I preferred to avoid any romantic entanglements."

Tulip turned to gaze out the window, for the street had truly come alive at this hour and she thought it was fascinating. "None at all?"

He came up behind her and put his arms around her. "No, nothing respectable or ever serious. Until you came along, I never thought I would marry."

She leaned back slightly, enjoying the warmth of his body and the strength of it. "Then you got entangled with me."

"I did not mind. In that moment when you bounded into my arms while in the Fullerton garden, I knew that I had a choice to make."

"How were you given the choice? Everything happened so fast."

"One always has a choice. Had I put my mind to it, I could have figured out a way to get you back into the ballroom with no one the wiser. I could have discredited Caruthers when he angrily claimed you were alone in the garden with him."

"And saved my reputation? If that is true, then why did you not do it?"

"I wanted more than one night with you," he said with surprising seriousness. "I realized in that moment that I needed *you*. That was my choice. One night with Tulip? Or a lifetime? I went for the lifetime."

She was rendered speechless by his admission.

Was it true?

Could he possibly want her?

Was there a chance of love between them?

He let out a breath. "You did not entrap me. If anything, I forced this on you. Well, now you know what really happened that night."

She looked up at him. "Did I not also have a choice? And I do not mean choosing you or Caruthers. I could have chosen neither of you and returned to Somerset. I have many friends there and would not have lacked for suitors. They might not have been dukes, but I never desired to be a duchess."

"Yet, you agreed to marry me. Why?"

"For the same inexplicable reasons you wanted me, I suppose. I don't know what drew me to you, but something changed for me in that moment. My instincts took over, perhaps. I had already been feeling badly about tossing you in with all the other Davenport wastrels and going out of my way to avoid you. It was wrong of me. The more I saw of you, the more I realized I had misjudged you."

"That's promising," he murmured.

"When you saved me from Caruthers and did it so valiantly, I knew you were a man to trust." She cast him an impish grin. "Also, your kiss was very persuasive."

His entire countenance lightened and he cast her another of his melting smiles. "Speaking of kisses…would you care for more?"

CHAPTER 9

WALKING AROUND FOR most of one's life expecting the Davenport demons to devour one's soul was an oppressive weight to carry, Alex knew. He worried about it because this had been his burden from the moment he was old enough to understand about good and evil.

And old enough to know the difference between devils and angels.

Davenports were devils.

Yet, he was standing in his bedchamber fortunate enough to be holding his very own angel in his arms. Tulip even looked the part, clad in white silk and studying him with her big, innocent eyes and breathtaking smile.

He worked to untie the tapes and lacings of her wedding gown, a lovely confection of silk and lace that now slipped off her shoulders and was about to slowly and sensually slide down the length of her body.

The two of them were halfway undressed, and he now purposely put out the candles so that the only illumination filtering into his bedchamber was the moon's delicate glow.

She looked so beautiful in this silver light.

He had expected to spend their wedding night sleeping on a pallet on the floor while she took the bed, but Tulip surprised him.

She was having none of it. "It does not feel right to start our marriage off by separating us."

"Then you are all right with having me share the bed?"

She nodded. "And I expect you to deliver on the promise of a wedding night."

He laughed, for he was achingly eager to oblige.

Too eager because he had wanted her for so long, and now she was his.

Fire surged through his blood in anticipation, but he kept himself in control because Tulip had never done this before.

He was experienced and knew how to pleasure her.

She was willing only because her cousins had told her that she ought to accept him. There was no unbound passion or urgent need of fulfillment on her part. Not that he minded, for she had never done this before and had no idea what would happen.

The burden was on him to ensure she would like it.

His only hesitation was that he had never bedded a virgin before.

How fast should he go when claiming her?

It could be said that this would be a first for both of them.

"Why did you put out the candles?" she asked. "We are now mere shadows to each other."

"This is for your sake, to heighten your pleasure." He wanted her to rely on senses other than merely the sense of sight.

"How will it be heightened if I cannot see you? Is there something I should not see?"

"No, Tulip. I have nothing to hide. Nor would I try to conceal anything from you. But your other senses are brought forward in the darkness and this will make for a more fulfilling experience for you." He had very few scars and women liked his body. "I want you to be aware of me in every way, to know my scent and the taste of me, to recognize my touch and the sound of my voice. The same as I wish to know yours."

"That deeper sense of recognition? Like wolves when they partner? Did you know they mate for life?"

"Yes," he said. "This is what I wish for us."

Once familiar with him, he hoped she would learn to trust him and be reassured by his presence.

He hoped there would be this very recognition and acceptance.

It was important for her to feel happiness and security in the warmth of his touch.

He wanted the same for himself, hoping they might work their way into each other's heart.

If they could bond in this way, then theirs would be a good life and a good marriage despite any obstacles that might be thrown in their way.

"Your ties are loosened, Tulip," he said with a husky rasp to his voice. "Take off your gown. Shall I help you?"

"Yes, please." She laughed lightly. "Silk slides rather easily, doesn't it? It is already pooling at my feet."

"It is a sensual fabric." He placed an arm around her hips and then bent to untangle her feet from the gown. Once free, he set the gown carefully across one of his chairs before attending to himself.

He removed his shirt that was the last of his clothing except for his trousers.

Since he was already aroused, he thought to keep those on because he wasn't certain how Tulip would respond to the sight of his maleness when she had no idea what was to happen next or whether she would like the act of coupling.

He could see she was already shy because she had placed her hands over her chest despite the lack of light beyond the silver streaks of moonlight.

She wore only her thin chemise, a garment of the sheerest gossamer, and she was quite conscious of its thinness.

"You don't need to hide yourself from me," he said softly. "That's why I put out the candles. It is enough for us to have shadowed glimpses of each other."

The mere outline of her body aroused him.

Even in the darkness, he could see that she was beautifully shaped.

Round in all the right places.

Lovely curves.

Yet, slender in aspect.

He cupped her face in his hands and kissed her gently on the lips. "Tulip, we do not need to do anything until you are ready."

She moaned lightly. "I am ready. I want this. I'm just not certain what *this* is. But my cousins told me I should trust you."

"And do you?" He placed tender kisses along her neck and shoulders, lingering kisses and gentle ones as he next nudged the chemise off her shoulders to bare more of her soft skin. His fingers grazed her bosom and he felt her slight shiver.

"Yes, I trust you," she said and leaned toward him.

"Good, love. I promise you will like this." He pressed his mouth to hers and kissed her long and slow.

She slid her hands up his chest and placed them to rest on his shoulders, clinging to them while he kissed her. "Your skin is hot," she said, running her hands along the muscle and sinew of his arms once he had ended the kiss.

"Because I am eager for you."

I burn for you.

Gad, he was on fire and aching to be inside of her.

"May we light the candles now? I would like to see your body."

"Not yet, Tulip. Be patient. You already know the look of me. It is the rest of me I want you to see first."

"So you've said. But how am I to do that?"

"Use all five senses, not merely your eyes. It is so easy to forget everything else and just rely on that sense."

"Oh, I see. I am to put my ears, nose, hands, and lips to work?"

He chuckled. "Yes, I want you to remember the rumble of my voice, the scent of my skin, the contours of my body, and the taste of my mouth on yours."

"Interesting."

"It is something I learned as an investigator. One's eyes can often deceive. It is best not to rely on that sense alone. I will light the candles afterward, I promise. Then you can inspect me to your heart's content."

"All right, I'll wait. I understand what you mean about my recognizing you beyond seeing your face or noticing the way you walk. You have a confident stride, by the way. A bit of a swagger. I'm sure your superiors found it arrogant. But now that *you* are *their* superior, they can have no quarrel with it."

He smiled and caressed her cheek again before wrapping his arms around her. "I'm sure I will still offend people. Becoming a duke hasn't changed me all that much. In truth, it is more of a burden. I enjoyed my work for the London magistrate."

"Gory and Julius will forever be indebted to you for solving her uncle's murder."

"And you? What are you thinking about me right now?"

She released a soft breath. "I'm thinking that I like the way you are holding me in your arms. Your hands feel nice on my body. They are big and rugged, but you are always gentle when you touch me. Is our talking like this a part of your seduction plan? You are also caressing my arms. Is that on purpose, too?"

"Yes and no. I just like touching you and holding you, but I also want you to be comfortable with me. This is your first time with a man." He wanted to make it an unforgettably good memory for her.

Time was his ally.

They had hours until dawn to enjoy each other.

Hours to explore each other and deepen their bonds.

The wolf and his mate.

This is what he wanted, that innate knowledge of each other branded into their memory.

Would she believe him if he murmured, *I love you*?

It was quite possible he felt this already, but dared not tell her yet.

Tulip was never going to believe him.

He hardly believed it himself because he had experienced so little affection in all his years, and yet had fallen so hard and fast for her.

For now, it was enough that she knew he had chosen to marry her.

His choice, he had told her.

She did not have to know it had been his fervent desire from the moment she first careened into him on Chipping Way. They had not even been properly introduced. He had no explanation for it, only that he knew she was meant for him. One look at her, and he was lost. His life would never be the same again.

When she had careened into him a second time in Lady Fullerton's garden, he realized they were fated to be together.

It was their destiny.

He had to have her.

"Let me unpin your hair," he said, his voice still husky and rasping.

Tulip assisted him with the pins. "Oh, it is a mess."

As moonlight fell upon them, he wrapped his fingers in her dark curls and caught his breath as those wavy tresses tumbled down her back and over her ample bosom. "No, love. It's beautiful. You are beautiful."

He led her to their bed, watching for any sign of hesitation as he slipped the chemise off her and then removed his trousers so that they would both be completely bare under the sheets.

If she wasn't ready, he would wait.

They could talk all night if this was all she wanted.

It would leave him in agony, but he would survive.

Despite their rushed wedding, she seemed determined to overcome her shyness and commit to their marriage.

She did not hesitate to open her arms to him once he had settled her onto her back on the mattress.

"What happens now?" she asked, sounding decidedly uncertain.

His dreams had been of hot passion and wild intimacy with Tulip, of him taking her on the bed. Against the wall. On his desk.

Their bodies locked together, hearts aflame and nothing held back.

But this was not going to happen tonight when she had never experienced any intimacy. If he came at her like a wild ape, she would scream and hit him over the head with the candlestick.

He propped on his elbows and slowly settled atop her so that she felt the press of his weight against her body but did not feel uncomfortable with it.

She gasped when she felt his arousal against her hip.

"That means I am ready for you," he said, "but now I need you to be ready for me."

"How does that happen? What do I need to do?"

"Nothing, it is up to me to get you ready. Close your eyes and enjoy. This night is for you, Tulip. Take in each sensation and let your body respond. It will respond, you needn't worry that it won't."

Because he knew how to touch a woman.

He knew how to make her gasp and pant with pleasure.

He was not lacking in this experience.

Of course, it would be different with Tulip, not only because everything was new to her.

This time, his heart was involved and she mattered to him.

He wanted her to know her importance and feel it in his every caress, his every kiss and every loving stroke.

He would give her his complete commitment, give all of his heart and all of his ardor, and touch her as though this was the last time they would ever be together and meant everything to him.

His first kisses had been soft and gentle, but he now pressed his mouth to hers with a more urgent and possessive heat.

Still tender.

Still cautious.

But he wanted her to know she was his.

He was also hers, and hoped to convey this, too.

He ran his hands over every part of her silken body, caressing her breasts and taking each tip in turn into his mouth, teasing and suckling. When he felt her responding, he expanded his onslaught, now sliding his hand to the intimate spot between her legs and beginning to stroke her there while still paying attention to her breasts.

She moaned and clutched his shoulders, then tugged on his hair. "Alex!"

"I have you, love. Close your eyes and let your body take over."

He wanted this night to be memorable for her in the best way.

He moved upward from her breasts to kiss her on the lips, but he continued to stroke her intimately, knowing just how to build the fire within her.

They both tasted of champagne, for it had flowed freely during the wedding breakfast and they had indulged.

She cried his name again, and it sounded soft and loving on her lips.

Alex.

"That's it, Tulip. Don't hold back." He kissed her mouth, her eyes, and then moved lower again to kiss and tease her breasts that were so beautiful to him.

She emitted little purring gasps, soft moans, and wriggled to push herself against his fingers because she did not understand what was happening to her body but was ready for more.

He held her as though she was the most precious thing to him.

"*Alex.*" She gasped his name again.

"Sweetheart, I'm going to claim you now. All right?"

She nodded and held onto his shoulders as he positioned himself over her, now wishing he had kept a candle burning so that he could see *her* and understand what she was thinking and feeling at this moment.

He sensed she had her eyes closed, her lips tightly pursed, and was holding her breath because she was uncertain what was to happen next.

But her nod meant that she trusted him.

Trusted him with the unknown.

He felt the moment her barrier broke, and heard her gasp.

He paused.

"No, don't stop," she said in a throaty whisper.

He didn't, but he purposely slowed down to give her time to absorb him and get used to these new sensations.

As his movements became more urgent, she started to open up and respond as he'd hoped...with innocence and mounting arousal.

She hugged him tighter and raised her hips to meet his thrusts.

Sweet heaven.

He wanted to bury himself so deep inside of her.

She was tight.

Blissfully and heavenly tight.

Her head was thrown back and her eyes were closed.

She licked her lips.

And once again raised her hips to fully take him in.

He released an aching groan and no longer held back.

All caution was tossed to the wind as mindless heat and

passion overcame them both, and they began to grasp at each other and move together like wild wolves who could not get enough of each other.

Fire roared through him.

He wanted to devour her.

Burn himself into her soul.

He inhaled her hot, sweet lavender scent.

He licked her breasts that were soft as cream.

Blessed saints.

What lovely breasts she had.

Ripe and full.

She brought out his savage hunger.

The air around them grew thick and damp, and the temperature soared around them as he thrust into her with growing urgency.

More fire tore through him, the flames scorching him to his core.

Tulip was moaning and crying out for him, her breaths short and ragged.

She clutched his shoulders again.

Her lush breasts molded to his chest as she drew him closer. "Alex...oh, Alex."

She was close now.

So close.

She called his name one last time as passion overwhelmed her and she shattered in an all-consuming pleasure that rippled through her like the wild currents after a storm.

They were so wrapped in each other that he felt her every thrum and vibration against his skin that was peeled to hers.

"I have you, sweetheart." He kissed her on the mouth to quiet her cries, but he mostly kissed her because she was so beautiful and he loved the way she had taken him in and responded to him.

It took all his determination to hold out just that little bit longer because he wanted to let her experience the full measure of her release before he followed with his own. Since he was already on the brink and had been holding back until this moment, it only took him two thrusts before he experienced his own shattering release and spilled himself into her warmth.

Blessed saints.

The passion poured out of him.

Heart, soul, and body into Tulip, forging this new bond between them.

Would it be unbreakable?

Would she ever grow to hate him?

Not now.

How could she after tonight?

No matter what happens, remember this moment.

He hoped she would always remember this night, and be able to forgive him if he turned into one of those abominable Davenport dukes.

She kissed him as he collapsed atop her, kissed his mouth, his closed eyes, and his jaw.

He opened his eyes and eased off her, grinning in conquest as he said, "Well, that was something nice."

She laughed. "Yes. Any more surprises in store for me?"

He gave her a light kiss on the nose. "Plenty, but not tonight. We had better sleep now or we'll never get up in the morning."

They needed to get an early start and travel as far as they could while the weather cooperated. It would take about a week to reach the seat of the Davenport dukes. Thornwycke Hall was an imposing fortress overlooking the Bristol Channel and filled with the ghosts of all the depraved dukes who had come before him.

After taking a breath, he reached out and drew her closer. "How do you feel, Tulip?"

She snuggled against him. "Good. I feel very good indeed."

He grinned. "Me, too."

"That was nice, Alex. Shocking, but also marvelous. Of course, you knew this would happen."

"I hoped it would." He gave her cheek a light caress. "I thought it might. There's more, but that's for us to explore over the next few weeks and months."

She nodded. "I'm looking forward to it."

"Me, too," he said with a rumbling chuckle.

"It will be odd returning to Somerset as your wife." She nestled closer as he absently caressed her arm.

"You'll be great. Everyone will love you."

She shook her head.

He felt the soft brush of her hair against his chest.

"I felt like a duck out of water when I first arrived in London. Everyone was very kind to me, especially my family, but it was all so overwhelming. Then I made friends here, and I loved being able to walk across the street to see Marigold or dash next door to visit Violet. I'll miss them very much. Yet, I don't think I will ever think of London as my home. That will always be Somerset for me."

"Things will be different for you there now that you have married me."

Once more, she nodded against his chest. "I know. My friends will treat me differently because I am your duchess. They'll try not to, but it will happen anyway. I hope my mother's family will still look upon me as one of their own."

"They won't stop loving you, but do not be surprised if they show you more deference. This is to be expected. Everyone is going to be more careful in what they say to you and around you. They'll think twice when talking about you to others, for you now hold all the power. Not that I expect your friends or family ever to say nasty things about you. They know you are a good person."

"I hope so. I try to be."

"You are, sweetheart. But do not be surprised if others are jealous and seek to undermine you. This is a problem we are bound to face, never knowing whom to trust and watch out for."

"Does one's character change all that much over time?"

"No, but how am I to judge a person's character when I don't know anyone from Somerset except for you and my idiot cousins? As we speak, they are probably drinking their way through their allowance at some *demi-monde* salon."

"It is better than having them sit at home and think up plots against you," she reminded him.

He grunted. "True."

Still, this would not address the problems he was bound to face in Somerset. Everyone would be a stranger to him. It was hard to take the measure of a person who had every reason to lie to him and try to impress him.

Alex was quite familiar with the petty nature of people, their jealously guarded aims and desires, since he often came across the worst of them in his investigations.

Everyone lied.

Everyone held back secrets.

"I will introduce you to all the townspeople I know," Tulip offered. "This is how I can be of help to you once we are at Thornwycke Hall. Of course, this is probably the major reason why you wanted to marry me."

She was diminishing herself in importance again.

How could she elevate that convenient coincidence and make it out to be anything beyond a minor significance?

"It is one *small* reason why you caught my attention. You had other things to recommend you. Beauty, wit, and brains for starters."

He sat up and lit one of the candles on his night table.

Tulip also sat up and drew the sheet to her bosom to cover herself.

"Don't be shy around me, love. I want to see you now in the light." At her nod, he reached out and gently slipped the covering off her.

"I knew you would be this beautiful," he said in a reverent whisper and kissed the swell of one breast.

She studied him, too.

He knew she would like his body.

He made love to her again by candlelight.

Tulip was as sweetly responsive to him as the first time.

She was also less awkward and frantic because she now understood this intimacy between a husband and wife.

But their first time would always be sweetest because he was her first and only, and this was something quite wonderful for him.

She brought out his every possessive and protective instinct.

Their second time was hotter and faster.

Oh, so good.

The friction between their bodies was pure, scorching heat.

They surrendered to the flames of passion, reaching their release together, and leaving their bodies in a tangle of limbs and perspiration.

It took them a few minutes to stop grinning and laughing.

Once their breaths calmed, they resumed their quiet conversation because neither of them could fall asleep yet.

Who could be sensible on a night like this?

Despite the temptation, Alex decided not to couple with Tulip again.

Twice in a night was enough for her, otherwise she would be sore come morning.

As Tulip lay quietly in his arms, looking as though she was ready for sleep, his thoughts drifted to other concerns.

What would they encounter upon reaching Thornwycke Hall?

Was there anyone in the household he could trust?

Was there anyone who needed to be watched?

He would not have cared so much were it only for himself, but he had Tulip to worry about now and he meant to keep her safe.

He mentioned this to Tulip when she gave him a gentle nudge to the ribs. "What is running through your mind, Alex?"

He smiled. "Just thinking ahead to Somerset."

"So, you have moved on from thinking of our coupling? I suppose it is ordinary course of business for you."

He caught her between his arms and gave her a scorching kiss on the lips before rolling back off her. "Nothing ordinary about you, Tulip. I meant it when I said this was very nice. Nothing better, frankly. You've left me exhilarated and my mind is now whirling ahead to our arrival at Thornwycke Hall. I don't know what we'll be facing there."

"Approach it as you would any investigation, with an open mind and reliance on those you know and trust. You know that you can trust me."

"For certain," he said and kissed her on the forehead.

"Having grown up near Thornwycke Hall, I am familiar with many of the people who work there or have had dealings with the estate," Tulip assured him. "I think they will open up to me when

I ask questions. I like the idea of your needing my help."

He grunted. "I'll be relying on you for more than just asking questions. I'll need your help in figuring how best to restore the estate."

"Never in my wildest dreams did I ever believe I would become mistress of Thornwycke Hall. I have never been inside the manor house, only seen it from afar. We used to sail past it on the hot, lazy days of summer. One of the Hester relatives had a beautiful sailboat and would take us out on the Bristol Channel."

"Sounds like fun."

"It was, but the waters around Thornwycke can be treacherous. The water levels change drastically between high tide and low tide, and the water surges come on fast and strong. This is something to keep in mind if ever you are walking along the salt marshes."

"Is there any reason I would be?"

"Yes, because your workers excavate the salt from there to be sold at market. You might have reason to walk across them when inspecting those operations or surveying your property. But the manor house itself is up on a hill and well protected from any flooding."

"What about the farmlands near Thornwycke? Are they susceptible to floods?"

"Only on extremely rare occasion. They are further inland and quite safe from the rising tides. Mr. Carver can tell you more about them, since he's managed the Davenport properties for years."

Alex grunted again.

"It will be nice to see him," Tulip said, sounding wistful. "He's a good friend to my Hester family, and a man you can trust."

"So you've mentioned before," he muttered, more to himself than an attempt at further conversation.

He would soon meet the man and assess his character for himself.

Alex kissed her once more on the forehead. "I'll rely on you to introduce me around. If you are of a mind, perhaps you could ride with me as I inspect the Davenport holdings."

"Yes, I would enjoy that," she said eagerly. "In truth, I would be disappointed if you left me behind to rattle around that big house all on my own."

"You would never be idle, even if I did leave you there. The house will require a major restoration, I'm sure. You'll have your hands full with that alone. Decorate it to your liking, Tulip. I want you to be happy living there. I have no idea what shape it is in."

"Or whether there will be funds enough to restore it," she remarked. "We can adjust our plans as necessary once you've taken a full account and decided upon the priorities. Will you leave all the decisions on decorating the house to me? I think we must agree on them together. After all, it is your home. You are the one with the rightful claim to it."

"Only by entailment. But I'll give my opinion when asked. However, I trust your judgment."

She laughed softly. "Do not be so hasty about that. I have never owned a house or ever decorated anything of importance. You have a good eye for detail, Alex. You've done a lovely job with this apartment."

He shrugged. "It is just an apartment."

"It is a lovely place, and you've made it a welcoming home. Thornwycke Hall is enormous. It was originally built to house a small army to serve and protect the duke. There will be structural issues that are beyond my comprehension. I would not be surprised if the older portions of the house are crumbling and might need to be closed off. As for its daily running, there must be a housekeeper who will attend to those duties. The manor is too big to function without one. The old housekeeper was a kindly woman by the name of Mrs. Dodge."

"I vaguely remember her," Alex said. "I'd see her marching briskly through the halls but she never paused to speak to me unless it was to caution me not to run about the house or my grandfather would spank my backside raw if I broke anything."

"She wasn't a bad sort, but caring for Thornwycke Hall meant everything to her. An exuberant eight-year-old boy running amok in the elegant parlor among priceless items must have given her a heart palpitation or two. She passed away several years ago and I don't know anything about her current replacement. Several housekeepers came and went in quick succession between then and now, some lasting no more than a day or two before hopping on the next mail coach out of Burnham."

"Not surprised," he said with a grunt.

"But I think the current one has been there since shortly before your grandfather died, so that's about five years. She could be helpful in providing us information."

"We'll find out soon enough." He gave her a light kiss on the lips. "All right, I mean it this time. We have an early start tomorrow and must get some sleep. Sweet dreams, Tulip."

"Do you mind if I curl up against you?"

He chuckled. "I don't mind at all. Give me a shove if I unwittingly squash you."

"You won't. Your protective instincts are too strong. You'll look out for me even in your sleep."

He hoped so.

He never wanted to hurt Tulip.

Would Thornwycke change him?

He tried to fall asleep, too.

But his thoughts were in a roil, so he remained awake a while longer and watched Tulip as she fell into a peaceful slumber.

Slivers of moonlight shone upon their bed and seemed to cradle her body.

She was a soft, little thing.

He liked that she was snuggled against his side, her head resting on his arm. Her hair was long and curled over her shoulders in a gentle cascade. He stroked her hair, brushing a few, stray strands off her cheek.

This was the last thing he remembered before he fell asleep himself.

The morning came too soon, and with it the glare of sunlight that had him squinting and blinking until his eyes adjusted to the brightness.

He started to shift off the bed, then realized Tulip was still nestled against him, so he slowly slipped his arm out from under her head and eased away. He was careful not to drag the covers along with him as he rose.

His arm began to tingle as he moved it.

No wonder the limb was numb, Tulip had been resting on it all night.

After taking care of his necessaries, he quietly shaved and washed up, then tossed on a fresh shirt and trousers. He would save the rest, the waistcoat, cravat, and jacket for later when they were about to leave.

He took a moment to watch Tulip sleeping like an angel in his bed.

The hour was early, and he had another few minutes before he needed to wake her.

"Beautiful," he whispered, feeling a quiet satisfaction as he studied his wife.

It was like watching a kitten sleep.

Curled body, pink and warm.

An occasional soft purr amid even breaths.

She must have sensed him watching, for she opened her eyes and stared first at the empty spot beside her on the bed. When she turned and looked up, she saw him standing by the foot of the bed and graced him with a glorious smile. "Good morning. Did I oversleep?"

"No, I was up early." The mattress dipped as he sank onto it to sit beside her. "You looked comfortable and I did not want to disturb you. Did you sleep well?"

"Divinely." She purred and stretched, then stopped herself upon remembering she had nothing on beneath the covers.

Gasping, she drew the sheet up to cover her chest.

"Here's your chemise." He handed over the delicate garment that was too sheer to be of much use. But if it made her feel more comfortable to have it on, then so be it.

It was not going to hide her perfect mounds or the rest of her beautifully shaped body.

Blessed saints.

He wanted her again.

But there wasn't time.

The memory of last night's coupling would have to do for now.

"Shall I leave you to your privacy?" he asked, now donning his boots and the rest of his attire. "Mrs. Gayle will arrive soon and I'll have her come up to assist you."

"Yes, that would be appreciated."

He walked downstairs and unlatched the front door, then took a moment to walk down his front steps.

The breeze was pleasantly light and cool since it was not yet seven o'clock in the morning.

The street was mostly quiet save for the vendors rolling their carts into place.

The shops and taverns were closed, but several would open within the hour.

He noticed a milkman's cart and saw the milkman delivering eggs, butter, and milk to the neighboring houses.

He was about to return indoors when he noticed his carriage coming down the street. Trent, as instructed, had picked up Mrs. Gayle and brought her here at the appointed hour.

He waved to her as she descended the carriage. "Good morning."

"Good morning, Your Grace." She wagged her finger at him as she approached. "I see by your grin that you had a good night."

He chuckled. "My wife is awake and will need some assistance in readying herself for our journey."

"I'll attend to her at once," she said then ran upstairs while he remained standing outside.

It wasn't long before there was more activity on the street.

Students started heading to classes, a few shopkeepers opened their shops, and the tavern across the street that was brisk with activity last night had opened again this morning, this time providing coffee and tea to their patrons instead of ale.

The aroma of freshly brewed coffee reached his nostrils.

He noticed that the men he had hired as porters to assist in loading their trunks and other belongings onto his carriage and the luggage cart had arrived a few minutes early and were now seated at the tavern, having their cups of coffee.

All that remained missing for their journey was the luggage cart.

He expected it would arrive shortly, for the man he'd hired to drive it was Trent's brother who was as reliable as Trent.

Since Mrs. Gayle's priority was to assist Tulip in getting herself ready, there would be no coffee made or breakfast ready for him this morning.

This was no problem.

If Tulip was hungry after last night's exertions, he would escort her to the tavern for a quick bite once she came downstairs.

They would have time while those porters loaded their trunks and other belongings.

His watch was attached to the small pocket of his waistcoat by a fancy fob he had purchased shortly after inheriting the dukedom. It wasn't anything too ornate, but seemed appropriately pretentious to wear now that he was a duke.

He checked his watch.

That cart was due at any moment.

His carriage was already out front since Trent was ever efficient and had delivered Mrs. Gayle here exactly on time.

Trent was now feeding and watering the horses in preparation for their journey.

A few minutes later, the luggage cart came around from the mews and made its way to the front of Alex's home.

The porters rose and walked across the street to begin their assignment. "Mornin', Your Grace," their foreman said in greeting as they approached.

"Good morning, Mr. Cullin. The trunks and furnishings are in the parlor. I'll see if my wife has anything more she wishes to pack away."

Tulip emerged from the townhouse just then.

Her hair was done up in a simple bun at the base of her neck, and a few stray curls fell over her brow. She had on a pert hat and wore a muslin gown in a shade of dark green that was sturdy and sensible for travel. She carried a matching pelisse over one arm and held her gloves and reticule in the other. "Good morning, gentlemen," she said, coming to stand beside Alex and the porters.

Her smile was pure sunshine.

The men were at first surprised by her friendliness, not certain what to make of her. Then they eased and smiled back, obviously pleased to have been noticed by the duchess...or the fact that she was beautiful no matter her rank.

Alex led them inside, showed them what was to be loaded, and then returned to Tulip's side as she waited for him by their carriage. "We can have coffee and a light breakfast while they work," he said, motioning to the tavern across the street.

"I'd love that, if it won't hold us up."

"It won't. We can sit at an outdoor table and watch them work. I know it won't take them long, but what does it matter? We are the ones to decide when we leave London."

Tulip had tea and a scone while he had his usual coffee and eggs.

It would have been a pleasant start to the day had Lord Caruthers not suddenly appeared before them, his shadow darkening their table.

Alex immediately rose and placed himself between Tulip and the oaf who looked as though he had been carousing all night and not yet found his bed. "What are you doing here, Caruthers?"

"Seeing you off properly, of course," he said with false cheer, his voice obviously slurred and so bellicose, everyone seated around them took notice. "You did not think I would forget, did you? Should I not be a good sport and wish you well on your journey, even though you *stole* my wife?"

Every patron was now looking at them, and several gasped.

The oaf's insincere smile turned venomous. "I wish you and your Jezebel *safe* travels...or perhaps you'll get what you deserve along the way."

Was that a threat?

No doubt an empty one because the man lived on borrowed funds and would not squander the precious little he had on paying scoundrels to accost them on the road to Somerset.

Alex was armed and so was Trent, if it came to that.

But he doubted it was anything more than the idle ranting of a sore loser because no scoundrel was going to agree to attack a duke for anything less than a king's ransom.

Caruthers had to borrow funds to have his boots shined.

"You are *unmarried*, Caruthers," Alex said in his most intimidating tone. "So how can you lose a wife you never had? But if I ever catch you near *my* wife or ever insult *my* wife again, I'll introduce your face to the cobblestone street before you catch your next breath."

Caruthers raised his fisted hands. "Just you go ahead and try it."

"No, Caruthers," he said with a sigh. "You are not worth the trouble."

"And your pretty wife? Was she worth the trouble? Or did she refuse to pleasure you last night?"

Several patrons gasped again.

"That tears it," Alex muttered and was about to toss him out of the tavern, but Tulip stood up and placed her hand on his arm to hold him back.

"He truly isn't worth it, my love. He is no gentleman, just a petulant loser. Punching him will only create scandal. This is what he hopes to achieve, although heaven knows why he is still bothering with you or me."

She now turned to Caruthers and spoke loud enough even for passers by to hear. "I rejected you, my lord. Everyone but you realizes it. Are you that deluded to believe I would ever marry a worthless fortune hunter such as yourself? What were you hoping to accomplish by coming here to see me and my husband off? To shame us? How can I ever be shamed when I have married the best man of all? Ours is a love match. You, on the other hand, are *meaningless* to me, so your effort is wasted. I would sooner marry a worm than ever marry you."

Well, that was a verbal kick in the nuts, Alex thought with some amusement.

He did not realize Tulip had it in her to stand up to the oaf, but was pleased he was mistaken.

Caruthers cursed them and stormed off.

Several patrons laughed and others began to clap.

Tulip nodded to acknowledge them, and then sat down again.

Alex sank into his chair and watched her with interest as she calmly finished her tea, although her cheeks were pink with ire and gave her away. "Are you all right, Tulip?"

She nodded. "Are you?"

He laughed. "Yes, little gladiator."

"I'm not all that brave," she admitted. "I would not have said anything were you not standing beside me. I knew you would protect me."

"Always, sweetheart." He leaned forward and caressed her cheek. "Tulip…"

"Truly, I am all right. You needn't fret about that cur upsetting me."

"It isn't only that." He regarded her with an investigative eye, his gaze sharp and intense. "You called me 'my love' and mentioned ours was a love match. Did you mean it? Or was it because you thought the situation called for it?"

"The situation called for it. But…would you mind if I did mean it?"

CHAPTER 10

TULIP STARED AT her handsome husband as they sat in his carriage and rode out of London.

She wished he had answered her question about theirs being a love match.

Would you mind if I did mean it?

He had said nothing, merely smiled and then escorted her to their carriage to begin the journey to Somerset.

She could have taken a seat beside him, but preferred to sit across from him in order to have a better look at him.

He returned her stare, once again casting her a soft smile, and his eyes held a glimmer of amusement.

She was curious as to what he found so humorous. "What are you thinking, Alex?"

"That I married the best lady of all," he said, mimicking what she had told Lord Caruthers when giving him a dressing down, "and I am congratulating myself for my wisdom and foresight."

She laughed, glad he thought so because she was developing very strong feelings for him. Perhaps it was love that she was feeling, but the true test would come once they reached Somerset and settled in at Thornwycke Hall.

They rode mostly in silence for the next several hours and were already a good distance outside of London when Trent drew their carriage to a halt at a coaching inn because the hour was coming upon noon. "Horses need to rest, Your Grace," he said, addressing Alex when they climbed down to stretch their legs.

The inn was crowded, for they were only one of hundreds on the road today.

Alex nodded and then turned to Tulip. "I'll secure a private dining room for us."

"All right, but we can also dine in the common room if there are no private ones available." When coming to London, she had taken her meals among the rabble of travelers. It felt so odd to now be returning as a duchess.

This would likely be the way they traveled from now on. Sleek ducal carriage. Private dining rooms. The best accommodations. All the privileges.

She bid a cheerful good day to a family comprised of a mother, father, and two young children who passed by as she stood near the entry waiting for Alex to make their dining arrangements. She was surprised when her pleasant greeting was met with resentment.

Her faith in people was restored when others who walked by smiled at her. But there were a surprising number who cast her resentful looks.

They made Tulip acutely aware her life had changed.

She was no longer a commoner.

It did not matter that her nature was always as it had been.

She breathed a sigh of relief when she noticed Alex striding toward her.

"Trent's given the horses over to the ostler's grooms for tending. He's having a bite to eat and an ale while he waits for us," he said, drawing her closer as the coaching inn began to fill up. He was obviously worried about her getting jostled or suddenly lost in the crowd.

She liked that he was naturally protective of her. "Oh, then we ought to hurry."

He noticed her look of disquiet. "What's wrong, Tulip?"

As they walked to the private dining room, she told him about the sneers and sullen looks cast her way by some of the travelers. The private dining room was a small, cramped chamber that held a table large enough to accommodate six patrons.

Perhaps it was decadent for them to have it all to themselves.

Alex held out a chair for her. "I've spent most of my career working for the London magistrate and getting hostile looks from the people I question. There's no avoiding it. Some will be cheerful and cooperative, but most will be evasive, resentful, and sometimes filled with bile. I'm sorry you have already encountered that sort. They'll dislike you no matter what you do."

They ate quickly and returned to the carriage to continue their journey.

Tulip climbed in and was about to resume her seat opposite him, but he drew her onto his seat bench. "Sit next to me, Tulip."

"All right."

He took her hand in his as the carriage rolled away from the coaching inn.

She glanced down as he entwined his fingers in hers. "Are we going to hold hands for the rest of the day?"

He chuckled. "Yes, if you don't mind."

"Are you doing this because you think I am upset that not everyone smiled at me at the coaching inn?"

He nodded.

Good heavens, that was a sweet thing to do.

She rested her head on his shoulder. "You are taking quite well to the role of husband, aren't you?"

"I hope so, but it is more about you. I don't want to see you hurt."

"I'll be fine, but this is nice. Isn't it, Alex?" She had been raised by good men who looked after their families, so this was not something completely new to her. But being looked after by a husband filled her with an unexpected warmth.

"It is nice," he said, furrowing his brow as he gave it some thought. "I've been on my own for so long. I thought it would be hard to adjust to having someone else to think about and worry about. So far, it has felt quite natural and easy."

"Well, it has only been one day of married life for us. I think how we handle settling in at Thornwycke Hall will prove to be more of a challenge." She felt him tense at the mention of the Davenport estate that held such bitter memories for him.

Since they had gotten very little sleep last night, Tulip found herself drifting off throughout the ride.

It was easy to relax when Alex held her in his arms.

That night, he took her in his arms again and made love to her.

He had an exquisite way of holding her and kissing her that touched her heart and made her feel treasured.

She did not think he loved her yet, but he knew how to make her *feel* loved. She dared not make too much of it. He was handsome and experienced, and knew how to send her soaring and shattering.

He could melt her with a mere smile.

She had never imagined anyone could be so beautifully formed. His body was sleek and powerful, his muscles rippling as he moved over her and pressed his weight lightly atop her. With his body coiled and tense, as any animal would be when hunting its prey, there was no mistaking he was the ravenous predator and she was the tender morsel he was eyeing for his supper.

She felt devoured whenever he kissed her.

"Tulip, how do you feel?" he always asked once he had pleasured her, and did so again now.

"Boneless. Weightless. Breathless," she responded while calming from the throes of their latest coupling.

"Yes," he said, taking her into his arms once they were done. "I thought it was nice, too."

They had fallen into a pleasant travel routine and were right on schedule to arrive at Thornwycke Hall by the end of the week.

Tulip sensed the tension rising within him as their travels drew to a close and they rode past the town of Burnham where she had been raised.

This was the last leg of their journey.

They would reach Thornwycke Hall within the hour now.

The grand manor house that served as the seat of the Davenport dukes stood a short distance beyond Burnham, past green hills and lush pastures. Over each rise they caught glimpses of miles and miles of salt marshes in the distance. It was not long before they caught sight of an impressive fortress perched atop a hill.

"Thornwycke, I presume," Alex muttered.

"Yes." As they drew closer, Tulip studied the place with an owner's eyes.

Much of the old turrets and original fortifications had survived, but over the years most of the original fortress had been replaced, expanded, and remodeled into a stately home fit for a duke who enjoyed his comforts.

Tulip poked Alex lightly in the ribs when she thought his tension was about to explode. "You are a married man who sleeps with his wife," she said. "You do not drink to excess. You do not gamble. I am sure we will settle into a very quiet, boring life here."

He laughed and drew her onto his lap. "I do not need you to reassure me that all will be well."

Yes, he did.

Despite his jovial laugh, his eyes remained darkened by dread as he now stared at the manor looming before them.

This was to be their home.

But it was a place he had always connected with misery.

She noticed more shadows marring his handsome features. "Alex, I know there will be a lot of work ahead for us. But we are in this together, are we not?"

"Sure," he said without conviction.

It was her turn to take his hand because she wanted to reassure him as their carriage drew up in the courtyard.

He stepped down first and assisted her to alight.

The massive front doors to Thornwycke Hall groaned open.

Alex glanced at their still clasped hands and arched an eyebrow in question.

She cast him a determined look. "I am not letting go of you. Is this not what a supportive wife should do?"

He grinned. "I thought it was you who needed my support."

"It works both ways," she said, watching as several servants scampered down the steps toward them.

The head butler, a tall, thin and rather dour-looking man, introduced himself. "I am Ernfield, Your Grace."

"Are you related to Samuel Ernfield?" Tulip asked, for Samuel was the local Burnham blacksmith, a jovial and gregarious fellow.

"He is my cousin," Ernfield intoned with all the gaiety of an undertaker.

Tulip choked back a laugh. "How lovely."

And how different these two Ernfield men were.

Could this fellow look any more morose without actually being dead himself?

A pretty woman who appeared to be in her early thirties stepped forward and introduced herself as their housekeeper. "I am Mrs. Granger," she said with far more cheer than Ernfield had exhibited. "Mrs. Eleanor Granger."

Tulip did not know any family in Burnham by that name, but this did not mean Mrs. Granger was a newcomer to these parts. Since the woman appeared friendly enough, Tulip knew she would have the chance to talk to her and find out more about her and her family in the coming days. "It is good to meet you, Mrs. Granger. I think we shall be relying on you considerably over these next few months."

"I look forward to it, Your Grace. It is good to have a Davenport duke once again in residence at Thornwycke Hall."

"And his charming duchess," Mr. Carver, the estate manager, called out gleefully to Tulip as he hurried out of the house toward them, all smiles. "Bless my soul! It is good to see you, Tulip...I mean, Your Grace."

"Mr. Carver!" Despite the gesture being completely outside of proper protocol, she gave him a hug. "It is so good to see you, too."

"Imagine my surprise when I learned you are the new Duchess of Davenport. Blow me over with a feather, said I to your aunt and uncle. But I could not be happier for you."

However, his voice sounded a little hollow.

No doubt, he was more worried than happy because he did not know Alex yet and had only the prior dukes and their horrible behavior to guide him.

Tulip knew everyone would come to admire Alex in time.

How could they not?

Tulip introduced Mr. Carver to Alex.

"We've corresponded a time or two," Alex said with cordiality. "It is good to finally meet you."

"In truth, we've met before. I don't expect you would recall, for I had not been working here long when you were a little boy. But I remember you well, though. Clever child you were. A pleasure to serve you now, Your Grace," Mr. Carver replied with apparent sincerity and a dollop of caution, no doubt because all the other dukes had turned out so poorly.

Then Ernfield and Mrs. Granger introduced them to the rest of the staff, most of whom appeared to be dutiful and friendly.

Tulip recognized several maids and footmen because their families lived in Burnham and they all attended the same house of worship as the Hesters.

She hoped their familiarity with her mother's family would help rather than hinder her and Alex as they settled in.

"Tulip," Alex said quietly, "you seem to be at ease here. May I leave you in Mrs. Granger's hands for a while?"

She was surprised by the request, but nodded. "Yes, of course."

"Good." He asked Mr. Carver to join him in the study. "There is a study in this house, is there not?"

"Yes, Your Grace," he replied. "I took the liberty of bringing all the estate ledgers over here yesterday and setting them on your desk. They are ready to be reviewed at your convenience."

"Oh, I think now is convenient."

Mr. Carver frowned. "Do you not wish to settle in first? Or have a tour of the house before we roll up our sleeves and get to work?"

"No, I'm fine." Alex turned to Tulip. "Let Mrs. Granger show you around the house while I am holed up with Mr. Carver for the next few hours."

She stifled her surprise once again, wondering why he would desire them to be apart for any length of time so soon upon their arrival. "All right."

He next turned to Mrs. Granger. "Is our bedchamber ready?"

"Yes, Your Grace. Both the duke's quarters and the duchess quarters are in readiness."

He turned to Tulip, his eyebrow arched. "Set us up however you wish."

"The duke's bedchamber is probably the largest and likely to have the best views. I'll have our belongings brought up there. It should be easy enough to move things around if we decide on any changes."

He nodded and strode into the house with Mr. Carver.

The housekeeper cast her a sympathetic smile. "It is obvious you are newly wed and much desiring to remain in his company. I felt this way about my husband throughout all the years of our marriage."

"Oh, then you are actually married?" She knew it was common for housekeepers to adopt the 'Mrs.' for purposes of respectability no matter whether they were spinsters or married ladies.

"Widowed early on," the woman explained with an obvious wistfulness to her voice and perhaps some resentment that her beloved was taken from her so soon. "Five years of wedded bliss before I lost him to a wicked fever."

"I am so sorry," Tulip said with genuine sympathy.

Mrs. Granger cast her a sad smile. "I started here shortly after he died. Work was a necessity if I was to survive in this world. Shall we go up to the bedchambers first? And then I will show you around the rest of the house. Are you thirsty, Your Grace? Or hungry? Shall I have refreshments brought up to you? And what about His Grace?"

"No refreshments necessary for either of us. We stopped at a nearby coaching inn for a bite to eat less than two hours ago. We were not certain of the preparations made in expectation of our arrival."

"Ah, you thought we might all be slovenly and lazy."

Tulip winced. "We hoped this would not be the situation, but did prepare ourselves for the worst."

"I think you will find us to be a very good staff. We are all pleased to welcome you here. Mr. Carver has had nothing but nice things to say about you."

"That is good to hear. He will come to admire my husband, as well. You all will, once you get to know him. He is incredibly intelligent and a very hard worker. I would not be surprised if he had this estate flourishing before the year is out."

Mrs. Granger regarded her dubiously. "I hope you are right. The prior dukes did quite some damage through their neglect and wastrel ways."

"Were you here through all four of the last dukes?" Tulip asked.

She nodded. "Yes, most of us were."

"You must have been only in your mid-twenties when you started here."

"Late twenties," she said with a sadness in her eyes. "I was desperate to find work and had to take whatever position I was first offered. It happened to be as housekeeper here. I was hired because I was pretty and for no other reason. It had nothing to do with my competence or years of experience. In truth, I had almost no experience. But I was eager to learn and caught on quickly. I think His Grace's grandfather, the old duke, was pleased with my services and appreciated seeing a smiling face."

A forced smile, Tulip imagined, because she must have been grieving the loss of her husband.

But one required food and shelter even while in the midst of grief.

Only the wealthy could afford to sit home and mourn without such life-threatening concerns.

Tulip had to admire the woman for showing strength despite her sorrow. "And what about the succeeding dukes? What were they like?"

Mrs. Granger's smile faded as they walked upstairs to the bedrooms. "They were a difficult bunch, I will admit. I did my job and tried to stay out of their way as much as I could. Some of the things that went on in this house are too shameful to speak of aloud."

"I heard rumors," Tulip murmured. "Gossip was rampant in Burnham. That's where I grew up and lived for most of my life."

Mrs. Granger sighed and shook her head. "Well, it is not my place to speak ill of the dead. I served them as dutifully as I served the old duke. It wasn't always easy."

"I think you will find my husband to be honest and fair. There won't be any such nonsense going on now that he is the duke. He is respectful of others, and a very good man."

They entered the duke's suite of rooms that at first glance appeared quite grand and impressively furnished. However, on closer inspection Tulip noticed the curtains were fraying and the walls looked as though they could use a fresh coat of paint.

The bed and the bed linens appeared to be in good shape, however.

Indeed, the linens looked new.

Mrs. Granger smiled when Tulip mentioned it. "Yes, we tossed out all the old ones, the mattress included, and purchased new. We thought His Grace would appreciate it and understand the reason for the added expenditure."

"Oh, he will," Tulip said, knowing Alex would burn down this entire place if given the choice because he blamed the old duke and his father for destroying his mother.

As far as Alex was concerned, they tainted everything they touched.

She walked to one of the windows to peer out. "The view is magnificent, Mrs. Granger."

"Yes, quite beautiful," the pleasant housekeeper agreed.

There was an expansive garden that sloped toward the waters of the Bristol Channel glistening in the distance. The shrubbery beside a willow tree in the garden's corner seemed a bit overrun. It encroached on the flower beds and pebble pathways, but a little pruning would easily fix that problem. "Look there, by the willow. This would be the perfect spot for a little reading nook. A bench would go perfectly right there."

To her surprise, Mrs. Granger became suddenly flustered. "Oh, we shouldn't. That is…Ernfield will not allow it. You see, it was the old duke's wishes to leave that spot untouched and Ernfield vowed it would remain so."

"Why?"

"Truthfully, I don't know. I think the old duke might have buried some of his favorite pets there when he was a child. Of course, you are in charge here now and can do whatever you wish. It would be a nice spot to sit and read."

Tulip thought it odd that a hard man like Alex's grandfather would be so devoted to his pets. "We shall leave it as it is for now. No reason to disrespect his wishes."

There was a fountain in the center of the garden, but Tulip could not tell from this distance whether it was working or not.

"The duchess bedchamber is next door, Your Grace," Mrs. Granger said, pointing to an interior door between the two rooms. "You mentioned that all the trunks were to be brought in here, but would you not prefer your privacy? How are you to dress or bathe while His Grace and his valet are about? And what of him? Is your lady's maid to be standing here while he traipses about half dressed?"

"What you say is sensible," Tulip admitted. "You can move my things into the duchess quarters since it makes sense not to have spectators while I am washing and dressing. But the door between our chambers is always to be left unlocked."

She marched into the duchess suite of rooms and found them a little shabby, too. Nothing too serious that could not be easily refreshed. The room was a good size. The furniture was more delicate than the duke's furniture, and obviously designed for the lady of the manor. The view was similar to that from the duke's chamber.

It looked as though no wives had spent time in here in over a decade. Well, this was not surprising. From the gossip she had heard while growing up in Burnham, the last five dukes had either been widowers or bachelors when they inherited the title.

The lack of feminine touches showed.

However, the bed linens appeared to be new.

"We purchased new linens for both bedchambers," Mrs. Granger confirmed as Tulip surveyed the room. "However, this mattress and everything else in the duchess quarters, from the furniture to the drapes, has been left in place since the time of your husband's great grandfather."

"That long? Has there been not a single lady of the house since his great grandfather's time?" Tulip was surprised.

"Well, your husband's grandfather was married and sired four sons. However, his wife had died by the time he inherited the title." She cleared her throat. "I expect having a wife would have interfered with his…er, habits. He did enjoy the ladies."

Oh, yes.

The exploits of Alex's grandfather were legendary.

This explained why the duchess quarters looked so very old and faded.

That debauched, old goat already had his heirs, all four sons, and saw no reason to take on another wife who might stifle his hedonistic pleasures.

No, the ladies who slept in here were merely temporary fixtures, and there was likely an endless parade of them.

Tulip felt a ripple of unease run up her spine.

She did not like this room.

"Your husband's grandfather had thought to fix it up about twenty years ago," Mrs. Granger commented. "He hired a young lady to decorate it and other portions of the house, but that plan fell aside."

"Perhaps the room held too many ghosts."

"Yes," Tulip's housekeeper said with a hint of sadness in her voice.

Did Mrs. Granger feel those cold prickles up her spine, too?

"We'll get around to properly restoring the duchess bedchamber eventually," Tulip remarked. "For now, I'll just use the dressing area and store my clothes in the wardrobe."

She was never going to sleep in here, however.

The mere thought of slipping under those bedcovers gave her the shivers.

She did not understand why this room left her feeling so cold, since Alex would never have anyone other than her reside in the duchess quarters.

And why should she care what the prior dukes had done with their ladies in here?

Perhaps it was the fact so many Davenport dukes had died tragic deaths in quick succession that rattled her.

But none of them had met their untimely end in here.

In fact, only Alex's grandfather had died in the house.

Each of the others had died outdoors.

"I think I have seen enough here, Mrs. Granger. What is on the upper floor?"

The color drained from the housekeeper's cheeks, but she quickly recovered. "Oh, nothing but the tower room," she said with a casual gesture of dismissal. "No doubt soldiers were posted up there as lookouts for marauding invaders back when this place was first built. No one's been up there in years."

The door leading up to the tower room was locked when Tulip tried it.

"Your Grace, no! We shouldn't go up there. Who knows what condition it is in? I'll have one of the footmen inspect it first to make certain no vermin have taken up residence there."

"All right," Tulip said, sensing there could be more to this tower chamber than Mrs. Granger cared to reveal.

She would mention this to Alex.

They returned downstairs.

Mrs. Granger, aside from her obvious distress about that locked chamber, was proving to be quite pleasant.

She gave Tulip a tour of the main floor of the house whose rooms were mostly used for entertaining guests. They were as elegant as any found in the finest English manors nestled in the countryside but looked careworn.

The main floor of the house included a spacious formal parlor and equally spacious dining room that must have served as the old banqueting hall centuries ago. There was also a library, a billiards room, a music room that was large enough to serve as a ballroom, and a visitor's salon just off the entry hall. The main hallways held portraits of the prior dukes dating back at least five hundred years.

Tulip paused in front of the portrait of Alex's grandfather to study it closely because his grandfather bore such a striking resemblance to Alex even down to the cut of his jaw and the sharp look in his dark eyes.

And yet, these two men were so different in character, one debauched and the other valorous.

She shook out of the thought and moved on with Mrs. Granger who now showed her two rooms of more practical use for her and Alex. These were a small dining room and a cozy lady's parlor that were far more inviting and would be much easier to heat once the cold weather arrived.

"We refer to these as the winter dining room and the winter parlor," Mrs. Granger remarked a moment later.

"I think we will use these smaller rooms throughout the year. My husband and I will not be ready to host formal dinners or other entertainments for a while yet. In truth, I do not see us hosting at all except for one dinner party for my friends and family. I hope to attend to this within the month. But for our daily routine, it makes no sense for the two of us to take our meals at a table large enough to fit a small army."

"As you wish," Mrs. Granger said with a nod.

Alex's study was also on the main floor, but his door was closed and Tulip did not want to disturb him. "We'll stop in here last. I'll have a look at the kitchen next."

"Very well, Your Grace." Mrs. Granger led her down a drab hallway that was long and narrow.

Tulip met the Thornwycke Hall cook, a surly woman by the name of Mrs. Crabbe. The name suited her, for she was short-tempered with her scullery maids and did not smile at all while they were being introduced or while giving Tulip a brief tour of the kitchen and pantry which was surprisingly well stocked for a manor house that was lived in by depraved dukes.

Well, Tulip supposed even depraved dukes had to eat.

And would they not be likely to hold extravagant parties?

"What are you preparing for supper?" Tulip asked, intrigued by the heavenly aroma emanating from the pot on the fire.

"I thought a hearty lamb stew would serve ye for this evening, Yer Grace. I've also made some fresh bread and an apple pie."

Tulip smiled at the cook. "Sounds perfect. I am quite impressed with your excellent kitchen."

The woman's lips did not so much as twitch at the corners to acknowledge the compliment, not even the hint of a smile.

Honestly, what a crab!

"I am certain His Grace will enjoy the meal," Tulip said, still holding out hope of a cheerful conversation from the woman. "I'll sit with Mrs. Granger tomorrow morning to go over the menus for the week. Please do let her know if you have any suggestions for us. I would appreciate your comments."

The woman's face remained expressionless. "Very well, Yer Grace."

Goodness, how did people do this?

Alex was good at this, too. This ability to look completely blank, so no one had any idea what he was thinking.

"As you may have heard, I was raised in Somerset. In Burnham, to be precise. My family resides there. Do you know the Hesters?"

"Can't say as I do, Yer Grace."

"We'll have them over as soon as His Grace and I get organized. How much notice will you need to prepare for guests? I also intend to hold afternoon teas for my friends and involve myself in social activities, and in the various clubs and church events held locally. But those won't be for a few months yet."

"Three day's notice is all I need, Yer Grace. Unless ye have special requests and I might then have to send to Bath or Taunton for any comestibles I cannot obtain nearby. I would need at least a week for those situations."

"Fair enough, Mrs. Crabbe."

"When do ye wish to dine tonight? And will ye wish to dine at a similar hour every night? I'll need yer schedule for the other meals."

"Let me ask His Grace about his preference." She turned to the housekeeper. "Shall we move on to the study? I think we've given the men enough time to discuss their pressing issues."

"Very good, Your Grace."

Were it up to Tulip, she would have run to the study and poked her head in to ask Alex what hour he liked to dine, and then run back to tell the cook. But Dillie had warned her about the protocol of a large house. The lady of the house spoke to the housekeeper who in turn delivered the instructions to the cook.

After today, she was not expected to step foot in the kitchen.

She really did not like that rule.

Shouldn't she know what was being purchased? What was spent. What was being pilfered, for this was another thing Dillie had warned her about. There was always someone sneaking out with an extra loaf of bread, eggs, or fresh meat. Some might be more brazen and attempt to sneak off with some of the silverware, which was why she needed to keep the silverware under lock and key, and keep an accurate count of the pieces.

Mostly, Dillie overlooked the petty pilfering. However, she made certain to let her staff know she was aware of it.

Action was taken in the rare instances it got out of hand.

Tulip intended to follow this advice.

However, she was pleased how this place was run. The cook, housekeeper, and head butler all seemed to be taking their positions in the household quite seriously. While the Davenport dukes were profligate, their staff was not.

She and Mrs. Granger left the kitchen and made their way back down the narrow hall, their next stop the study.

The door was still closed, which meant the men were probably still working.

She knocked anyway.

"Enter," Alex called out with ducal authority.

She could not help but smile when she saw him with his jacket off and his expression serious as he made a notation in what appeared to be a ledger book. He still had on his waistcoat that accentuated his broad shoulders and trim torso, and she thought he looked very handsome indeed.

He remained immersed in the ledgers a moment longer, studying them with a sharp-eyed look.

When he finally glanced up, he smiled with genuine warmth upon realizing she had been the one to knock and not the butler. "Did you enjoy your tour?"

She nodded. "Yes, very much."

He rose to come around to the front of his desk. "Good, then you can show me around later and point out what you particularly liked."

"All right." It seemed an odd request since this house was as new to her as it was to him. Well, he had lived here as a boy, but so much must have changed since that time.

Back then, he was looking at Thornwycke through the eyes of a child.

He clearly was not asking for either Mrs. Granger or Mr. Carver to accompany them and serve as guides. "Our cook, Mrs. Crabbe, asked when we would like supper served. She also wanted to know when we would like to take our other meals."

Alex shrugged. "What is your preference?"

Tulip responded with a shrug of her own. "Oh, it makes no difference to me. Whatever suits you."

"Newly married and you are already being difficult," he teased, chuckling lightly. "Very well, how about supper at seven o'clock in the evening. Breakfast at eight o'clock in the morning. And one o'clock for a midday meal?"

She smiled. "Sounds perfect."

"But it ought to be nothing elaborate for the midday meal these next few weeks because it is likely I'll be riding out with Mr. Carver every day for the foreseeable future."

Tulip turned to Mrs. Granger. "Would you please relay this information to Mrs. Crabbe?"

She bobbed a curtsy. "If I am not needed here, I'll take care of it now."

Alex dismissed her with a nod.

Once their housekeeper had walked out, Alex drew out one of the chairs beside his desk and motioned for her to take the seat. "Join us, Tulip. I'm sorry I abandoned you, but I was eager to attack these ledgers without delay."

"Not at all, I know you meant to arrive here days earlier."

And without a wife, she could have added.

Their need for a hasty wedding had been the reason for his delay.

But was it not better to let the staff believe for now theirs was a proper courtship leading to a well-planned wedding? The truth would eventually come out. By then, she hoped the staff would respect her. "I had a nice chat with Mrs. Granger in the meanwhile."

"Good." He motioned for Mr. Carver to resume his seat, too.

But Alex remained standing, casually leaning a hip against the solid desk. He folded his arms across the lovely expanse of his chest and faced her. "What did you think of the house?"

She glanced at the kindly estate manager who was trying to be discreet and not give hint of his feelings about Thornwycke Hall. "I only saw the main rooms and the upstairs bedchambers, so I cannot speak to its foundations or what work might be needed on the roof and such. I'm sure Mr. Carver has reported on those."

"We touched upon it," Mr. Carver confirmed.

Tulip nodded and continued. "The house could be beautiful if freshened up. I saw very few spots where the rain had seeped in through the walls and needed to be patched. The windows all looked to be sound. No cracks."

Mr. Carver now spoke up, his expression one of pride. "I've tried my best to maintain this place in good order, not that the last three dukes cared a whit. Your grandfather cared, however. Despite his…" He sighed. "Despite his utter lack of propriety in his style of living, he did love this estate. It became more difficult to care for the manor house as his mind grew feeble and he began to gamble recklessly. But until then, despite his eccentric ways, he took excellent care of all his properties."

Tulip knew of the old duke's sad decline, for it had been no secret in Burnham that the old duke was losing his marbles. Her impression of the old duke was that he was an odd mix of intelligence and hedonism. She had overheard her uncle, William Hester, talking to Mr. Carver about the debauched goings on here. Wild parties. Women running around half naked on the grounds. Lewd games. Outrageous wagers placed on the stupidest dares.

No wonder all the next dukes had been wastrels.

How were they ever to grow up decent when the patriarch of their powerful family was openly lecherous, immoral, and indulging in sin?

Of course, their conversations were never meant for her delicate ears.

They would never have discussed the duke's depravities in front of her or anywhere within her hearing. They never knew she'd had her ear to the door and was listening in on their every word.

How sad that Alex's mother had walked into a house run like a brothel and gaming hell, unsuspecting of all the embarrassments she would have to endure while her father-in-law ran a libertine household.

Had Alex's father broken his wife's heart by openly partaking in those sinful indulgences along with his father and brothers?

How brave of her to escape and make certain her son was kept away from all those bad influences.

"Now tell me what you were *not* shown," Alex said.

The question surprised her, but she had quickly caught on to the workings of his mind. He approached everything with an investigative eye, something certainly warranted under these circumstances. "Well, I did not see the tower room. Mrs. Granger said no one has been up there in years."

Alex arched an eyebrow as he turned to Mr. Carver. "Is that so?"

"Aye, Your Grace. Your grandfather would not allow anyone up there, nor would the subsequent dukes. I think they continued the practice for no other reason than the old duke had done it, so they would, too. It was my intention to ask your permission to inspect it because there must be some upkeep required on the walls by now." He cleared his throat and cast Tulip a sheepish glance. "I would not recommend Her Grace joining us until we know what is to be found up there."

Alex let out a breath as he nodded. "Agreed. Is there a door to the tower wing? Is it kept locked?"

"Yes, Your Grace." Much like Mrs. Granger, he had a belt with several keys on it. "I happen to have the key right here."

"Good, let's go up now."

Tulip's eyes widened in surprise.

Alex did not waste a moment when in pursuit of answers, did he?

"Is that a good idea?" she asked. "What if you find something upsetting?"

"All the more reason to address it immediately," he reasoned, which showed how different their minds worked.

She would have put it off until morning because the thought of finding something gruesome as evening approached would have given her tormented dreams. This assumed she would be able to fall asleep at all and not spend the night tossing up her accounts if the tower room proved to be a prison of horrors.

"Stay here, Tulip. We won't be gone long." Alex motioned toward the bookshelves that actually had some books on them. "Find yourself something interesting to read."

"All right." But she was too agitated to concentrate and had no intention of attempting to do so.

Pacing impatiently is what she was going to do.

But as the minutes passed, she did become curious and decided to browse those bookshelves. The books were mostly guides on farming, no doubt acquired when the old duke still retained some common sense and looked after the ducal properties.

There were also a few books pertaining to the Davenport family history that would be of interest to read. As she drew several off the shelf, she noticed something tucked behind them. It turned out to be a journal that belonged to Alex's grandfather, judging by the dates written at the start of each entry.

He must have kept it hidden behind the other books.

Obviously, it had gone unnoticed all these years because none of the succeeding dukes had ever bothered with reading material.

"Definitely worth a closer look," Tulip murmured and plucked it off the shelf along with others pertaining to the family's history.

She had just settled in one of the plump, cushioned chairs beside the hearth when she heard Alex and Mr. Carver talking in the hall.

"What happened?" she asked, hopping to her feet and keeping the journal clutched in her hands as they strode in. "What did you find?"

She was surprised by their quick return.

"Nothing." Alex smiled, but it felt to her like a forced smile.

She eyed him in confusion. "You found nothing at all?"

"The room was empty. There were scuff marks and patterns of shading on the floor. Also scratches and small holes on the wall. There might have been furniture up there at one time."

"And?"

"And nothing." Yet, his eyes were shadowed.

She knew Alex had to suspect something more.

"Do you think someone was kept up there against their will?"

His eyes widened, and then he let out a breath. "Yes, it is possible. Or more likely that one of the earlier duchesses meant to turn it into a sewing room for herself. There's no reason to believe anything sinister occurred up there. Truly, no evidence of it at all."

"Even if something had occurred, it would have been ages ago," Mr. Carver said. "Certainly before the old housekeeper, Mrs. Dodge, came into her position or before Ernfield became head butler."

"What if it was not all that long ago?" Tulip asked.

Mr. Carver frowned. "You mean, in recent history? Someone would have heard noises up there or cries for help, or odors of decay. I never gave that old tower room a thought, not even once the next dukes began dying in quick succession. In fact, neither Mrs. Granger nor I had the key or ever had permission to go up there. We hunted for it and found it after the last duke died."

Tulip was surprised. "And you did not think to go up there until now? Why wait?"

He cleared his throat. "There was no sign of activity up there. It wasn't our place to trespass."

Of course, the entire staff held their positions at the pleasure of whoever happened to be the current duke. None of them could afford to gain said duke's displeasure and lose their means of livelihood, all the more dire if they had a family to support.

Perhaps they were terrified of what they might find beyond that tower door.

Or they merely respected the odd quirks of each duke. If Alex's grandfather wanted no one in the tower room and no one sitting under the willow tree, then so be it as far as the staff was concerned.

No questions asked.

They believed it was their duty to comply with their master's wishes, even if they were odd.

She let out a shaky breath. "Is there a dungeon in this place?"

Mr. Carver's expression lightened. "There was, but for the last hundred years it has been used as nothing more sinister than a larder. You'll find potatoes and an assortment of root vegetables, preserved fruits, dried meats, grains, and the like stored there. Mrs. Crabbe keeps a tight account of whatever is in there."

"Good, perhaps the ghosts will not be so angry then," she said in jest, but there was a kernel of truth to her remark.

This place felt haunted to her, as though something sinister had happened in the past and needed to come to light.

"There are no ghosts here," Mr. Carver insisted. "You need not concern yourself, Your Grace. You might hear the wind howling outside your window and echoing through the chimneys, but that is all."

"I see," she said.

But if that were all, then why did Alex look troubled?

He sensed something, she was certain of it.

So did she.

Why were cold tingles racing up her spine?

CHAPTER 11

ALEX LOOKED FORWARD to an evening spent alone with Tulip.

It was their first night at Thornwycke Hall and there were so many questions still to be answered. However, one concern could clearly be checked off the list because their cook was a marvel. The lamb stew he was now polishing off was among the best he had ever tasted.

Tulip smiled as they sat beside each other at the small table in the cozy winter dining room. "Mrs. Crabbe is a crusty, old crab, but she cooks divinely, doesn't she?" she mentioned between mouthfuls.

Alex gave an enthusiastic nod. "I'll say. Beats the tavern fare I used to have or anything Mrs. Gayle ever prepared for me."

Tulip set down her fork, for she had devoured the contents of her plate and now patted her stomach as though she could not manage another bite. "What is our plan for tomorrow? Where are we going first?"

He arched an eyebrow. "Would it not be more efficient if we split our tasks?"

She frowned, obviously not liking the suggestion. "As we did within minutes of our arrival?"

He placed his hand over hers again, realizing he had to stop thinking efficiently and start thinking like a married man with a capable wife who wanted to be with him. "That wasn't fair of me to do that to you, was it? But you knew Mr. Carver and seemed to be familiar with several of the servants, so I thought it would be all right if I left you in Mrs. Granger's care. She seemed friendly enough, and I knew she would confide in you if it was just the two of you chatting."

Tulip nodded. "You're probably right. I did learn more about her and the goings on in this house. She suggested I keep my belongings in the duchess quarters, so we unpacked them there and placed your belongings in the duke's bedchamber. I'll need to hire a lady's maid and you will need a valet, so it would be awkward to have us preparing for the day together. How will either of us wash or dress while having both maid and valet in the room?"

He cut himself a chunk of the freshly made bread. "Yes, I see."

"However, there is a door between our rooms that I instructed must always be kept unlocked."

"So that we may visit each other during the night?"

"I don't want visits," she insisted. "I would like to permanently share a bed with you. *Yours.* Not mine. I get odd sensations whenever I look at that duchess bed. I don't know why, but cold shivers run up my spine."

He gave her hand a light squeeze. "That's all right then. You'll sleep with me. I want you beside me every night, anyway. You are my wife, Tulip. You belong with me."

She cast him a sweet smile. "I feel the same."

"Well, that was easily resolved," he said with a sense of contentment, for this was what he had hoped for in their marriage and had not expected to achieve it so fast.

That she did not like the duchess bed gave him little concern. It was likely the feeling of separation from him that she did not like, and not some ghostly presence.

He would have been willing to give Tulip the time she needed to get accustomed to him and their married life. Fortunately, it had not taken her any time at all to get comfortable with him.

In truth, a wedding night was all it took.

Perhaps this is what came of her having good and honest men in her life, for she approached their marriage with the intention of trusting him until he gave her a reason not to trust.

He never would.

Marrying Tulip was the best thing he could have done for himself.

On the other hand, he had been raised to trust no one, especially not his male relatives who would stab him in the back if he were ever to drop his guard.

But trusting no one was quite isolating and he had felt that starvation in his soul.

He was no hermit and wanted a family life as well as a circle of good friends. He had found those friends in Julius Thorne and his brothers, and had also grown to admire their wives. Perhaps this was why he had ached for a wife for himself.

But who could he trust, especially once it became known he was the new Duke of Davenport? Every debutante had a reason to lie to him to gain his favor.

Only one had ever run from him.

That was Tulip.

An inconvenience because he had fallen in love with her at first sight. Her every action in the ensuing months had shown his instincts were right and that he could trust her.

She was the wife he wanted.

At the moment, she did not look all that pleased with him because he was trying to be logical and efficient by dividing their tasks.

Was this not a good way of working together? Accomplishing twice as much in half the time.

Apparently, Tulip took 'working together' to mean they would actually stick to each other as they went about learning how this estate functioned.

"I can meet with Mrs. Gayle and review the running of the household any time over this coming week," she argued when he foolishly tried to explain the logic in dividing their chores. "It doesn't have to be done tomorrow. She is quite capable. I can leave her to continue things as they are."

"While you tour the farms with me?"

She nodded. "This was our plan originally, wasn't it?"

"Yes, because I did not expect Mr. Carver to be so competent. Fine, Tulip. So be it. You'll join us. We'll need to get an early start on the day because there is much to do. How about we retire to our quarters now?"

"Yes, I would like that. I have some reading to do."

His eyebrow shot up. "That journal you were clutching in a death grip earlier in the study? Do you really think you will find anything of interest written in it?"

"I hope so. Actually, I am sure of it. At the very least, it will give us an idea of the workings of your grandfather's mind."

He grunted.

If this was his grandfather's journal, it could consist of pages and pages of depraved thoughts and descriptions of orgies. He did not know if there would be descriptions of more sinister acts. The man was a renowned libertine, but had he gone beyond mere womanizing? Taking willing ladies to bed was one thing, yet was there a darker side to him?

The locals called him eccentric, and he had been quite the charmer in his younger days. But had he done things that would have gotten him imprisoned or hanged if he were not a duke? "Tulip, perhaps I ought to read it first. There could be something upsetting written in that journal. In truth, lots of upsetting secrets confessed."

"I'll stop reading if it gets too lurid."

He sighed. "You cannot *unread* something after you've read it. You were queasy at the mere idea of our inspecting the tower room in the afternoon, and now you think to lie in bed at night and read the journal of a man we know was the very definition of immoral? No, I'll read it first."

She frowned, but nodded. "All right."

He leaned over and kissed her. "Do not be angry because I wish to protect you from a darker side of life."

"I'm not angry, merely…I don't know. It's just that I thought of the journal as *my* find. But it would upset me if there were horrible things written in it. Well, now I will have to find something else to read."

"You noticed other books on our family history. Read those. They'll be helpful to me, yet not so luridly descriptive of my ancestors as to weigh on your heart. I like that softness about you.

I never want to see it destroyed."

They retired upstairs, Tulip disappearing into the duchess quarters with Mrs. Granger who would assist her for this evening since she had yet to engage a lady's maid.

Alex felt a tug to his heart when the door clicked shut between their bedchambers.

It was a stupid response because Tulip would open it up again in a few minutes.

And yet, it felt like an eternity.

Living here was going to be so vastly different than living in London, he realized while waiting for her to return.

It was obvious Tulip would require a maid assigned to attend to her daily needs. He would require a valet, but not to assist him in dressing or washing or shaving. He could manage those himself as he had always done. But someone needed to attend to his clothes, make certain they were cleaned and pressed, and see that his boots were polished. Those chores had been easily handled by Mrs. Gayle herself or by any number of nearby shopkeepers when he lived in London.

Thornwycke Hall was miles away from the nearest village, so he could not simply take a five minute walk to the local laundress or shoemaker.

He was himself partly undressed and had washed up by the time the door opened again and Tulip walked into his bedchamber.

She looked pretty with her hair down, and wearing a thin nightgown and robe. In her hands was one of the books on the Davenport family history.

Obviously, she wanted to hop into bed and read it.

He had taken off all but his shirt and trousers, for the hour was still early by London standards. He hoped Tulip would prefer to sit with him beside the hearth and talk about their plans first. "All right, I like that idea. Mrs. Granger thoughtfully ordered a pot of hot cocoa delivered to me. It's in the duchess quarters. Let me bring it in. Would you like to share it with me?"

"No, I have a bottle of brandy for myself."

But he did not bother with the brandy this evening, for his

mind was already in a spin and he did not need it to spin further with drink.

He watched Tulip pour the cocoa for herself. "Do you have the journal, Alex?"

He nodded. "It's by the bed. Speaking of which, do you have a preference for a particular side of the bed to sleep on?"

She laughed. "No, you choose."

"I'll take the right side since it is closest to the door. But let's not leap into bed yet."

She had just taken a sip of her cocoa and coughed mirthfully. "I did not think I would ever hear you say that."

"Oh, I am still hot for you," he said with a chuckle. "Never doubt it. In fact, there is a very strong possibility we will do something other than reading once we slip under the sheets."

He sank onto one of the cushioned chairs positioned by the hearth. "But let's talk for a few minutes first."

"Just talk?" She set aside her cup and came to his side.

He drew her onto his lap. "Yes, shouldn't we?"

"Very well." She put her arms around his neck, obviously feeling quite comfortable nestled in his arms.

He decided to kiss her first because she was so soft and tempting.

And kiss her again.

"Alex!" She laughed as he untied the belt of her robe. "Is this your idea of talking?"

"No, but you are irresistible." He loved the way her body felt against his, the pertness of her round bottom and the softness of her breasts pressed against his chest. But she was right, they would never accomplish anything if he did not keep his hands off her.

Still, he kept her on his lap.

"Tulip, I think we need to find building plans to this house as soon as possible. I asked Mr. Carver, and he told me he had placed them in the top drawer of the desk in the study last month, but they're gone now."

"Perhaps he forgot and stored them somewhere else."

"He wondered about that, too. But he does not strike me as the sort to forget something as important as that."

She nodded. "He isn't at all foggy-headed. He is very organized and his mind is very sharp."

"Then isn't it odd that we cannot find the plans?"

"I'm sure they will turn up eventually. Why must you have them immediately? You haven't the funds to undertake major renovations, do you? And aren't we planning on touring the farms first?"

"Yes, the farms first because they are our primary source of income. But we also need to survey the structure of this house that was built centuries ago. There must have been secret passageways built into the walls to provide escape routes if ever Thornwycke Hall were attacked. It also follows that there must also be secret passages between some of these rooms that would allow someone with knowledge of them to slip through the house without being seen. Our bedchamber door can be latched to keep others out, but it will not keep out someone who knows a secret way into this room."

"Do you think anyone on the staff knows of these secret passageways?"

He shrugged. "Possibly, but they won't ever confess this to us."

Tulip stiffened in his arms. "Should we start looking for those hidden doors now?"

"No, I'm just being a cynical clot and thinking aloud. I like to be in control of a situation, know where everything is, that's all. But I've scared you, haven't I?"

She pursed her lips. "A little. This house is already daunting, and made more so because so many dukes in succession have died here."

"The last three did not die in this bedchamber or even in the house. As for my grandfather, he was old, sickly, and bedridden. It is likely he died of natural causes."

"But you still have your doubts about the other deaths."

He winced. "Only because they happened within so short a span of time. That is the only reason. I know they were ruled accidental and no one has proven otherwise."

"But you could do it."

"Assuming there is anything sinister to prove about them. I'll keep my eyes open and ask questions. Anyone can fall off a horse while out riding, especially if they are riding recklessly fast. Anyone can drown, especially if they are wandering around drunk at night and stumbled onto the salt marshes as the tide came in."

Tulip nodded. "It is extremely dangerous to be caught up in a changing tide even if one is sober and walking about in broad daylight. Surely, the predecessor dukes had to have known this since they'd lived here most of their lives."

"My grandfather kept his sons and grandsons firmly under his thumb while he was alive. Once he died, who was to hold them back from all the destructive behaviors they learned from him?"

"I suppose." She studied his features. "What are you thinking, Alex?"

He shrugged. "Nothing that makes any sense yet. Let's worry about the estate and getting it back in order. Mr. Carver is going to give us a tour of the farms and dairy tomorrow. That could turn into a long day for us."

"We haven't talked about your findings yet. Anything surprising turn up in the ledgers you were studying earlier?"

He grunted. "Yes, but it was a good surprise. The farms and dairy are actually turning a small profit. The bad news is that my predecessors spent the income faster than it came in."

"So we have to rebuild starting from nothing?"

"Yes, pretty much. But we do have the prospect of income, and that is important. We'll need some luck to build up the Davenport coffers to any significance. A bad year would set us back and force us to pile on more debt. So, let us pray for good weather over the next few years to get us back on our feet."

"What about the old cheesemaking works?"

"I would like to revive that, but I don't know if it can be done this year. The estate has too little income coming in just yet. Not sure if there is enough to spare in getting that project started."

"I knew Mr. Carver was a good man and could keep this estate going no matter how badly your predecessor dukes ravaged the assets."

"I am vastly relieved you turned out to be right. Half the battle is reining in the profligate spending, and that ought to be fairly easy for us to do."

"Yes, I agree," Tulip said. "Our needs are not extravagant. I can sew new drapes and make my own gowns, if necessary."

Blessed saints.

There was no pretense to the girl, just compassion and a desire to be helpful. No wonder his instincts had gone wild at the first sight of her and screamed at him to marry her. She was ready to be a true partner to him in every essence.

Gad, that felt nice.

"No," Alex said with a gentle laugh. "I will not have my *duchess* wife reduced to a seamstress. But I appreciate the offer. What we need to do is decide upon the priorities and address them with proper budgeting. We'll need to carefully allocate the income already coming in. Which problems are most urgent? I have my opinion on the top three."

"And what are they?"

His expression turned serious. "Reducing the debt that has been run up. Maintaining the house and farms in good repair. And giving you a sufficient budget to do whatever you wish with this house."

"As in redecorating?"

He nodded. "I want you to be happy here."

"So you have made me a priority?" She kissed his cheek. "I would be happy living with you in a barn if we were to have moments like this. In truth, I think you would be happier in a barn, too. This house is twenty times more than we'll ever need."

"It is a bit of a monstrosity," he acknowledged.

"And holds such unhappy memories for you, Alex. Would time and a bit of redecoration ever change your dislike of this place?"

"I don't know," he said with a tinge of bitterness.

Tulip cast him a soft look. "We don't have to stay here. Once Thornwycke is put back in shape, we can return to London or go anywhere you like. You can see Mr. Carver is efficiently running this place and does not require constant supervision."

"But you love being in Somerset, you've always said so."

"Yes, but I lo–" Her eyes widened and she stared at him for the longest moment.

What was she about to say?

That she loved him more?

He held his breath, hoping to hear those words.

But as the air continued to hang thick between them, he knew she was not yet ready to make such a claim.

"Somerset is a lovely place," she finally said, still wide-eyed, "but it is just a place. My home is with you, wherever you wish to be."

He kissed her again. "Let's go to bed."

He eased her off his lap and rose, but took hold of her hand. "Our first night here. I'm glad that mattress and the linens are all new."

"Me, too." She stared at the bed. "New life. New start."

Tulip removed her robe and he removed the last of his clothes before they settled under the covers.

Tulip regarded him expectantly once they were tucked in.

"What?" he muttered with a soft laugh. "Do you think I cannot control the beast in me? Let's read first."

"Just read?" She smiled. "Isn't this nice? We are like an old, married couple."

He rolled her atop him, grinning as she gasped in surprise.

"Perhaps I am not quite ready to control the beast yet. There's still a bit of life left in me, and you are quite delicious." He clamped his arms around her so that their bodies were pressed to each other. He felt her lush bosom mold to his chest, and her hips rest against his. "Gad, you are distracting."

He kissed her again because she had the sweetest lips, but then he set her back on her side of the bed and picked up the journal to read. "I really need to get to this tonight."

She nestled against him and took up her book on his family's history.

They must have been reading in silence for only a few minutes before Tulip yawned and set her book aside. "I'm suddenly so tired, Alex."

He frowned. "All right, love. We accomplished a lot today."

"Not all that much. It wasn't very strenuous, but my eyes suddenly feel unbearably heavy. I cannot keep them open another minute."

He was surprised that her exhaustion had come on so rapidly, but this could be explained logically. This first day may not have been physically strenuous, but it held a wealth of feelings that roiled her and must have drained her strength. Who would not feel the same when returning home a duchess and finding oneself mistress of a garishly large manor house with an unsavory history and a mysterious tower room that quite possibly held dark secrets?

Since Tulip appeared comfortable enough while snuggled against him, he dismissed his worries and remained awake reading his grandfather's journal well into the night.

He was glad Tulip hadn't been awake to pry and ask to read the lurid entries.

She would have been shocked by the goings on his grandfather had described.

What a lecherous, old goat.

Surprisingly, there was nothing cruel or seriously depraved mentioned in the pages.

It became clear the old man was a proponent of living freely and following one's spirit animal.

What utter tripe.

His grandfather's spirit animal was a wolf, apparently.

Which really meant the lecherous, old goat, who merely thought himself a wolf, invited beautiful young ladies to stay at Thornwycke Hall and encouraged them to remove their clothes whenever the impulse struck, even if it came over them while walking around the grounds.

And if they had an impulse to do more, he was ready to oblige.

Gad, the dirty, old man.

What had the staff thought of this behavior?

They could not have approved, although some of the men might have thought it amusing at first and gawked at whatever was being shown. He had been too young at the time to understand or even see much of this behavior going on. Also, his mother had done all she could to keep him away from it.

They had left Thornwycke when he was eight years old.

Before then and since, there had not been any shortage of young ladies willing to engage in these romps. By his grandfather's description, one would think these buxom sprites were happy creatures who were never coerced into doing anything against their will.

Well, this was his grandfather's version.

He would question the staff and find out what really went on.

The journal only covered the years *after* his grandmother's death, so he did not know if this nonsense went on during the poor woman's lifetime. He thought it might have done because his father and uncles had obviously been indoctrinated into this style of living and had no qualms about carrying on the depraved Davenport traditions.

This must have been why his mother took him away before he was old enough to have embedded memories of any of these goings on.

But the impact on him had been deep and severe.

There were a few references to his father within the journal that Alex read with extreme interest.

He despised the man for treating his mother as shabbily as he had, but Alex got the impression his father was a sad figure who had loved his wife but been too weak to pull himself away from the old man's influence.

Still, Alex had no pity for him.

Was it not the responsibility of a husband and father to fight for and protect his wife and child?

But something else became clear while reading the passages his grandfather had written closer to the end of his life. The old man was harboring a terrible secret, something that had happened years earlier in that tower room, and weighed heavily on his heart.

His guilt and need for absolution became evident as he reached his end of life.

Whether the secret sin was his or another's, Alex could not tell yet.

He continued reading late into the night, hoping to find more answers, but the journal contained no further hint of what the secret was, only that a young woman by the name of Elspeth was involved, and it was something that needed to be buried deep and forgotten.

Except, his grandfather had not been able to forget it.

He'd been haunted by the Elspeth incident.

He'd written it in his journal in the hope of expunging it from his mind.

Had he confessed the sin to someone as he lay upon his deathbed? And with that confession set off a string of revenge deaths on the Davenport dukes?

Alex placed the journal aside, now troubled.

This shed new light on the accidental deaths of the last three dukes.

Perhaps these deaths were not so innocent after all.

Who had learned of his grandfather's secret? And what was this awful truth he'd needed to confess?

"Bloody hell," he muttered, gazing down at Tulip's sleeping form. He should never have brought her here. That the deaths of three prior dukes were ruled accidental should not have swayed him.

He was the trained investigator and ought to have known better.

But he'd wanted Tulip so badly, ached to marry her and make her his wife, that he'd lied to himself about the danger.

After reading this journal, could there be a doubt the deaths of his three predecessors had been murder?

Perhaps his grandfather's death had also been a murder, and the simplest to accomplish because the old man was already sick and frail.

Everyone would believe he had died of natural causes, but what if he had been slowly poisoned?

That would make four deaths.

Was he next?

CHAPTER 12

SUNSHINE PERMEATED ALEX'S bedchamber and warmed his face to stir him awake early the following morning. He could not have managed more than three or four hours of sleep, but it was enough for him. However, the solid eight hours Tulip had received appeared to be not enough for her.

It troubled Alex that she seemed groggy even after he gently shook her awake.

He had grown used to seeing her bright smile and having her reach up to kiss him when she awoke, but she appeared to have trouble even lifting her head this morning.

He shook her again gently.

"Tulip," he whispered, kissing her lightly on her warm, pink cheek.

She finally cast him an achingly sweet smile. "Is it time to wake up already? I feel as though I have just closed my eyes."

Even her movements were sluggish as she drew the covers over herself to bargain for a few more minutes of sleep.

"Love, we need to get an early start. I thought you wanted to come with me."

And after reading his grandfather's journal, was there a doubt he needed to keep her close to him today on the chance she was also in danger?

"I did want to, Alex. I *do* want to. But I can hardly lift my head. Why don't you go on ahead with Mr. Carver?"

"No, Tulip. I need you with me."

She snorted. "Weren't you the one who originally suggested we divide and conquer? You heading off to the farms while I inventory the household silver and work out the weekly menus with Mrs. Granger? This will occupy much of my day."

Oh, sure.

It would occupy her for about five minutes.

He frowned, but spoke gently to her. "And weren't you the one who insisted on joining me in touring those farms? If memory serves me correctly, you were quite vocal about it. Come on, Tulip. This isn't like you."

Indeed, her lethargy was concerning and nothing like her usual behavior.

True, they had only been married a week, so how was he to know what was usual and what was not?

But every morning since their wedding day, she had bounded out of bed all smiles and chatty, and eager to kiss him.

No, this was not his Tulip at all.

"Love, come on," he insisted, drawing the covers off her.

She groaned and tried to tug them back over her head. "Why?"

"I'll tell you as we ride to the farms."

"All right." She finally sat up with a gaping yawn. "Give me a minute and I'll ring for Mrs. Granger."

"No, let me help you dress."

"And style my hair?"

"Yes." He gestured airily with his hands. "I'll help you pin it up in a simple…I don't know, that *thing* ladies do with their hair."

She rose and shuffled into the duchess quarters.

Alex was already washed and dressed, so he followed her in and went straight to her wardrobe. "Here, this looks like a sturdy gown."

It was a bluish-gray muslin that would suit her to perfection.

"Not that one, Alex. It will show all the mud stains."

He hadn't thought of that. "Or better, this one then."

He drew out a dark brown muslin for her.

He must have looked perplexed, for Tulip was grinning at him. "Yes, that one's a much better choice. Give me a moment and I'll get myself ready. I'll call you in when I need help with the laces."

"All right." Since she was obviously asking for privacy, he retreated to his own bedchamber but kept the door slightly ajar between them because he could not bear to actually shut that door.

It was stupid and nonsensical to want no barrier between them even for something so innocent as getting dressed.

He supposed it was foolish to equate a shut door between them as being shut out of her heart.

"Idiot," he muttered, and went to the pot of cocoa that sat atop one of the small tables in his bedchamber.

Was it possible Tulip had been drugged?

He lifted the pot's lid and inhaled, but his nose did not pick up the scent of anything other than cocoa.

He next gave Tulip's cup a sniff and found nothing odd there, either.

Not ready to give up yet, he poured a little of the cocoa remaining in the pot into Tulip's cup and took a careful sip.

The cocoa tasted fine, just cold.

What in blazes?

Why was she so lethargic this morning then?

And why had that exhaustion come on so rapidly last night?

He set aside the cocoa and spent the next few minutes examining his bedroom walls for a secret entrance, but he noticed no tell-tale crevices to indicate a discreet opening. Nor was there a servants stairs since this was part of the old fortress built at a time when defense was most important and not the 'inconvenience' of seeing servants moving from room to room as they cleaned.

Perhaps there was a passage hidden in the fireplace, he mused.

He took hold of one of the fire irons and used it to press along the brickwork on its back wall. Despite the ashes having been properly cleaned out, the fireplace was far from spotless, so he did no more than poke at the bricks.

Nothing.

He wanted to step into the massive fireplace and check it out more thoroughly, but he had just washed up and could not risk getting covered in soot.

A more thorough inspection would have to wait for another time.

"Alex," Tulip called to him in her sweet voice. "I'm ready for help with my laces."

He strode into her bedchamber, turning breathless at the sight of her standing there with a smile on her face and her gown slipping off her shoulders. She had done up her hair herself, simply drawing it back and pinning it in a braided bun at the nape of her neck.

Gad, she was a pretty thing.

He'd be a happy man if she smiled at him this way each morning.

But how many mornings would he have if there was a killer on the loose determined to dispatch him as efficiently and cleverly as he had done the prior dukes?

Would the killer harm Tulip, too?

Or had she been purposely drugged to keep her out of the way?

Yes, that was likely.

Why else bother putting her to sleep?

Blessed saints.

Perhaps he was meant to be drugged, too.

But he hadn't taken any brandy last night, instead eager to read his grandfather's journal while lying in bed with Tulip. Had his remaining awake reading the journal into the wee hours thrown off the killer's plans?

What irony that his wretched grandfather might have saved his life.

"Tulip, did you have something other than the hot cocoa last night?"

"No, nothing more after our supper. Why do you ask?"

He shrugged. "You were unusually slow to wake up this morning. I thought you might have eaten something or had a drink of something that upset your stomach."

"No," she repeated, so he let the matter drop.

She might have taken something during their meal then.

He easily recalled what each of them had eaten because the meal was a single course and rather simple.

Delicious, too.

But they ate the same thing.

They even drank the same wine at supper.

Alex had investigated hundreds of crimes in his relatively short career, succeeding in solving many of them because of his cool demeanor and ability to concentrate on the facts instead of getting caught up in *his* emotions concerning the crime.

How was he to dismiss all feeling and think with cool clarity in this situation?

"You are frowning," Tulip remarked as he stood in front of her.

"Just a little distracted, that's all. Turn around, love."

Her eyes lit up and she cast him a devastatingly beautiful smile.

Oh, gad.

He had been calling her 'love' ever since their wedding night, accidentally having it slip out a time or two because it felt so natural and appropriate.

She was taking to it like a kitten given a bowl of sweet cream.

And now, she smiled every time he used the endearment.

Well, she was becoming his 'love' wasn't she?

"Stop tempting me and turn around," he said with a chuckle, kissing her on the nose and then taking her by the shoulders to turn her away from him.

He gave her a hot kiss on the neck because he simply could not resist.

She giggled as he tied her laces and took his time about it. "Alex! Are you lacing me up or undressing me?"

His knuckles kept grazing sensitive spots on her body, but who could blame him when she looked so delicious and he genuinely adored being married to her? He readily admitted to working at cross purposes in getting her dressed.

Finally, with a silent chiding to himself, he tied the last of her laces. "There."

"You are very good at this, Alex."

"Am I?" He was not about to comment further since he refused to discuss his previous intimate experiences.

He had gained this skill by assisting other ladies back into their clothing after romantic assignations, often in the dark, and when all due haste was required.

There had been nothing romantic about those encounters.

They were merely convenient releases of lust for both participants because he did not choose ladies of sterling character.

They were usually married, unhappily so.

Or widows who enjoyed their independence and intended never to remarry.

These were casual liaisons.

Nothing permanent and certainly no hearts involved.

But that was before he'd met Tulip.

He had not been with another woman since setting eyes on her because there was nothing casual about his feelings for her.

He wanted *her*.

No one else would ever do.

"Mr. Carver will be along soon," he said, giving her a softer kiss on the neck before releasing her.

She donned her walking boots, grabbed her bonnet and a shawl, and walked downstairs with him just as a clock in the hall bonged the eight o'clock hour.

Alex was pleased to find their breakfast salvers set out in the winter dining room.

Tulip inhaled deeply. "Oh, my. That's heavenly."

"Yes, for certain." He quietly tasted everything Tulip had served herself, piling a spoonful of each of her choices onto his own plate.

Nothing tasted amiss.

He also pretended to take an interest in the tea poured for her by a footman, taking a sip out of her cup before she'd had the chance to drink it herself. "Ah, that's good."

"Alex," she said, laughing. "You could have asked for a cup of your own."

"Would you care for tea, Your Grace?" the footman asked, holding out the teapot in his hand.

"No, just curious. I'll have coffee."

Once poured, he drank it slowly, trying to discern anything odd about the taste, but there was nothing wrong with the coffee, either.

In fact, it was quite good.

What was going on here?

Not that he should be irritated that a hearty breakfast had been served.

So what had Tulip taken last night to knock her out cold?

He did not like puzzles he could not solve.

Mr. Carver was waiting for them by the carriage when he and Tulip walked out of the manor house a short while later. "Climb in with us, Carver."

"Thank you, Your Grace." He scampered in after them and took a seat across from him and Tulip.

It was a blustery morning, but the sun was still shining and the sky was a vivid blue. There was no threat of rain anywhere in sight, but English weather was always unpredictable. It was best to complete their tour of the local Davenport farms as soon as possible.

Alex kept the conversation light and pleasant as they rode toward the first farm.

He stared out of the carriage window as Mr. Carver and Tulip pointed to various places of interest.

For the most part, however, their carriage rolled swiftly along these rural roads that were fairly isolated.

The scenery was beautiful, a refreshing change from the crowded London streets, but the quiet was a bit disconcerting to Alex.

He'd grown used to the noises and odors of London.

He looked north and saw glistening water in the distance, the sun-dappled gleam of the Bristol Channel.

They rode past salt marshes and streams that were offshoots of the channel.

But as their carriage moved further inland, the terrain became lush and green. Those salt marshes were replaced by rolling hills and flower-dotted meadows.

Pastures were plentiful and divided by ancient stone fences.

Some of these pastures held sheep grazing on the grass while others had cows wandering in them.

He noticed several apple orchards on their approach to the first of his farms.

"Here we are, Your Grace. Lollibridge Farm," his estate manager said with obvious pride, and then proceeded to give them a tour. "This one's your largest and best producer."

The farmer who ran the place came out to greet them as they began to walk around the grounds that were comprised mostly of apple orchards.

"This is Mr. Rawlings," said Mr. Carver.

Tulip apparently knew him from church, for she stepped forward to greet him warmly. "How lovely to see you again, Mr. Rawlings."

The man's smile was from ear to ear. "And you, Miss Tulip…that is, er…Your Grace. Your uncle said you'd gone to London to find yourself a husband."

"I got the best," she replied, smiling up at Alex.

After a round of genial conversation and a brief tour, Rawlings returned to his tasks while they continued to have a look around. There was a cider press that appeared to be in good order, and a small chicken coop on the property as well as a barn that held a substantial number of milking cows. "But this is not the Davenport dairy," Mr. Carver explained. "This farm is known primarily for its apple orchards. We sell the apples and cider come autumn. The apples will be at their best in about a month. That's when we'll hire day laborers to pick them, press some into cider, and take our wares to market."

"What is done with the milking cows?" Alex asked.

"These pastures have the best grass feed and our Somerset milk is particularly creamy because our cows are so well treated. Their milk is perfect for churning into butter or making the best cheese. We supply milk to the town of Cheddar where their cheeses have become quite popular because of their distinctive, deep yellow color. That is a sign of healthy cows. We also sell our milk to markets as far south as Exeter and as far north as Bristol. Of course, we are close to Bath and regularly sell all our products there. These farms supply not only milk, butter, and eggs, but salt, apples, and cider, too. Extracting salt from the marshes is another important use of the land."

The next two farms were similarly run, their primary products being milk, cream, cider, and apples. But there were also some plum trees, acres of vegetable patches, and blackberries and strawberries growing wild on these two farms.

The fourth farm was where the Davenport cheeses were once produced and Alex was most interested in touring that farm next and seeing what could be done about reviving the abandoned cheesemaking operation.

Mr. Carver was delighted when he mentioned it. "Aye, Your Grace. I would love to have us make our own cheeses again. We have everything we need for it, starting with the excellent grass feed for our cows. Milk, rennet, salt, but it will take time for the cheese to properly age and ripen. You would be sinking money into the production without seeing any financial return for several years."

"How much do you think it will cost to get the cheese works running again?"

"Not sure, Your Grace. Depends on how badly the machinery has fallen into disrepair."

They completed a cursory inspection of the cheesemaking machinery that did, unfortunately, require significant repair.

Alex felt some disappointment, but all in all the morning had gone well. "Let's get those cost estimates as soon as possible, and we'll decide what to do once we have the answer."

Tulip tugged on his jacket sleeve to hold him back while Mr. Carver walked ahead to say farewell to the pleasant, older fellow who ran this fourth farm they had been touring. "There's also my dowry," she said quietly. "Uncle John will have it paid over to you before the end of the month."

He placed his hand over hers as it rested on his arm. "No, that is to be preserved for you and our children."

"But what is the point of a dowry if you will not put it to good use?"

"It is being put to good use, protecting you and our children. Those funds will be placed in your name alone so that no subsequent Davenport duke can ever get his grasping hands on it.

If the cheese production proves successful, then I will consider investing some of your dowry funds into it, but that ownership interest will remain in *your* name. However, I will not allow it until I know this will be a profitable venture."

"Did Uncle John insist on your holding my dowry apart?"

"No," he said, smiling wryly. "I demanded that this be done. Whatever comes to you from your family shall remain yours always."

She cast him a heartwarming smile. "I knew I liked you for a reason."

He laughed. "Shall we move on to the dairy?"

It was the fifth and final Davenport asset they were to visit today.

"It is only a mile from here," Mr. Carver said when they approached the carriage.

They all climbed back in.

However, this time his estate manager sat up front with Trent to show him the way. "There are a few turns that are easy to miss," he explained.

Alex did not mind, for it gave him time alone with Tulip.

"How are you feeling?" he asked, settling beside her and taking her hand.

"Much more alert," she assured him. "I don't know what came over me this morning. My entire body felt like stone."

He was almost certain she had been drugged.

But how?

And why?

Well, the answer to the 'why' was easy. The villain did not want her waking up while he…or she…tried to kill Alex. But why attack him in the bedchamber? It would look too much like murder if he were found dead in his bed.

Why not keep to what had worked in the past? Killings made to look like accidental deaths.

The perfect crimes.

A sabotaged carriage wheel would do the trick. A drowning. Falling off a horse.

Perhaps that last idea had been used too much.

Two of the last dukes had fallen off their horses.

Two dead dukes. Two broken necks.

A third duke dying of a broken neck while out riding would raise too many questions.

Another problem to be addressed by the killer was Alex's manner of living. He was not profligate like his predecessors. Anyone who knew him would never believe he was drunk or reckless.

So, how would the killer do him in?

More important, who was the killer?

And how was Alex to stop him?

Of course, this still assumed there was an actual killer and an actual threat, not just his instincts on fire and sensing danger.

He needed to find out more as fast as possible.

"Tulip, would you mind if we rode to Burnham after we tour the dairy?"

Her eyes widened. "Not at all. Are we to visit my Hester family?"

He nodded. "I know it is not polite to drop in on them unannounced, but they must be eager to see you. And I know you are eager to see them. We would not stay long, just a quick visit."

She nodded enthusiastically. "They would love it. So would I. They'll invite us to stay for supper."

Alex shook his head. "Would you mind if we refused? Trent is not familiar with the roads yet and I prefer to have him navigate them in daylight. Also, I expect Mr. Carver would like to return to his home at a decent hour. He'll need a ride back to Thornwycke Hall where he's left his horse."

She raised her eyebrows and smiled at him. "Mr. Carver lives in Burnham. On the same street as my aunt and uncle, in fact. He has only to walk down the street to arrive at his home. Oh, but his horse is at Thornwycke, that is true. He'll need to retrieve his mount or else he'll have to walk there tomorrow morning. But I'm sure someone will give him a ride, if it comes to that. Uncle William would do him the favor."

"Good, then it is settled. We ride to Burnham after we tour the dairy."

He saw the brightness in Tulip's eyes and her satisfied smile. Indeed, the smile never left her face the entire while they toured the dairy and visited the cow pens.

Alex even tried milking a cow.

Tulip took a turn, as well, and was obviously experienced because every drop she squeezed went straight into her bucket, while he got more milk on his boots than in his bucket when he'd taken his turn.

"Burham next," he said after grabbing a cloth and wiping the milk off his boots.

Tulip cast him a beautiful smile. "You'll adore my Uncle William and Aunt Perty. Won't he, Mr. Carver?"

"For certain," he said with a hearty chuckle. "Your Grace, you won't find better people than the Hesters."

This light exchange pleased him, not only because it meant Tulip had been raised in a loving home. It also meant he could send Tulip to the Hesters if she needed to be placed out of harm's way while he figured out what was going on at Thornwycke Hall.

Of course, this assumed something sinister was happening there.

He had no actual proof, for Tulip feeling particularly exhausted this morning could easily be explained away.

As for his bottle of brandy, would anything show up once he had it tested?

His grandfather's journal revealed a concerning incident, but what was the secret he'd been hiding about a young woman called Elspeth? Was it not likely he'd taken that secret to his grave?

Yet, Alex had a bad feeling in the pit of his stomach that simply would not go away.

He silently cursed himself for being too besotted with Tulip to accept the obvious warning signs about Thornwycke Hall. Instead, he'd barreled ahead and made her his. She had even suggested they wait to be married, but this was the last thing he ever wanted.

It was selfish of him to bring her back to Somerset.

Well, they were here now and he did not think Tulip would ever accept to be sent back to London.

Nor did he wish it, for he truly liked having her in his life.

But he would have her stay with the Hesters for a few days, a week, or a month, if necessary to keep her out of the way while he caught a killer.

Tulip continued to smile at him as they rode toward Burnham, but he was glad when she turned away to gaze at the passing scenery that was so familiar to her.

He needed to think logically about all that had happened at Thornwycke Hall, and this included thinking about Tulip's dislike of the duchess bedchamber.

She had felt too unsettled to sleep there.

In fact, she would not go near her bed.

He ought to have questioned her more thoroughly about this because Tulip had excellent instincts, perhaps even better than his own. If the sight of that bed curdled her stomach, was it possible this terrible incident his grandfather had written about so cryptically had happened there?

This was another mystery to pursue…and possibly connect to Elspeth.

He ought to have considered Tulip's instincts sooner. It was stupid of him to dismiss her unease simply because he was glad she wanted to sleep with him in his bed.

He would question her further about it tonight, and also ask questions of the long-time household retainers. Ernfield was the head butler and had to know plenty about what went on in the past. For years, he had been standing at the front door and seen everyone who traipsed in and out.

There was also the cook, Mrs. Crabbe. And Mr. Carver. Possibly others…grooms, gardeners, household maids.

However, he set aside the thought as they reached Burnham.

Their visit to the Hesters was a friendly call for Tulip, but it was a hunt for information for him. These Hesters had grown up here and had to know something of what went on at Thornwycke Hall.

He might dig up a lot of useful information by engaging them in casual conversation.

Yes, getting them to talk first made the most sense. Their

livelihoods were not linked to Thornwycke Hall, which meant he was more likely to get the truth out of them than his estate manager, Carver, or his head butler, Ernfield.

He trusted Carver as far as it came to running the Davenport properties. As for Ernfield, he was a bit enigmatic, but weren't all head butlers trained to keep their mouths shut about what they saw?

Both men had reasons to hold something back, especially if their silence reflected badly on them.

Well, maybe the Hesters would shed sufficient light to get him started.

He smiled at Tulip as their carriage drew to a halt. "Seems we have arrived."

She cast him a heartwarming smile. "Thank you for this, Alex."

He merely nodded, for he refused to take credit for a kind gesture when his true purpose was to investigate.

Where to start?

There were so many lines of inquiry whirling in his head.

But he sensed that he needed to start in the past and find out more about this Elspeth hinted at in his grandfather's journal.

She had to have been the dark secret that scared the dying, old man and later set off a chain of vengeance killings.

His grandfather wrote that she had gone missing about twenty years ago, maybe more or maybe less...the timing was not precisely written down.

Had she been held in that tower room at Thornwycke Hall?

Were there rumors of a young woman held prisoner there at the time?

Of course, he could have asked Carver or Ernfield, perhaps even Mrs. Crabbe about it. But it was possible these long-time retainers had been involved in some way. Not in actually harming her, but had seen something or later learned something that they kept to themselves even after the death of Alex's grandfather.

He raked a hand through his hair in consternation.

Interrogating Carver would not be easy because Tulip adored him and trusted him.

But Alex had mixed feelings about his estate manager.

The man was obviously competent and had handled management of the Davenport estate with diligence and devotion.

He wanted to like Carver.

However, it was not a stretch to imagine Carver would keep silent about his grandfather's misdeeds in order to preserve his position as estate manager.

Estate managers were well paid and often held in high regard.

Would Carver toss it all away to tell the truth about a girl who had gone missing two decades ago?

William Hester was the man to question first, for certain.

Better yet, Perty Hester was the one to engage in casual conversation.

Women knew everything that went on in their village.

She would remember the details of any scandals or mysteries about a young woman's disappearance.

The Hester residence was a pleasant house built of golden stone situated on a quiet square just off the town's high street. Ivy covered the facade of the house and there was an abundance of flowers in the garden.

Alex noticed a woman bent over a rose bush with pruning shears.

The woman turned out to be Perty Hester herself.

She dropped her shears and rushed toward the carriage the moment she spotted Tulip descend from it. "Tulip! My sweetheart! Oh, what a joy it is to see you!"

Tulip ran to her aunt and the two of them embraced with fierce delight. "I missed you so much, Aunt Perty!"

Alex marveled at the depth of love between them.

When they ended their joyful reunion, Tulip introduced her aunt to Alex.

"Your Grace," Perty said, her eyes wide as she bobbed a curtsy, obviously daunted to be addressing a duke.

He gave a nod in return. "It is a pleasure to finally meet you, Mrs. Hester. My wife has said nothing but good things about you and your husband."

The woman's expression turned to one of dismay. "Oh, Tulip! You are now a duchess. How am I to address you?"

"As you always have," she insisted. "And you are not to treat me any differently, unless we are in public and formality demands it. But even then…"

"Don't you worry, love," her aunt said. "I know my place in your heart and in society, too. Don't ever worry that you might slight me or your Uncle William. We know we shall always hold a place in your heart, even if the silly rules of etiquette forbid you to show it. Now, come in the pair of you and I'll put the kettle on for us."

She called over one of the boys who obviously did odd chores around the house. "Peter, run to the shop and let Mr. Hester know his niece has come to visit."

"Right away, ma'am." The lad took off down the street.

She next turned to Mr. Carver and asked if he would join them.

"No, Perty. I shall take full advantage of these few hours off and enjoy the quiet of my own home."

Alex watched him march down the street and enter a house similar to that owned by the Hesters, same golden stone and ivy, although the garden was not as nicely maintained.

"Poor man," Mrs. Hester said as they watched him disappear into his house. "He hasn't been the same since his dear Martha passed on."

"His wife?" Alex asked.

"No, his daughter," Mrs. Hester replied. "She died suddenly a few years ago. About five years, I think it was."

Alex's heart beat a little faster, for unexpected occurrences tended to be linked, did they not? "The same time my grandfather died? Was it before or after his death?"

Perty pursed her lips in thought. "Shortly afterward, I'm fairly certain. Came as a surprise to us all, for Martha was a cheerful, hearty girl. Never sick a day in her life, and suddenly she began to waste away. Not sure what she died of. Mr. Carver's wife had passed over a decade ago by then, poor woman died of a lung fever. Ever since then, it was just him and Martha. What a bright, sweet girl she was. Poor man, he is quite alone now."

"They never did learn what illness killed Martha, did they?" Tulip asked as they ambled into the house and settled in the parlor.

Perty took a moment to leave their side to put on the kettle.

It did not take long before she was back with cakes and delicate plates. She was followed by a maid who carried a tray with teapot and cups. Once the maid had set it down, Perty poured each of them a cup of tea while responding to Tulip's question. "What killed poor Martha? No, it remains quite the mystery."

Alex frowned, but this was just his natural instinct to question anything sudden and unexpected leading to death. "Where was she when she came down with this mysterious disease?"

Mrs. Hester shrugged. "Oh, she had been to Thornwycke Hall to see her father. But no one at Thornwycke got sick afterward, so that was ruled out. Mrs. Granger was so kind and thoughtful to them. She had soups and easily digested stews delivered to Martha daily, but nothing seemed to help."

"That is sad," Alex said, the hairs on the back of his neck beginning to prickle.

What had Mr. Carver's daughter noticed at Thornwycke?

Whatever it was, he'd wager it got her poisoned.

By the ever-helpful Mrs. Granger?

Or was his cynical mind looking for something sinister where it did not exist? Martha obviously was not the girl mentioned in his grandfather's journal.

And the killer had not done away with any of the Davenport dukes yet…unless his grandfather had been helped along to an earlier death, one also hastened by slow poisoning.

And how was Mrs. Granger involved in any of this when she was new on the job at the time?

"What do you know about Mrs. Granger," Alex asked. "She seems rather young to be a housekeeper for a manor house as large as Thornwycke Hall."

Tulip's eyes widened and she stared at him, no doubt wondering why he was curious about their housekeeper.

"Did you know her, Aunt Perty? I don't remember ever seeing her in Burnham before."

"She rarely comes into town. Odd, one would think that she would."

"Why do you find it odd?" Tulip asked.

Perty Hester shrugged. "Her family is from around here. Your uncle and I, and Mr. Carver, grew up with Mrs. Granger's mother and aunt. The mother's name was Margaret and the aunt was Elspeth."

Alex choked on his tea, but quickly recovered. "Do go on, Mrs. Hester. Forgive me, but I felt a sudden urge to sneeze. It has passed. I am fine."

"Where was I? Oh, yes. Margaret and Elspeth, both of them were such pretty girls. Margaret was the elder. She married and moved away with her husband. They had a little girl, and that is your current housekeeper, Eleanor Granger. But I don't think they were blessed with any more children."

"And Elspeth?" Alex prodded.

She sighed and continued. "There was something quite special about her. She was so flawlessly beautiful, she seemed almost magical. All the boys adored her. The girls did, too. She was always very kind and never put on airs. Their parents, the Palters, who are Mrs. Granger's grandparents, went to live with Margaret shortly after Elspeth disappeared."

Tulip gasped. "She disappeared?"

Alex tensed.

Dear heaven.

She had to be the girl named in his grandfather's diary.

He continued to listen intently as Perty rambled on.

"Yes, my dear. She vanished without a trace," her aunt replied, shaking her head and frowning. "We were all quite shocked by it and worried that something bad had happened to her. Then a rumor began circulating that Elspeth had run off with a handsome navy officer."

"And did she?" Tulip asked.

"Well, I had my doubts. She was a beautiful girl, and we all could see how a man might fall in love with her on the spot. But there were no naval officers anywhere around here at the time."

"Then you don't believe she ran off?"

Perty shrugged. "Well, not with a naval officer. That seemed unlikely, but we thought it was possible she had eloped with someone else. You see, Elspeth had confided to us about a romantic interest but never told us who the man was. We were sure it was a local gent, someone of importance in our village and perhaps married. But she was a good girl and I could not see her ruining her prospects by consorting with a married man."

"Then why else bother with all the secrecy?" Tulip asked.

"I truly don't know, my dear," her aunt said after taking a sip of her tea.

Alex was eager to pursue this questioning. "Did any gentleman go missing at this same time?"

"No," Perty replied. "And that's the bother of it, for everyone here knows everyone else's business. Well, the parents were frantic with worry at first, but then they seemed to have received news to allay their fears."

"A letter from Elspeth?"

Her aunt shrugged. "Possibly. That's when the gossip about her running off with a handsome naval officer began to spread, and they did not deny it. A few months later, the parents came into some money and moved away to live closer to their other daughter, Margaret. That was the end of it. We never heard from any of them again."

"And Margaret was Mrs. Granger's mother?" Alex asked, merely confirming the family relations.

"Yes. Anyway, none of us ever heard from them or Mrs. Granger's aunt, Elspeth, again."

She sipped the last of her tea and continued. "We were quite happy when we learned Mrs. Granger had sought employment at Thornwycke Hall. Of course, we weren't sure it was such a good idea for her to work there considering she was young and beautiful, and the old duke was such a lecherous devil. Oh, I do beg your pardon, Your Grace. I…"

Alex shook his head. "I know how awful my family is, Mrs. Hester. Rest assured, I am as appalled as you are. Do go on, I am eager to hear more."

Tulip's aunt poured more tea for all of them and picked up where she had left off. "As I was saying, Mrs. Granger seemed an odd choice for the position of housekeeper, but the duke always liked pretty faces around him. I heard from Mr. Carver that they got along well enough. Your grandfather did not push himself on her. In fact, seems he was quite respectful of her."

"That's a surprise," Alex muttered.

Perty arched an eyebrow. "Yes, but I think his exploits were exaggerated. Despite all you may have heard, he was not really the sort to push himself on anyone. Why should he when he was a very handsome fellow in his younger days and women came to him willingly?"

She turned to her niece. "Tulip, dear...it is the way of things. Handsome dukes get what they want and hardly need to lift a finger to get it. But I understand from Mr. Carver that it was never like that between Mrs. Granger and the old duke. Of course, he could not do much of anything by that time, seeing as he was becoming so frail and sickly. Anyway, there was no need to foist unwanted attention on Mrs. Granger. He still had dozens of scantily clad ladies running about the place even as he lay on his deathbed."

Tulip's aunt now turned to Alex, frowning. "You aren't anything like your grandfather, are you?"

"No, I assure you. My first act upon becoming duke was to write to Mr. Carver and have him send away these...um, unwanted guests."

Tulip's eyes widened. "You did?"

"Of course."

She nodded. "You see, Aunt Perty? Alex is the most decent person you will ever meet. He is nothing like his horrible relatives. He is smart and kind and considerate. And–"

Her aunt laughed. "I am delighted to hear it. I did not think John Farthingale would ever approve of the marriage unless he thought highly of His Grace. Of course, we all know your story and are relieved you turned out nothing like your predecessors."

"You know my story?" Alex leaned forward, eager to hear Perty Hester's version of it.

"Oh, yes. It was all anyone spoke of for months afterward. Your mother was very wise to take you away from Thornwycke Hall."

"I am very well aware," Alex assured her.

"Very brave of her, too," she added.

Alex looked forward to Tulip's aunt telling him more about his mother, but those were questions for another time. His priority was to discover whether there was a killer on the loose who intended to strike again.

"Where was I?" Perty muttered, serving each of them another slice of cake while preparing to spill more gossip that Alex was eager to hear.

"You mentioned Mrs. Granger," he said, definitely interested in learning more about her now that Perty had made the connection between his housekeeper and Elspeth who was likely the girl his grandfather had mentioned in his journal.

"Oh, yes. She managed the old duke quite well and learned how to maneuver herself around those…er, free-spirited ladies of his. She never complained about the old duke or any of his successors, as far as I know. But I don't think the succeeding dukes were as nice as the old man. They took on all of his vices, but had none of his charm."

Alex grunted.

The Davenport dukes were all depraved and everyone knew it. Even his 'kindly' grandfather was a wretched specimen of a man. That he did not force himself on women was a point in his favor, but he was reprehensible in so many other ways.

The local residents just did not openly state it.

"We hoped you would turn out different, Your Grace," she continued. "I'm so glad your mother was able to save you from your grandfather's influence."

The conversation stopped when Mr. Hester rushed in. "Tulip! Dear girl!"

She leaped to her feet. "Uncle William!"

He was a big, jovial bear of a man, and obviously sentimental. He swallowed Tulip in his beefy arms. "My sweet girl! How good of you to stop by to see us."

Tulip laughed and hugged him back. "We'll have you and Aunt Perty to Thornwycke Hall very soon. We only arrived yesterday and have yet to get our bearings."

She quickly introduced him to Alex.

William Hester regarded him warily, unlike his wife who seemed to accept him without hesitation. But William was probably aware of the depths of the depravity that went on at Thornwycke, things Mr. Carver had told him about that he would never repeat to his wife.

"You are going to adore my husband," Tulip insisted. "He is nothing like his horrible ancestors. In fact, he is wonderful in every way. Just ask Mr. Carver if you do not believe me."

William managed a smile. "Glad to hear it."

"He is," Tulip insisted with a vehemence that made Alex feel warm inside.

They did not stay long afterward, for the clouds were beginning to thicken and the sky had turned gray. "We had better start for home," Alex said, thanking them for their hospitality and promising they would receive an invitation shortly.

William kissed his niece's cheek. "I see that you are happy, Tulip. I pray it shall always be this way," he said quietly in her ear.

She tipped her chin up. "You will soon find out what a marvel he is. Rest assured, my husband is the best of men."

They climbed back in their carriage and made haste toward Thornwycke before they were caught in a downpour.

Tulip was full of questions for him during the ride back. "What was all that about? Were you investigating Mr. Carver and Mrs. Granger? You had Aunt Perty going on and on about them."

"Why should I not know more about them? They are in our employ and in important positions within our household."

"Do you think one of them is a murderer?"

Alex did not immediately answer.

Tulip gasped. "You think one of them might have killed your predecessors?"

"Their deaths were ruled accidental, and there is nothing to contradict those findings."

"Nothing but your unfailing instincts," she said. "You do believe those deaths were intentional, don't you? That's why you wanted us to visit my aunt and uncle, and why you were asking all those questions. You choked on your tea at the mention of Mrs. Granger's mother and aunt. What have they to do with anything? Or Mr. Carver for that matter. I shall never believe Mr. Carver is capable of murder."

"Nor do I believe it, frankly. But his daughter died of a mysterious illness shortly after my grandfather's death. She might have seen something and the killer was afraid the truth would come out."

"What truth? And need I point out that she did not die instantly? She had weeks to tell someone about what she saw, assuming she had discovered anything."

"Carver's daughter might not have realized the significance of what she had noticed. My grandfather was on his deathbed and none of the successor dukes had passed away yet. But the killer knew he or she had been caught doing something suspicious. They had to dispose of Martha before she could put it all together and report her finding to Mr. Carver or the authorities."

"Well, Mr. Carver would never hurt his own daughter. That rules him out."

Alex rubbed a hand across the nape of his neck. "Maybe."

"Alex, he would *never* harm his own daughter. He adored her. She was the light of his life."

"Fine," he said, knowing Tulip was probably right. "Then that leaves Mrs. Granger."

"Why her?"

He quickly told her of what he had read about Elspeth in his grandfather's journal. "Together with what your aunt told us this afternoon, how can we not believe something sinister happened? I doubt Elspeth eloped. She was murdered…well, possibly an accidental death that was covered up. Then her parents were bribed to keep their mouths shut and go along with the rumor that Elspeth had run off with a naval officer."

"You think Mrs. Granger learned the truth and is now here to seek vengeance on every Davenport duke?"

"Why would she come back here unless it was to avenge her aunt's disappearance? Who knows what her own mother told her about the goings on at Thornwycke? What if Elspeth had been held captive in the tower room? Who would know? Who would ever hear her cries for help while locked away in there? What if she were held there bound and gagged?"

"You are giving me the shivers."

"Sorry, love. But my grandfather could have got away with just about anything with the cooperation of a few loyal household retainers. His old housekeeper for one."

"Mrs. Dodge? How is it possible? Surely, word would have gotten around, even in a big house like Thornwycke. A butler or footman would have seen Elspeth go in but not come out."

"Was Ernfield in service as a butler at the time? He merely needed to be the one duty when Elspeth went missing. Does he seem like a chatty fellow to you?"

"Being quiet does not mean he would keep silent about an innocent girl's abduction. And there had to be maids going in and out of the upstairs bedchambers. They would have heard scuffling sounds above their heads, or cries for help, or wondered at the extra food brought up to the duke. You found nothing in the tower room when you searched it yesterday."

"Doesn't mean there was nothing in there back in my grandfather's time. The furniture and a body could have been moved at any time."

"And where would they have carried a young woman's body? Or buried it?"

Alex thought of the salt marshes and how barren they were. It would be easy enough to bury a body in the mud, or not bury it at all and let it wash out to sea with the tide.

He could not reveal this thought to Tulip, for it would upset her even further.

Tulip frowned. "Someone would talk, especially if it was Elspeth's body being moved."

"Not necessarily. Dukes are powerful. Sometimes, it is easier to pretend to see nothing."

"But she was known in Burnham, had friends who would worry about her. Do you really think she was murdered by your grandfather? Did he have it in him to commit that depraved act?"

"I have no idea, Tulip. Truly, I know nothing about him other than he was someone my mother risked everything to avoid." Perhaps his mother had been there when Elspeth suddenly went missing and knew more than she had ever let on.

Is this what had prompted her to leave Thornwycke Hall with him and never return?

Had his grandfather and father allowed her to live apart from them in return for her silence? Perhaps the money he had inherited upon her death was not from her or her own family but from his father and grandfather, bribes to buy her silence.

He raked a hand through his hair.

And he, an eight-year-old boy at the time, had been oblivious to it all.

This was all conjecture.

He would have to dig deeper and determine an accurate time line of events.

Tulip cleared her throat, drawing him out of his thoughts. "Do you think your grandfather knew of Mrs. Granger's connection to Elspeth when he hired her?"

"I expect she hid that bit of information from him. He was already ill and dying when he hired her. It is also possible he confessed his secret to her, never realizing her connection to Elspeth."

"And Mrs. Granger was so enraged by his confession that she sped up his death?"

Alex nodded. "It is quite possible."

"But why harm the succeeding dukes?"

"Perhaps because they were as depraved and lecherous as the old man. Or I am wrong about all of it and each died accidental deaths because they drank too much and were sinful, reckless idiots."

He thought about Harold Havers and his idiot brothers.

He had suspected them at first glance of bettering their odds by doing away with the next heirs in the Davenport line.

But this was too sophisticated for Harold and his brothers.

If anything, they would be next in line to die unless Alex figured out what was going on and how to stop it.

Tulip had been drugged last night, he was certain of it now.

This meant the vengeance against his family was not going to stop.

He really needed to get that brandy bottle in his bedchamber tested. After all, he was the one the killer was after.

But the testing would have to wait, for he doubted anyone in Burnham had the capability to run tests at this level of sophistication. Otherwise, wouldn't the local coroner have found something when examining the bodies?

Alex had read the coroner's reports and knew they were thorough…but obviously not thorough enough.

He would have to take his brandy bottle to Bath or Taunton, have it tested in a true laboratory.

Unfortunately, he did not have the time to attend to it just now.

Even if tested, would anything turn up?

His own amateur testing had turned up nothing when he'd taken a sip of Tulip's cocoa and sniffed it.

If the drug was in the cocoa, then it was odorless and not discernable by taste, either.

But if the drug wasn't in the cocoa, then how had Tulip ingested it?

CHAPTER 13

A WEEK HAD passed since their arrival at Thornwycke Hall, and Tulip remained insistent on helping Alex figure out what had happened to the predecessor dukes and finding the culprit responsible for doing them in.

They went into town to speak to the coroner, a man by the name of Dr. Harding, who also happened to be the only doctor in the vicinity. He had an earful to relate about Alex's predecessors who had indulged in the old duke's debauched ways among other sins of sloth and excess, but he firmly believed their deaths had been accidental. "Many people had reason to do away with them," he said with obvious moral indignation, "but they did the work of others by cutting their own lives short with their outrageous behavior."

As they walked out of his infirmary, Tulip brought up the matter of Alex's untouched bottle of brandy. "Why did you not mention it to Dr. Harding? You might have changed his mind if he found something in it."

"No, love. He has already made up his mind about the string of deaths and that brandy bottle isn't going to change it. The poison is going to be something quite subtle that ordinary test instruments will not pick up. Dr. Harding would only become more entrenched in his opinion if his results turned up nothing."

Tulip thought giving the bottle over to the doctor was worth a try, but respected Alex's judgment. "All right, you're the expert investigator and would know best."

"I don't know about that," he said with a grunt. "Perhaps I am losing my touch. I can't even find my watch fob. Haven't seen it since yesterday."

She looked up at him in surprise. "Truly? You are always so meticulous."

"I know, but this mystery must have me more distracted than I realized. You haven't seen it, have you?"

"No, Alex. But I will keep an eye out for it."

They next met with Lord Farnhum, the local magistrate, whose feelings were much the same as the doctor's about the prior dukes. "Your Grace, I am glad to see you are nothing like them," he said, smiling in approval of Alex's polite manner around Tulip. "As suspicious as those rapid deaths in succession may be, I saw no proof at all to rule them as other than accidental."

Next, they spent time poring through newspaper accounts, the pages yellowed from age, that were maintained by the town's bookshop owner, Miss Adela Keane. "It is my civic duty to hold onto these vital records since neither the magistrate nor the newspaper office appear to deem preservation of old news necessary," the middle-aged spinster had declared.

They spent hours reading those newspapers, taking care to keep them from crumbling under their hands. Unfortunately they came across nothing helpful because the volumes in the bookshop's storage did not go all the way back to Elspeth's time.

Alex seemed convinced the deaths of his predecessors were related to Elspeth, but they had come to a complete dead end because there were no records or subsequent clues to be found, not even in the local church registry.

Tulip could feel Alex's tension mounting daily.

Each night, he would inspect the walls, the fireplaces, and even the flooring in search of a hidden doorway, but never found one. He would then wash up and retire to their bed with his grandfather's journal and read portions of it over and over again. "I am missing something obvious, Tulip," he said with frustration as they climbed into bed at the end of another long day.

"It cannot be obvious if it is eluding someone as clever as you," she replied. "What if I read it? Maybe it will help to view it from a woman's perspective."

"No, sweetheart. I know what's written in these pages will upset you. It upsets me and my heart is made of stone."

She snuggled against him, knowing that he had the softest heart for her.

Well, she would insist on reading that journal if nothing came to light within the next few days.

She fell asleep in Alex's solid arms, soothed by the strong, steady beat of his heart.

Had she claimed his heart?

Neither of them had admitted their love yet.

Perhaps it was still too soon to make such declarations even if they were husband and wife.

Tulip awoke early the following morning refreshed for another day and with a battle plan in mind. She hoped to gain information from friends and family who would attend the dinner party she and Alex were hosting tonight. "We haven't questioned Mrs. Crabbe yet," she casually mentioned while she and Alex prepared for the day.

"We?" He shook his head. "Tulip, leave it alone. I don't want you interrogating anyone, and especially not Mrs. Crabbe who will be in worse humor today of all days because of our party."

She donned her walking boots. "I can go into the kitchen pretending to check whether all is in readiness for this evening. Is this not an excellent excuse?"

"No."

"But this would be the perfect opportunity for me to hold a casual conversation with her."

"Again, no," Alex said, shrugging into his jacket as they were preparing to go downstairs for breakfast. "She's a surly old bat even on the best of days. I'm serious about not wanting you to poke your nose in this investigation. This is no game." He then grunted. "Assuming there is even anything nefarious to be found out. All we have are disconnected facts."

"A young woman gone missing about twenty years ago. Another who died under mysterious circumstances about five years ago. And a string of Davenport dukes who met their untimely ends. That's more than mere 'disconnected' facts. We must take Uncle William and Aunt Perty aside and question them more closely again tonight."

He kissed her on the forehead. "No, not tonight. This party is to celebrate our marriage."

"But, Alex—"

He kissed her again. "They were immensely helpful, but we still have no proof those deaths were murders and no proof that Elspeth died."

"Of course, she died!"

"All we have is gossip, suspicious circumstances, and some old stories that gave rise to them. I agree with you that something bad happened to Elspeth, but you cannot go blurting it around. Are we agreed? No talk of her or Martha or the dukes tonight."

She frowned. "Why are you suddenly so reluctant?"

"I'm not. What I am is methodical. I cannot go out there and hurl cannonballs when the coroner, the magistrate, and even the newspaper reports all indicate the deaths were accidental. I am sorry we hit a dead end with those old newspapers."

"Yes, me too. If only they had gone back more than fifteen years."

He grunted. "We'll figure out what happened to Elspeth eventually. Her death will not always remain a mystery."

She took his arm as they walked downstairs to have their breakfast. "I like that we are spending so much time together, but I think you are purposely keeping me close and it has nothing to do with your being enamored of me. We'll never draw the killer out if we are attached at the hip."

He paused and held her back as they were about to enter the dining room. "I am trying to be a good husband and spend time with my wife, especially since I feel badly that we haven't taken a proper honeymoon."

"Oh, Alex. It wasn't a proper courtship or wedding, either. But we are married now and I am rather enjoying being your wife."

He chuckled. "I'm liking it, too. Are you meeting with Mrs. Granger this morning?"

She nodded. "Yes, as always. Right after breakfast."

"I'll join you."

"Fine," she said with a sigh, "but you ought to go away soon afterward and leave me to talk to her alone. She will never open up to me if you are always hovering close by. I can do this, Alex. Trust me."

"Stop, Tulip." She could see the worry in his eyes as he said, "I have every faith in you. It is Mrs. Granger that concerns me. I do not trust her."

"I'll be sitting with her in the ladies parlor and that is within earshot of the formal dining room where a half dozen maids and butlers will be working to polish the silver and set up the dinner table for tonight's party. If your gut is telling you that she is somehow involved in the deaths of your predecessors, then let me see what information I can coax out of her. She won't be on her guard around me. I expect she believes I am naive and stupid."

He arched an eyebrow. "You? Yes, you are naive but never stupid. In fact, your mind is surprisingly sharp. I…"

She cast him a smug smile. "Yes, sharp enough to get her to reveal something about her past and possibly about her feelings for your immediate predecessors."

Alex had been going around quietly questioning everyone who had served in the household during his grandfather's day, but he could only get so far with them because they considered him a stranger and he was *the* duke.

He was very smooth about asking his questions, but he could not dig as deeply as he wished without giving his purpose away.

She, on the other hand, was known in the area and her family was very well liked. If anyone was to open up and gossip or confess some secret, it would be to her.

For the past week, Alex had made a point of sitting with her and Mrs. Granger while they reviewed the household accounts, went over the weekly menu, and other matters related to the running of the household that traditionally were in the sole the domain of the mistress of the house.

Mrs. Granger found this quite irritating, although she never openly expressed her displeasure. It irritated Tulip, as well. She and Mrs. Granger had real work to do in preparation for this evening's dinner party. But it was also clear that Mrs. Granger would never confide in her while her duke of a husband was lurking close by.

"Do you have any specific questions for me to ask Mrs. Granger?" Tulip asked before leaving her husband's side after they'd finished their meal.

"No, I mean it, Tulip. She will immediately become suspicious if you mention Elspeth." He sighed. "If you must, then pretend to be curious about my grandfather and the other Davenport dukes, but only because you wish to get a better sense of my life growing up as a child here. That ought to be safe enough."

"I can do that." Tulip would be working very closely with her housekeeper all morning long because this was to be the first party held by her and Alex, and Mrs. Granger knew that she wanted it to be perfect.

Alex had suggested inviting not only Tulip's relatives but a few of her friends, as well. On the surface, it seemed a generous gesture to bring together friends and family in celebration of their marriage and settling in at Thornwycke.

But it was also a convenient and not so obvious way to pump information out of others who knew Elspeth and might have something new to reveal.

Although Alex refused to openly admit it, Tulip knew this was his primary purpose in hosting this party.

She also knew he considered Mrs. Granger his main suspect in the deaths of his predecessors and Mr. Carver's daughter, Martha.

Well, she thought this was what Alex felt.

She could not know for certain because Alex kept his suspicions to himself.

At the very least, he had to feel their housekeeper was the key to solving these possible murders because of her connection to Elspeth, her access as housekeeper to everything in the house, and her cleverness.

It took skill and finesse to execute a string of perfect crimes...which had yet to be shown were crimes at all.

Tulip now summoned her housekeeper to the parlor.

"I have arranged the seating chart for your approval, Your

Grace," Mrs. Granger said, bustling in with papers in hand.

"Excellent, I'll have a look at it now."

Alex walked in while they were perusing the table seating.

Tulip glanced up at him in annoyance because he was supposed to leave them alone to chat, and now he was here again and undermining the entire purpose. But she wondered what was on his mind, for she noticed a flicker of something in his eyes.

"Mrs. Granger, I understand your family used to reside here," Alex said, his manner light and pleasant.

Alex was never light and pleasant.

What was he up to?

Mrs. Granger looked up at him, obviously wary. "Yes, they did."

"Then do join us when we host my wife's family and friends this evening. I learned quite by chance that your mother and aunt were great friends with William and Perty Hester. I'm sure they would be delighted for your company."

Heat shot into Mrs. Granger's cheeks. "Oh, Your Grace. That is most generous, but I couldn't. It isn't my place."

Alex shook his head. "Ah, but you must. I have invited Mr. Carver to dine with us, too. I understand they were all good friends. This will help me very much as you are all far more familiar with the Davenport history than I am."

"But I will add nothing. How can I know anything about your history when I wasn't raised here and did not know them at all?" she said, her voice sounding the littlest bit shrill.

"Well, this will be your chance to get to know them better." He slapped his hands to his thighs, indicating the discussion was at an end. "I'll leave you to work out the modifications to the table seating with Her Grace."

Tulip smiled sweetly as he strode off to his study.

What in blazes?

He had told her *not* to mention Elspeth, and here he was tossing her memory right in Mrs. Granger's face.

Mrs. Granger let out a heavy breath. "He is not serious about having me join you, is he? Please, Your Grace...I would be so embarrassed."

"Don't be, for he is quite serious and means to do you a kindness. Would it not be rude of us to leave you out when your family was great friends with my own? Why did you not tell me?"

"I did not think you would care. And why should you? My family was nothing special. It never occurred to me to mention them."

"Well, no matter. Mr. Carver will be joining us, as will some of my friends and their parents. Of course, you know this," she said with a light trill of laughter, "since you've helped me organize this party from start to finish."

"But I am merely your housekeeper."

"And Mr. Carver is our estate manager. And my uncle runs a mercantile shop in Burnham. What is your point? And there is not an ounce of blue blood in my family."

"But you are now a duchess. I should not be sitting with you," she insisted.

Tulip shook her head. "Tonight, you are a friend. I cannot pretend our dining together will be a common occurrence. Obviously, it will not. Our next round of parties will be for the purpose of introducing ourselves to the local landed gentry and those of rank who reside in the area. Enjoy yourself as our guest this one time."

She placed her hand over Mrs. Granger's as though to soothe her, but her real purpose was to measure her reaction to the invitation.

Her hand was cold and trembling.

"Mrs. Granger, is something wrong? Why are you so afraid of sharing a meal among friends?"

"I am not friendly with any of your family or friends," she repeated with insistence, her features now pale and her composure quite fragile. "They do not know me."

Goodness, she certainly did not look like a killer just now.

More like someone painfully shy about meeting strangers.

Actually, someone scared.

Alex had her at the top of his list of suspects, so Tulip could not allow her to avoid the party. "You will love them all, especially my Uncle William and Aunt Perty. They are the kindest people you will ever meet. I'm sure they will be eager to know you better. From what I hear, your family was well liked. Aren't you the least bit curious to meet your mother's old friends?"

"No," she said, visibly shaking. "I have worked here for over five years and purposely made no effort to make their acquaintance. Why should I do so now?"

And wasn't that odd?

Did this not sound guilty? Why come here if not to ingratiate herself among her mother's old friends?

Tulip sighed. "You can confide in me, Mrs. Granger. Why are you so afraid to join our dinner party?"

"I am not frightened…it's just…" Her eyes began to well with tears. "Being with them will bring up unhappy memories."

Tulip kept her hand gently over her housekeeper's clenched fist, patting it to calm her. "What unhappy memories? Please tell me. I am a good listener and will keep anything you tell me confidential."

"I cannot. You will tell your husband and then he will pry into my private affairs. He was London's top investigator, so I've been told by Mr. Carver."

"Yes, he was. No one was better at the job." So, their genteel housekeeper had been asking questions about Alex.

Tulip supposed this was to be expected.

Everyone had to be curious about the new duke.

Perhaps this also meant she was reassessing her vengeance tactics because Alex was too sharp to approach with her usual ploys. This explained why the entire week had passed without incident beyond her possibly being drugged that first night.

Despite finding no hint of any opiate traces or poisons in her cocoa, Alex remained convinced she had been given something to knock her out.

Tulip believed she must have been, too.

But how was it done?

She had not eaten or imbibed anything after supper, only the cocoa, and Alex had found nothing harmful in it.

"Discharge me, if you must," Mrs. Granger insisted, surging to her feet, "but I will not sit at your table."

Tulip rose, as well. "I thought our invitation would please you, but it has left you obviously distraught. Who is it in this seating chart that you dread seeing? You must tell me, Mrs. Granger. I am not going to dismiss you until I hear the truth. What you are saying is nonsensical. Why come here in the first place if you had no interest in finding out more about your family's past? And if there is some secret you wish to uncover, then let us do it together. His Grace and I will help you. We are not your enemies."

Mrs. Granger stared at her for a long moment. "You wouldn't understand."

"Oh, I think I would. In fact, I am already convinced some very bad things went on when my husband was just a child and lived here. This is why his mother took him away."

Tulip had assured Alex that she would not specifically mention Elspeth, but she had to say something to evoke a response from her housekeeper. "Answer me truthfully, Mrs. Granger. Something tragic happened in the past…was it connected to your family? Is this why you came to Thornwycke? To discover the truth about your aunt, Elspeth? Please, let us do it together."

Mrs. Granger at first appeared stunned, and then her shoulders sagged. "You will not like what I am about to tell you," she said, releasing a long, defeated breath.

"Perhaps not, but I will not punish you for telling me the truth. So many strange things went on in the past. Is it not time to put them out in the open?"

There was a long pause, and then Mrs. Granger sank back into her chair, defeated. "I did come here to learn about my family. It was all innocent, at first. Well, I was innocently unaware of the horrible goings on here. I mean about the ladies the old duke had wandering about the place, and the debaucheries that went on nightly. All of the Davenport men were involved, all of them scoundrels and wastrels. Suddenly, I felt trapped."

Tulip gasped. "Did anything happen against your will?"

"To me? No, nothing like that. Why would they bother with me when there were plenty of beautiful ladies sponging off the duke's largesse and prancing around the grounds scantily clad? None of them were ever held against their will, as far as I am aware. They had no qualms about engaging in intimacies with the Davenport men in exchange for expensive gifts and the chance of living in luxury."

"I see."

"As for His Grace's grandfather, he might have indulged in his younger days. But he was old and frail by the time I came to work here. He did not take any ladies into his bed…and, if it is any consolation to His Grace," she said, referring to Alex, "I do not believe his father ever participated in those sort of revels, either."

"He didn't? How can you know this for certain when his father died years before you ever arrived here?" This was important to Tulip because she knew it would mean a lot to Alex.

"His Grace's grandfather and I used to have long chats toward the end. He confessed his regrets to me, one of those being how he had kept his sons too much under his thumb. He felt they had turned out weak because of it. He called them all useless wastrels, except for the one son who had married for love. He blamed himself for poisoning that marriage and believed his son had died of a broken heart after the wife left and took their little boy with him. The old duke would not allow his son to follow them."

Tulip struggled to hold back her tears. "My husband was that little boy."

"Please tell him what I have told you. He deserves to know the truth about his father, just as I deserve to know what really happened to my aunt, Elspeth." Mrs. Granger took a deep breath and continued by telling Tulip much that she already knew.

Tulip did not interrupt or stop her because it was important to hear whatever her housekeeper had to say. "Do go on, Mrs. Granger."

"I arrived here about five years ago, hoping to land a good position in a respectable household and start conducting my investigations on my afternoons off. But I quickly saw my mistake. I think whatever happened to Elspeth must have occurred right here at Thornwycke Hall."

Tulip gripped the arms of her chair.

Was this the evidence Alex had been hoping for?

"I was scared to death. How could I stay here with all of *that* debauchery going on? But that was the least of it. I thought it possible your husband's grandfather had killed Elspeth. Or perhaps one of his sons had done it and he'd helped cover it up."

"Did the old duke confess this?"

She shook her head. "No, he actually seemed to have no involvement in her disappearance. If anything, I got the impression he genuinely adored her."

Tulip's head began to spin.

How did this make sense?

If the old duke and the other Davenports had nothing to do with Elspeth's disappearance, then why were they killed off?

She refused to believe those deaths were accidental.

But Mrs. Granger would have no motive for plotting their deaths.

"I was in over my head, but I had no funds and where was I to go? I intended to keep my head down, mind my own business, and get out of here as soon as I had saved sufficient wages. But then, I began to hear things."

Tulip edged closer. "What things?"

Mrs. Granger let out a ragged breath. "Oh, I cannot tell you."

"You must. Let us work on this together. You mustn't view my husband and me as enemies. Let us help you find out the truth. Do you believe your Aunt Elspeth was kept prisoner here? In the tower room?"

"No! The old duke would never have imprisoned her. But I don't believe she ever eloped with a naval officer. Someone killed her. I am convinced of it." She placed a hand over her stomach as though in pain. "It is a terrible thing to discover my sweet, beautiful aunt never made it out of here alive."

Tulip could hardly breathe, for her heart was overcome by anguish. "Oh, Mrs. Granger. I am so very sorry. Please, go on. What else do you know?"

"Little else. I had never met Elspeth. My mother and grandparents were always so mysterious about her. Why had they suddenly moved away from here? Who had given them their sudden inheritance? I knew the story they gave was a lie, for we had no wealthy relatives. I think the old duke must have paid them off to buy their silence."

"But why would he do this if he had nothing to do with her death?"

"I don't know. Perhaps he thought one of his sons had done something. As father, he might have wanted to protect that son. I think now I should never have come here. My mother, on her deathbed, warned me to keep away. I should have listened."

"It took great courage for you to seek out the truth." Tulip might have done the same if she had no one left in the world and sensed a terrible thing had happened to her family in the one place she was warned never to go.

"No, it was foolish. But I had to learn the truth about Elspeth. I began to ask questions. Ernfield was most helpful because he was around back then and knew my mother and Elspeth."

"You got him to talk to you?"

She laughed softly and nodded. "Yes, he surprised me by being most forthcoming."

"What did he tell you?"

"Nothing particularly helpful...except..."

"Except what?" Tulip prodded.

"He'd served the Davenport dukes all of his life and was not going to give away their secrets. But he did warn me about others..."

"What others, Mrs. Granger? You must tell me. More important, you must *trust* me."

"Your Grace, I do trust you. Is this not odd? For I have every reason to be afraid of you."

"Of me? Why?"

Mrs. Granger released another long breath. "Because your uncle, William Hester, was involved in Elspeth's disappearance. Ernfield warned me to keep away from him at all costs."

"That is ridiculous," Tulip said with insistence, her head now in a complete and utter spin. "Did Ernfield tell you straight out that my uncle had harmed her?"

"No, but he merely alluded to..." She appeared to struggle for words. "I think William Hester...perhaps did not kill her, but might have had a hand in covering up Elspeth's death. There might have been others involved in hiding her body. Even Mr. Carver, perhaps. Weren't he and your uncle best friends? And now you are asking me to sit at your dinner table with these men?"

The accusation against her uncle and even Mr. Carver had caught Tulip by surprise, and it took her another moment to make sense of it. "Ernfield has to be mistaken. Trust me, Mrs. Granger. My uncle would never do this. He is a truly decent soul."

Mrs. Granger stared at her. "Is he? Is this what he has everyone believing? And now that I have told you all of it, will my own life be forfeit? In truth, I no longer care, for I know my husband and parents will be waiting for me at heaven's door."

She knocked the papers off the small table where they had been spread out for Tulip's review. As those papers floated to the floor, Mrs. Granger let out a sob and rushed out of the parlor without waiting to be dismissed.

Tulip scooped up the papers and sat in stunned silence a moment before hurrying to the study in the hope of finding Alex there.

The door was shut, but she burst in without knocking. "Alex!"

He set aside his quill pen, and almost tipped over his chair as he rose abruptly to come to her side. "What is it, Tulip?"

"Mrs. Granger claims to be in dread fear of Uncle William. *My uncle.* Can you believe it? This is why she refuses to join our party tonight. Ernfield told her that my uncle and possibly Mr. Carver were involved in Elspeth's disappearance. Well, he did not come right out and accuse them of her murder, but he intimated that something terrible had happened to Elspeth and those two were involved in covering it up."

"She told you this?" he asked, frowning.

She nodded.

"And you believed her?"

"Well, I did find it odd that Ernfield should be the one to tell her all this when he hasn't said more than two words to us since we arrived here. But she was genuinely overset and I don't believe she was lying to me."

He cast her a doubting look. "Tulip, where is she now?"

"She ran off into the garden in tears. I saw her heading toward the willow tree. You know, the one I think would have been a perfect spot to place a bench. Perhaps it is time to add one there, even if the old duke did not agree."

Alex sighed. "Tulip, what do I care about benches or that willow tree? Go on about Mrs. Granger."

"Well, I thought I would give her some time alone to have a good cry."

"And you don't think her hysterics were part of an act?" He sighed again and ran a hand through his hair. "Everyone lies under questioning. Did you not think for a moment she was cleverly insinuating Ernfield into this? Do you really believe that stoic man suddenly felt compelled to reveal to her that William and Carver were to blame? Or is it more likely she made it all up?"

"But she was so convincing. Shall we go look for her?"

"I'll go look for her in a moment. I'm glad you came to me first." He took her hand and marched out with her, striding down the narrow hall toward the kitchen.

Tulip had to scamper twice as fast to keep up with him. "Why are we going to the kitchen when Mrs. Granger ran into the garden?"

"To stop her from getting anywhere near our food."

Tulip tugged on his arm to hold him back a moment. "Seriously? Are you worried *she* means to poison us all?"

"I have no idea if she does or not. But why take the risk? Anyway, it is probably just me she is thinking to poison...or perhaps you, too." He paused a moment and took her gently by the shoulders. "Or perhaps it is William she means to harm. This would be her best chance, would it not? How can I not be wary of her, especially after what you've just told me?"

"But she sounded so innocent, and she told me more..." She took a deep breath. "Oh, Alex, she told me about your father. He did love your mother very much. She said so."

"Oh, and you believed her? Can you not see she was manipulating you? What a good little actress she is."

Tulip stared up at him. "You think she was lying to me?"

"My father *abandoned* my mother and never gave a second thought to me. So, yes. What she told you was utter nonsense. But more to the point, if she won't dine with us tonight, then she's not going to supervise tonight's meal preparation. Mrs. Crabbe is more than capable of handling it all on her own."

"Dear heaven." But this made sense, especially if he thought their housekeeper was a murderess who poisoned her victims.

Was she that sly and conniving?

Tulip had been completely taken in, falling for her tears and for her stories.

Or was Alex wrong about their housekeeper?

He marched into the kitchen with all the authority of a man born to be a duke. "Mrs. Crabbe, has Mrs. Granger come in here recently?"

Their cook was as tough as nails, but even she was intimidated by Alex and his fierce scowl. "No, Yer Grace. Not since early this morning."

"What was she doing in here in the morning?"

"Reviewing the menus with me, as she does every day." Her usually surly demeanor was gone and she was surprisingly deferential to Alex.

Well, he was the duke.

And he did look quite fierce at the moment.

His gaze remained on Mrs. Crabbe. "Just reviewing or did she go near the food?"

"None of the food was out yet, Yer Grace." Mrs. Crabbe frowned. "Has she reported a problem? My food is fresh and I will not have anyone accusing me otherwise."

Since their cook looked ready to grab a rolling pin and go after the housekeeper, Tulip spoke up. "No accusations, Mrs. Crabbe. But are you certain she did not go anywhere near the food today?"

"Quite certain," she said with a nod.

Alex appeared a little calmer as he said, "She was looking quite peaked just now and it seemed as though her stomach was upset. I have no doubt everything you put out tonight will be flawless and make us proud. But if she is coming down with something, then it is best she stay out of here for the rest of the day. If she touched something, then throw it out. I won't have our guests getting ill because she has contaminated your finest preparations."

That seemed to mollify the woman. "If Mrs. Granger is ill, I'll make up some broth for her. Never ye worry, Yer Grace. I will not let her into my kitchen until she has recovered from whatever ails her. As ye said, I do not need her breathing on my food or coughing in here. My scullery girls don't need to be getting sick, either."

She then turned to the girls. "Did ye hear that, loves? Mrs. Granger is not to step foot in here until I say so."

The girls, who were huddled together and listening to their exchange with wild-eyed looks of fear, bobbed their heads.

Alex nodded in satisfaction and strode out.

Tulip thanked Mrs. Crabbe and then scrambled after him. "Where are you going next?"

"Where do you think?" he asked, his expression daunting. "I'm going to find Mrs. Granger and question her thoroughly. She cannot simply hurl an accusation about your uncle and then go on her merry way."

Tulip cleared her throat. "Um, she was scared, Alex. Not in the least arrogant or irreverent. In fact, we might have this all wrong. If your predecessors were murdered, then I do not think it was her."

"Oh, really? That is quite an abrupt change of heart." He folded his arms across his chest and stared down at her. "If that is so, then let me confirm it. This doesn't change a thing. I still need to find her. I'm also going to search her quarters."

"For evidence of poisons? All right, but let me be the one to check her quarters. The staff will talk if they see you go in there. They'll think...well, you know. They'll think you are as lecherous as the prior Davenport dukes."

He let out a breath. "That is ridiculous."

"Is it?"

He let his arms drop to his sides. "Fine, search her room while I look for her in the garden."

They parted ways, each walking in opposite directions.

Perhaps Alex was right to pursue this immediately, for this

was quite a serious allegation against her uncle.

Why would Mrs. Granger consider her Uncle William a villain? Merely on Ernfield's cryptic warning?

Had Ernfield even said something to her or was that a lie, too?

Tulip hurried to the staff quarters.

Mrs. Granger had her own room, larger than the rest and set apart from the other bedchambers in a sort of alcove to afford her more privacy.

Tulip knocked on the door. "Mrs. Granger, are you in there?"

No answer.

She knocked louder.

Still no response.

Tulip let out a breath and tried the door handle.

She was relieved when it opened easily and the door swung open to reveal a tidy chamber.

An empty one, too.

"Oh, heaven forgive me," Tulip said, quietly shutting the door and immediately proceeding to open her housekeeper's bureau drawers.

She did not know exactly what she was looking for, only that she would recognize it when she came across it.

A diary, perhaps.

But she found none.

Well, someone smart enough to murder three or four dukes and avoid suspicion would not be stupid enough to write down the details of each crime.

Nor did Tulip find a suspicious vial containing pills or any unfamiliar liquids.

In fact, there was absolutely nothing to be found in here.

Not even letters from her family.

No remembrance of her deceased husband, assuming he ever existed.

Not a single personal item.

That seemed odd in itself.

Tulip made certain to leave everything exactly as she had found it and hurried off to search for Alex.

He stood by the willow tree, a hand shaded over his eyes as he gazed toward the distant salt marshes.

She hurried forward and called out to him.

He turned and strode toward her. "Anything, Tulip?"

"No, but I think this might be something in itself."

"What do you mean?"

She quickly told him about her search. "She had absolutely nothing in her bedchamber. Not a letter from a friend. Not old letters from family. No remembrance of her husband. No bible. No records whatsoever of her life before coming to Thornwycke Hall."

"I am not surprised."

"You aren't?"

"Because her entire identity might be a ruse."

Now, Tulip was really confused. "Are you saying she is not Mrs. Granger? And not related to Elspeth, the girl who disappeared all those years ago?"

He raked a hand through his hair, something he did whenever he was perplexed. "I don't know. Anything is possible. She could be completely innocent, or possibly guilty of three or four murders. We don't even know if these were murders."

"Oh, Alex. My head is now in a complete muddle."

"So is mine," he admitted with a wince. "Let me find her and get this cleared up. One of the gardeners thought he saw someone heading toward the salt marshes. Could be her. Go back to the house and stay within sight of the staff until I return."

"No, I'd rather stay close to you."

"Why?"

"Because I don't want you searching alone along the salt marshes. I know these tides and you do not. Besides, am I not safer with you, at least until we find her? What if she went back into the house? How will I be protected while you are out here searching for her?"

He grunted, obviously not pleased that her reasoning made sense.

After a moment, he nodded. "All right, stay close. But you must do exactly as I say and the instant I say it. No questioning and no hesitating."

"Got it. If you say hide, I hide. If you tell me to run, I'll run."

He cast her a wry smile. "And will you run even if you believe I am in danger?"

She cleared her throat and glanced down at her toes.

"This is important, Tulip. I am the one who has vowed to protect you. It does not work the other way around."

Honestly, did he have to be so marvelously apish about this? She would run and she would hide, but she was not going to keep running or hiding if he were in danger and she could do something to save him.

Mr. Carver happened to be walking back from the salt marshes with some of his workers. Alex stopped them. "Have you seen Mrs. Granger?"

Mr. Carver frowned in thought a moment. "Perhaps, Your Grace. We noticed someone in the marshes and thought it odd because the tide was coming in. I just assumed it was a fisherman, but didn't get a good look." He turned to his workers. "Anyone notice who was out there?"

"No," a few replied.

But one of the men regarded him uncertainly. "Didn't look like no lady, but I only got a glimpse so I could be wrong. I thought it was a fisherman carrying his nets over his shoulder. Looked like a man hauling a bundle. Why would Mrs. Granger ever be out here?"

"No idea," Alex said smoothly. "But she seemed out of sorts this morning and my wife is worried about her."

Tulip put a hand to her throat. "The tide comes in fast and she may be too distraught to realize it."

"I'll come search with you, Your Grace. Er...with your permission," Mr. Carver said, handing his shovel to one of his men at Alex's nod. "Lads, escort Her Grace back to the house and then gather rope and rowboats, and come help us search."

"Yes, take my wife back. Two of you stay with her until I return." Alex now turned to Tulip. "Mr. Carver's right. You need to go back to the house. I don't want you getting caught up in the tide and drowning."

She shook her head. "But I know my way around these

marshes and you do not."

"I expect Mr. Carver knows them better than both of us. I'll be safe enough." He gave her cheek a light caress. "Please, I don't want to be worrying about you, too. We'll return shortly."

Tulip did not like this one bit, but she supposed he was right.

She was not dressed for wading through the marshes, not to mention she had to prepare for this evening's party. "All right, but stay close to Mr. Carver and do not stray from the path or you'll sink into the mud and could get stuck. If you feel the ground begin to give way beneath your feet, immediately lie flat and crawl toward firmer ground."

Alex cast her a soft smile. "I will, Tulip. Thank you for the good advice."

The tide was beginning to rise, already covering some of the distant sedges and reeds that lined the marshes. Everything would be underwater within the next quarter hour as the water surged.

Tulip watched her husband head off with Mr. Carver.

One of the workmen approached her. "Please, Your Grace. We need to get you away from here now."

She nodded, for she was only delaying them in getting their rescue equipment. And was this not most important, especially if Alex and Mr. Carver were the ones who would ultimately need rescuing?

She spared a last look at Alex making his way along the marshes. "All right."

The workers hurriedly escorted her as far as the terrace before all but two headed off toward the barn to stow their tools and grab ropes. The boats were stowed in a shed beside the barn and needed several men to carry each down.

The two men assigned to her remained standing in the garden with their eyes on her while she stood on the terrace in their full view. She was busy peering out toward the salt marshes when Ernfield approached her. "Your Grace," he said, slightly out of breath and his boots squishing as he climbed the few steps toward her, "I do beg your pardon. Has something happened?"

"Yes," she replied, wondering why he was not at his post by the front door, "Mrs. Granger was rather upset and ran off in the direction of the marshes. His Grace and Mr. Carver are searching for her now."

His eyes rounded. "Oh, dear. I had better go help them."

Tulip glanced in the distance and saw the water level rising dangerously fast. "No, Ernfield," she said in impulse. "They have it managed."

"But Your Grace, I know these marshes and can help. I *must* help. Is it not my responsibility as head butler to protect His Grace?"

She ought to have let him go, but something held her back. Perhaps it was the note of agitation in his voice. This stoic man, who had not shown so much as a glimmer of feeling in the week they had been here, was suddenly awash in it.

Was she sensing worry? Or concern?

In truth, she sensed some anger in him.

Was this not very odd?

Well, she could be wrong.

This entire day was turning out odd.

Besides, she was peeved with Ernfield.

Had he really accused her uncle and Mr. Carver of covering up Elspeth's disappearance?

Even if he had not, she did not change her mind about allowing him to go to the salt marshes.

Something simply felt *off* about him...or perhaps it was her. But it felt like *him*.

Oh, her stupid intuition.

The poor man was probably secretly in love with Mrs. Granger and wanted to help the men find her.

She heard the distant roar of an incoming wave and then another immediately following it that crashed dangerously close to where Alex and Mr. Carver were searching. "Stay here, Ernfield. The tide is already too high. It is bad enough His Grace and Mr. Carver are out there getting soaked and will likely need rescuing."

Ernfield appeared about to say something to her, but the rest of Mr. Carver's workers came around the side of the house at just that moment. "See, they are already preparing to help out. Leave them to it, Ernfield. Anyway, should you not be supervising the preparations for tonight's dinner party?"

"That is Mrs. Granger's role, Your Grace. I can assure you, the staff is experienced and has it all in hand. Is this rescue not more important? I ought to lend assistance."

"No," Tulip said, more firmly.

Gad, why did she feel so compelled to stop him?

He seemed quite fidgety and not at all happy, but she was the duchess and he had no choice but to obey her command if he wished to retain his coveted position as head butler.

Tulip could not blame him, she supposed.

It was quite frustrating to be held back when one wanted to help.

Did she not feel this same frustration?

"Oh, look!" she cried a moment later, for Ernfield had remained on the terrace with her and was now pacing like an agitated lion. She felt bad about forbidding him to join the search when she had wanted to do the same. But she had accepted Alex's instructions while Ernfield appeared ready to leap off the terrace…or leap at her in frustration.

She was glad Carver's two men had their eyes on her.

"I see them! They've found her!" she called down to her two guards.

They all hurried to the garden's edge, Ernfield loping along beside her, and watched eagerly as Alex and Mr. Carver slogged their way toward them while waist deep through the quickly rising water. "Come on," she whispered. "Don't stray off the path."

She let out a breath as Alex, who was holding an unconscious Mrs. Granger in his arms, closely followed Mr. Carver's guiding steps onto dry land.

Several of Mr. Carver's men dropped their ropes and hurried forward. Others who had been in the midst of hauling out rowboats from the shed now set them down and also raced forward while cheering.

Both Alex and Mr. Carver were breathing heavily by the time they reached the garden and everyone surrounded them to offer their congratulations.

Alex managed a special smile for her.

Tulip smiled back.

She wanted to tell him that she was so very proud of him, and was ready to tell him that she loved him. But he still carried Mrs. Granger and was obviously eager to make his way back into the house. Also, they were surrounded by their workers, so nothing of a romantic nature could be said just now.

Ernfield reached out his arms. "You must be exhausted, Your Grace. Let me carry Mrs. Granger into the staff quarters for you."

Alex drew back. "No, Ernfield. I have her."

"But your clothes, Your Grace. You and Mr. Carver are soaking wet. May I not relieve you while you change into dry garments?"

"Not necessary," Alex insisted and started toward the house.

Everyone followed him.

"Your Grace, may I ask…what happened?" Ernfield's eyes were wide and his mouth tensely pinched as he studied the dark-gowned bundle lying limp in Alex's arms.

"She must have tripped and hit her head on something," Mr. Carver replied. "Good thing we found her or the tide would have swallowed her up and washed her out to sea within minutes. It was a very close call." He then turned to his workers. "Put the ropes and boats back where they belong."

"Aye, Mr. Carver," one of them said. "But will you let us know if Mrs. Granger is all right?"

"Of course, Dougal," he said to the man who had asked. "His Grace and I will let everyone know as soon as we ourselves learn what happened."

Ernfield trailed after them as Alex carried the poor woman into the servants wing of the house through the kitchen entrance since everyone's boots were wet and possibly muddy. As they squished along the flooring, Tulip realized what had felt off about Ernfield.

He'd squished, too.

His boots had been wet.

But how was it possible while indoors supervising the staff's party preparations?

Alex stopped abruptly and turned to their head butler in

obvious exasperation, for the man was practically breathing down Alex's neck. "Ernfield, if you insist on being useful, then ride into town and summon the doctor."

"Very well, Your Grace. I'll assign one of the footmen to–"

"No, *you* are to do it," Alex insisted. "My wife needs the footmen here to prepare for our dinner party." Then he softened his tone. "Do not take this badly, Ernfield. I saw how you stood beside my wife as I carried Mrs. Granger back to the house. Your instincts are protective. I know you are the only one I can trust to diligently search for the doctor, since he may not be in his infirmary. Find him as quickly as possible. I fear time is of the essence. Mrs. Granger may not survive, for she took a fair amount of water into her lungs."

Tulip was surprised Alex had assigned the chore to Ernfield specifically.

Wasn't it an insult to send the head butler off as a messenger, even if her husband gave a flattering reason?

She would ask Alex about this later.

Hadn't she insulted poor Ernfield herself when commanding him to remain beside her and not go in search of Mrs. Granger?

Odd that she and Alex both felt the need to put Ernfield off.

But did his squishing boots signify anything? He might have stepped outside as delivery wagons came up the drive and inadvertently walked into a puddle.

Well, now was not the time to think about it.

Tulip skittered in front of Alex and Mr. Carver to lead the way down the narrow hall toward the housekeeper's bedchamber that she had searched only a short while ago. "Mr. Carver, please ask two of the maids to come in here to help me change her out of her wet clothes. And also ask Mrs. Crabbe to bring her some broth."

"At once, Your Grace," he said and hurried off to the kitchen.

"She'll have to wake up first or you won't be able to ladle anything down her throat," Alex remarked, pointing out the obvious.

"What happened to her? Did she trip and hit her head on a rock?"

Alex had been frowning and his frown now deepened.

"Unlikely. I'm thinking she got bashed on the back of her head."

Tulip gaped at him. "Why would you think that?"

"Because if this were just an accident, she would have fallen backward and that's how she could have hit the back of her head on a rock. But she fell *forward*, her body sprawled face down on the ground when we found her. How does one end up that way unless struck from behind? That's the only explanation for the position of her body. One has to be falling *backward* to strike the back of one's head, but would fall *forward* if struck from behind by someone else. Again, no accident. Someone attacked her. We'll learn more when she regains consciousness."

"Do you think she will?"

"Actually, yes. I think we got to her before any water got into her lungs. But no one has to know this yet. Let them all think she is at death's door."

"Who could have attacked her?"

"I don't know, love. But it could not have been Mr. Carver because he was with his men when it happened. I'll question them closely once we have Mrs. Granger safely settled. One of them mentioned noticing a fisherman carrying his nets or some sort of bundle. It could have been the villain carrying Mrs. Granger after he'd struck her on the head."

"And intending to toss her into the salt marshes to drown?"

"Yes." He still had their housekeeper in his arms, but obviously could not settle her on the bed because her gown was soaking wet. "Pull out a change of clothing for her, will you, Tulip?"

"All right. The maids should be along shortly to assist me. I–" She broke off suddenly. "Alex! Oh, my goodness! This isn't possible. Look!" She held up two vials filled with liquid that would no doubt be found to contain an opiate or perhaps poison. "These weren't here when I searched her room earlier. What was it, maybe fifteen or twenty minutes ago? There is no way she could have returned to her bedchamber between then and now to put those vials in her drawer."

He stared at her, saying nothing, but she could see the ideas whirling in his investigative brain.

Then his expression shifted ever so slightly and he let out a soft breath.

Tulip gasped. "Oh, Alex! You've figured it out, haven't you?"

He quirked an eyebrow.

"Yes, you have! Tell me, who did this to Mrs. Granger? And is this attack in any way related to the deaths of the predecessor dukes?"

CHAPTER 14

ALEX COULD NOT be sure he had figured out anything, but when one stripped away all the excess chatter and concentrated on the essential, it became obvious there was one person within Thornwycke Hall present from the beginning, manipulating the clues, and doing his best to focus suspicion on others.

One name alone stood out among the rest.

But Alex needed to be certain before he said anything, for there was more information to be gathered.

First, what was this suspect's motivation for harming Mrs. Granger?

Having come up with a name, he could now probe backwards to find out what had made the man desperate or angry enough to harm her and beyond this, to commit murder...assuming his predecessors had been murdered.

However, having a motive was not enough.

Alex needed to figure out how each murder was accomplished.

Who had the means and intelligence to carry out these villainous acts? And to cleverly position Mrs. Granger's body in the salt marshes to make it look like an accidental drowning once the tide ebbed and her body was found?

And what of Mr. Carver's daughter, Martha, and poor Elspeth?

Well, Elspeth's disappearance and probable death might have been at someone else's hand...his grandfather's, Alex would guess, even though the old man had supposedly denied it to Mrs. Granger.

But who could trust that wily hound?

What was certain was that Elspeth's unfortunate end was the inciting incident that had led to all of these revenge killings.

Yes, they must have been killings.

His instincts were never wrong…even if the evidence said otherwise.

He could wrap this all up before tonight's dinner party, he realized with much relief.

As soon as Mrs. Granger was properly settled, he would start interrogating the elder staff members who had been in service here longest. He intended to start with Mrs. Crabbe, ready to endure her taking a rolling pin to him for distracting her from her meal preparations.

Yes, she had an important feast to cook for tonight. But he wanted to start with her because it was her food delivered to Mr. Carver's daughter when the poor girl became ill. Mrs. Granger had requested this be done, but he doubted the housekeeper ever delivered the food herself because her own duties would have kept her tied to the house.

Both women had the opportunity to tamper with the meals prepared, but they weren't the only ones. Besides, he knew from Perty Hester and even from Mrs. Granger's own mouth that she rarely went into Burnham.

So, she must have arranged for someone to deliver the food to the Carver residence.

Who next had the opportunity to tamper with it before it got to poor Martha Carver?

Mrs. Granger had started to figure this out. The killer must have noticed, got scared, and tried to kill Mrs. Granger only a few minutes ago.

Which confirmed the killer was in their midst.

Lurking dangerously close.

And desperate to complete what he hoped would be another perfect crime.

Alex had to admit that knocking Mrs. Granger unconscious and letting the incoming tide swallow her up was quite clever. The coroner would easily dismiss the gash to the back of her head as an accidental occurrence and conclude death by drowning, for her lungs would have been filled with water when examined.

And everyone would believe she was a distraught woman who had been too overset to realize the tide was coming in…or who intentionally meant to drown herself.

A good plan, except Alex and Mr. Carver had foiled it.

His suspected killer also had to be someone who had time to plant those vials in Mrs. Granger's drawer in order to make it appear as though she was the one who had drugged Tulip's food and next meant to poison her…or poison *him*.

That part was foiled by Tulip who had searched Mrs. Granger's room earlier and knew for a certainty that those vials had not been in the drawer.

But the killer did not know this.

Mr. Carver returned with two maids in tow. "Is there anything more you need of me, Your Grace? If not, I'll get the men back to work."

"I do have another request of you," Alex said. "I need you to ride to Burnham and summon the magistrate. Have him bring along two constables."

"Yes, of course. I should have thought to suggest it when you sent Ernfield off. He could have attended to both."

Alex gave Mrs. Granger over to the two maids who were built like bulls and could easily manage the unconscious woman, ordered them to remain in the room to guard her and not leave her side until further notice, and then steered his estate manager out of the room.

He was not surprised when Tulip scampered after him as he marched down the hall to his study with Mr. Carver.

"I want you to be very careful and avoid being seen by Ernfield while in Burnham," he instructed his estate manager as soon as the three of them were ensconced in his study.

Tulip gasped.

She then *eeped*, obviously bursting to ask questions.

But she knew better than to interfere.

Mr. Carver also appeared puzzled. "Your Grace, may I ask why?"

Alex sighed. "I want the magistrate and his constables to be present before I say more. Do not tell anyone where you are going. *No one*, Mr. Carver. This is vitally important. You are the only one I can trust to accomplish this task."

Mr. Carver eyed him warily. "This is about more than Mrs. Granger's near drowning, isn't it? Your Grace, I beg you to be honest with me. Do you think I am the guilty party? Is this why you are sending me off on this task? Hoping to keep me out of the way while you set your trap for me?"

Alex gave a curt, bitter laugh. "You? No. You are the only one I can trust without doubt or hesitation. You have Tulip to thank for that. Her faith in you is unwavering. We know you were not involved in any of the deaths connected to Thornwycke Hall. More important, upon your return, I will ask you to guard Tulip while I am busy interrogating the staff."

"Of course," he said with affection while staring at Tulip.

She smiled back at Mr. Carver but frowned lightly at Alex. "Should I not remain beside *you* while you question our staff? Have I not been immensely helpful so far?"

"Yes, you have," he said, tossing her a wry smile in return. "But you are my wife and I will not have you anywhere near a murderer as I unmask him."

"Can you not simply tell us who it is? Why keep it a mystery?" She was obviously frustrated that he was not providing her more information.

He regarded her soberly. "Accusing someone of multiple murders is no light matter, Tulip. I need to be certain before I charge the man who will face certain hanging upon his conviction. Also, I must rule out any accomplices. It is important to have all my facts straight before presenting the evidence to the magistrate."

He gave her a surprisingly tender kiss on the cheek. "Let me go about my business without interference. I am trained for this, not only for putting all the clues together, but keeping others out of harm's way – and that means *you* in particular, my lovely but snoopy Farthingale. I need you to remain safe while I gather the evidence necessary to convict this villain."

"Snoopy! Do not think giving me a gentle kiss on the cheek absolves you of this insult." But Alex saw she was not really angry with him, for she was laughing softly as she spoke.

Mr. Carver grinned, but quickly turned serious. "Let me change into dry clothes and I'll be off."

Alex took Tulip's hand as they watched him leave. "I need to change out of these wet clothes, too. Come upstairs and help me."

"I don't think you need my help so much as want to keep me in your sight," she muttered as they walked upstairs.

"And why not? Aren't you the most beautiful vision a man can behold? And am I not the luckiest man to wake up to your smile every morning?"

"You do not have to flatter me because you are about to shut me out of your investigation. But you really ought to confide in me."

"I will, Tulip. Just give me a moment to gather my thoughts."

But she knew he already had his ideas in place and it was time for him to share his knowledge with her.

"Who do you think is the killer?" she asked as soon as they entered their bedchamber. "I suppose this incident now rules out Mrs. Granger. I told you she seemed innocent to me. Do you really believe it was not Mr. Carver, or were you sending him off as you did Ernfield because you believe it is him? Or perhaps you think those two colluded? Him and Ernfield working together? I will never believe it of–"

"I trust Carver. Everything I told him was true. And I fully intend to have him guard you upon his return."

Tulip let out a breath. "I'm glad you have faith in him. He's the soul of kindness. Nor could it be Uncle William, even though Mrs. Granger seemed to be scared of him. He is a good and loving man, and I will never, *ever* believe he could do anything evil, no matter what Ernfield told her. Besides, Uncle William has a busy mercantile to run and everyone would notice if he were gone even for a few minutes much less the hour or two it would have taken him to come here, set up an elaborate murder of a duke, and get back. And someone would have noticed if he returned to his mercantile all wet just now."

"The tide had not come in yet, so he would have got out of the marshes with only his boots wet. But he is off my suspect list, as well. He was not the one to harm Mrs. Granger this morning."

He busied himself by removing his own wet boots as she continued to toss questions at him. "Nor do I believe Mrs. Crabbe was ever anyone's accomplice, Tulip. I only mention this since you seem to be curious about all the old retainers."

Tulip nodded. "I agree that she could not have been involved. She is a complete curmudgeon and does not hold back if she is irritated with you. A killer or his accomplice would be sly and never reveal their feelings, is that not so?"

"Yes, love," he said softly, now unbuttoning his shirt.

"So…that leaves Ernfield. Am I right? He was the only other staff member in service back in Elspeth's day, still working here now, and who could move about the house without suspicion raised. It must be Ernfield. But why would he harm his employers? And how? What is his possible connection to all the murders? Yet, who else but Ernfield could ever get so close to any of them that easily? It is him. Isn't it? I sensed it as he stood beside me and watched you carry Mrs. Granger back to the house. He wasn't concerned so much as agitated, no doubt worried she was going to wake up and accuse him. Oh, we must protect her. Tell me, Alex. I've guessed it, haven't I? It's Ernfield."

He sighed as he studied her determined expression. "Yes. Why else would I send him off to find the doctor? I needed him out of the house while I gather the evidence against him. But Tulip, you cannot let on to anyone else that he is the guilty party."

"I'll try my best," she said in earnest.

He gave her a light kiss on the lips. "That's the hard part for you, isn't it? You cannot help but show your feelings."

"I'm sorry, Alex. I will try, I promise."

"I know, love. Nor am I complaining about it. I like that you are soft and compassionate. Just try to remain stoic while I interrogate the long-time retainers. I'll start with the ladies first because they tend to notice details and share information among themselves. Men don't."

Her eyes bulged when he took off his shirt.

He frowned. "What's wrong? Why are you gaping at me?"

"You're shirtless."

He shook his head and laughed. "Too distracting for you?"

She blushed profusely. "Yes."

He grinned. "Then turn around, love. I'm about to drop my trousers."

CHAPTER 15

TO ALEX'S SLIGHT disappointment, Tulip did turn away and marched to the window to look out of it. "I always thought you were an extremely handsome man," she said, her gaze intent upon the view, "but you manage to get even handsomer by the day. Why is that, do you think?"

"Is it not obvious, Tulip?"

She still had her back to him, but nodded. "I suppose. But is it not too soon to feel a thing so deeply? To form an abiding and powerful connection within a matter of days, barely a fortnight, and not even a full month yet?"

"A bond of love," he said softly.

She nodded again. "Yes, that. I adore your intelligence and your strength. Your charm and quiet wit. I love that you hold me in your arms each night, and include me in your tours of the Davenport farms. I love that we are a part of each other's lives."

"So do I, Tulip."

She turned back to face him now that he had changed into dry clothes and was about to don a pair of dry boots. "Alex, I meant to tell you this after tonight's dinner party...but I think I must say it now."

"What, sweetheart?" He sank onto a chair and was in the midst of donning the first of his dry boots when he heard her take a deep breath.

Was she going to reveal more of her conversation with Mrs. Granger? Or mention Ernfield again? His heart had taken a sudden lurch when he saw the head butler standing on the terrace beside her as he'd slogged out of the salt marsh.

No reason why apprehension had surged through him.

Just instinct.

He now understood why.

The man was a killer.

What would Ernfield have done if Carver's two workers had not been keeping watch over Tulip?

Blessed saints.

He did not want to think of it.

Tulip took another deep breath. "I love you, Alex. I love you so much."

Her words jarred him out of his dismal thoughts, but it took him a moment to realize what she had just said.

"And I am fine with your not feeling the same yet," she hastily added when he did not immediately respond with a similar admission to her. "I know it is too soon. But after Mrs. Granger's near drowning, I could not hide my feelings any longer. Whatever happens next, I do not want you ever to doubt that I love you."

A slow smile spread across his lips.

I love you.

She had no idea how desperately he'd longed to hear those sweet words tumble from her lips.

Lord, he loved her so much.

And *hide* her feelings?

Tulip was an open book.

Her beautiful smiles, her welcoming response to his touch, the way she looked at him in gentle adoration.

She made him feel so good.

He hastily donned his second boot and rose to take her in his arms. "Tulip…sweetheart…"

A pounding at the door interrupted his next words, which would have been to admit he loved her, too.

But the pounding was persistent.

He hurriedly opened the door and saw one of the maids assigned to watch over Mrs. Granger looking quite overset as she bobbed a hasty curtsy. "Oh, Your Grace! Mrs. Granger is awake and insisting on talking to you and Her Grace. She won't lie still and says it is urgent."

He took Tulip's hand. "Yes, we'll come at once. Thank you, Mary."

They raced down the stairs, then along the narrow hall leading to the servants quarters, and burst into their housekeeper's room.

The maids had changed her out of her wet clothes and into her nightgown and robe.

The poor woman looked quite frail as she struggled to sit up. "Help me, Hortense," she said to one of the beefy maids.

"Aye, Mrs. Granger. There ye go."

Alex dismissed the maids once they had made Mrs. Granger comfortable. "But stay close, for I'll have you return shortly to watch over her."

"Aye, Your Grace," they said in unison and scampered out.

Alex closed the door after them, and motioned for Tulip to take the lone, rickety chair beside the housekeeper's bed. "Who did this to you, Mrs. Granger?"

Tears ran down her cheeks. "It was Ernfield."

"I knew it," Tulip mumbled, then immediately shook her head in dismay, obviously realizing she should not have said anything. "Do go on, Mrs. Granger. Tell us what happened."

"I was overset after our morning conversation," she said, her gaze on Tulip. "I ran out into the garden, but hadn't gone far before I realized I should not be seen crying by the staff. It isn't seemly. So I made my way to the salt marshes, intending to walk off my distress. I was only there a few minutes and had every intention of returning to the house because the tide was coming in and I felt my boots getting wet. Suddenly, Ernfield was there, cudgel in hand, and staring at me with such a demonic look upon his face."

"So, you turned and ran?" Tulip asked.

She nodded. "But before I could take a step, he hit me across the back of my head. I fell to my knees. I was too dazed to scream, although I tried. But I couldn't catch my breath and I felt myself passing out. He lifted me over his shoulder and carried me deeper into the marshes. The tide was coming in. I started to struggle, but he tossed me onto the ground, laughing as I landed face first in the mud. He must have struck me again to make certain I would not get up. That's the last I remember until waking up just now."

"Why do you think he came after you?" Alex asked, because there had to be a connection to Ernfield's sudden determination to be rid of her.

"I saw him earlier in the day remove something from one of the decorative vases in the parlor. I didn't see what it was, only that it was something small that he immediately tucked into his pocket. Perhaps two small things because I heard a light, tinkling sound, like glasses clinking together."

Tulip stared at Alex.

"The vials," she mouthed.

He nodded.

"I asked him what he was doing," Mrs. Granger continued, "but he said nothing and merely strode out. The next time I saw him, he was coming at me with a cudgel. I think he is deranged and dangerous."

"We know," Tulip said, and Alex sent her a silent warning not to say more.

He wanted to hear the housekeeper's own words and not have Tulip commiserating and telling the woman what *they* knew.

But he also wanted to learn more about Martha's death which he expected was indeed by slow poisoning. "Tell me about Martha Carver. She had come to Thornwycke Hall and got sick shortly thereafter."

"Yes," she said with a nod, casting them both a look of confusion because she had to be wondering why they were asking about Carver's daughter. "It was such a sad time for poor Mr. Carver. He was beside himself with grief."

"I remember," Tulip said. "I understand you had food sent to her daily."

She nodded. "Oddly, it was Ernfield who suggested it. How could he be so kind one moment and then completely mad now?"

"Tell me about that arrangement…the food delivery. Take me through every step," Alex said, bending on one knee beside Tulip as they listened to their housekeeper speak from her bed.

"Well, Mrs. Crabbe prepared the daily meals and stowed them in a basket. I would take the basket to Ernfield who then arranged for one of the stable boys to take it down to Martha's house. She lived with her father in Burnham, as you know. Her father would return the basket the following morning and Mrs. Crabbe would load it up again. That's all I can tell you. It was a simple arrangement, each of us doing our little part to try to restore her to health."

"Thank you, Mrs. Granger. That's very helpful. Was there one stable boy in particular assigned the chore?"

"Yes, young Edward Wilcox. Poor lad. He was a little slow-witted but so proud he'd been given this responsibility."

"Edward?" Tulip gasped, and then turned to Alex with a groan. "How utterly, utterly stupid of me never to make the connection. The lad died shortly after Martha passed on. We all thought it might have been of the same wasting sickness and he might have caught it from Martha. But it turned out not to be contagious because no one else suffered similar symptoms afterward."

He took hold of Tulip's hand, hoping to soothe her.

They were dealing with a madman here, one crazed enough to kill an innocent boy.

Mrs. Granger now realized the purpose of his questions and gasped. "Oh, no! Do you think Ernfield killed poor Edward? And Martha? No...oh, no. And none of us ever had a suspicion. Is it possible he harmed your grandfather, too?"

"Not only my grandfather, but the next three dukes in the line of succession," Alex said. "But start with my grandfather. Why mention him when he was already old and frail?"

She let out a breath. "Because Ernfield brought up warm milk and biscuits for your grandfather nightly. To me, it appeared there was a friendship between the two of them that I thought was quite endearing. The old duke and his ever-faithful servant fondly reminiscing about their younger days. This is why I was surprised when your grandfather started talking to me, confessing things to me, and not to Ernfield."

"Yes, about that...what did he confess, exactly?" Alex asked.

"And did his confession have anything to do with your aunt, Elspeth?"

Her eyes widened. "Yes, how did you know? Oh, your wife must have told you what we discussed."

"I already suspected something before you said anything to my wife this morning. Mrs. Granger, I am fairly certain everything that has happened at Thornwycke is connected to Elspeth. What did my grandfather tell you?"

"He did not confess to her murder, if that is what you are thinking."

He was, but did not allow it to show. "I am merely trying to collect information and assess the facts. Do go on. My grandfather did not confess to her murder, and…"

"Quite the opposite," she insisted. "I think he loved her and was considering marrying her."

Tulip turned to him, her eyes wide. "Marriage?"

Alex's stomach was now in a roil.

What was going on here?

This was turning what he'd been told about the old man upside down.

Was it possible his grandfather actually had a heart?

No, he was mostly depraved, as well as ruthless in controlling his family.

"Why did you not tell me this morning?" Tulip asked Mrs. Granger, bringing his own attention back to the present.

Mrs. Granger appeared distressed. "I wanted to. I don't know why I did not say anything then. But please know, I did feel I could trust you. However, I feared this was too much to reveal all in one sitting. Who would ever believe me? The old duke had such a debauched reputation and it was deserved. There were women all around the place, shamelessly offering their bodies not only to the duke but to his offspring."

"My father, uncle, and cousins," Alex said with much disgust.

"Not your father," Mrs. Granger insisted. "I know you won't believe this, but your father adored your mother and it broke his heart when you and she left. Just as I think your grandfather's heart was broken when Elspeth disappeared. I believe my aunt and the old duke were having a true courtship, one that was intended to lead to their marriage."

"He told you this?" Alex asked.

"Yes, he confessed that he was her secret beau and not some mysterious naval officer. He told me that his intentions were serious. And why not? He was in his forties, still hale and virile, and Elspeth probably loved him sincerely. I think it would have been a love match."

Her eyes began to tear. "I never believed what my mother and grandparents told me about Elspeth. Even if she had run off with someone, my grandparents loved her too much ever to disown her. They missed her very much. Elspeth was also a warm, loving girl. She would have written to them. Visited them. They had to know she was not alive."

"Do you think the inheritance they supposedly received was actually a bribe on my grandfather's part to keep them silent?" Alex asked.

"No, Your Grace. Not a bribe. Never that. But yes, I think he quietly helped them move away because living in Burnham was too painful for them. He took care of them because he loved Elspeth and this was how he chose to honor her."

Alex struggled with this. "But if he loved her, then why not move heaven and earth to find her when she disappeared? He had to know she would never willingly leave him if they did love each other. And yet, there is no hint he ever insisted on an investigation or ever participated in one."

To Alex, this meant his grandfather had to know she was dead.

But who would he protect with his silence?

One of his heirs?

Three heirs had ascended to the dukedom and all of them had died, no doubt by Ernfield's hand.

"Yes, all you say is true," Mrs. Granger muttered. "But I am now convinced the truth lies with Ernfield. I think he knows what happened that night of her disappearance, and his nightly visits to your grandfather were not about two old friends chatting, but served as a warning to your grandfather to keep quiet about Elspeth."

"Except, he didn't," Tulip remarked. "He began to confide in you."

"Yes, and this is why I am convinced your grandfather did not harm Elspeth. But she died, somehow. Perhaps it was by accident. I think he would have told me if he knew she had been murdered. He would have given me a name. But he accused no one."

Alex raked a hand through his hair.

Did this mean Elspeth killed herself?

Why would she do this if she believed she was going to marry a duke?

He shook back to the present, for more was needed to resolve the confusion surrounding Elspeth's death.

There was enough evidence to imprison Ernfield for attempting to kill Mrs. Granger, but still not enough to link him to any other deaths. One might build a circumstantial case around poisoning Martha, and now young Edward Wilcox could be added to his list of victims. But Elspeth? Or his three predecessors?

Well, perhaps he would have to settle for this one crime, and even that was Mrs. Granger's word against Ernfield's. Would it be enough to have him imprisoned for the rest of his life? Or hanged? "Too bad no one got a better look at him coming after you on the marshes."

Tulip pursed her lips. "Why? Wouldn't Mrs. Granger's testimony be enough for a conviction?"

He shrugged. "Possibly, but it depends on whether Ernfield, a long time resident of Burnham whose family is well-liked and trusted, or Mrs. Granger, a stranger to these parts whose family left suddenly and under mysterious circumstances, is to be believed. Having additional evidence to bolster her claim could be the difference between Ernfield being found guilty or not guilty."

"I can testify," Tulip said.

Alex arched an eyebrow. "You? What proof can you offer?"

"His boots squished."

Alex laughed. "What?"

"Ernfield came up to me as I stood on the terrace and I thought it was odd that his boots squished, which means they were wet.

How do boots get wet when you are the Davenport head butler and your role is to stand indoors? So, obviously he was outdoors and the soles of his boots might still hold traces of marsh reeds and sedges. The fresh mud and grasses would link him to the salt marshes at the time Mrs. Granger was attacked."

Alex smiled. "Thank you, Tulip. That was a clever observation."

She cast him a delicious smile. "Shall we question Mrs. Crabbe next? Never mind about tonight's dinner party. If we have to send word it is cancelled, my friends and family will understand."

"No, let's not cancel anything just yet. Let's talk to Mrs. Crabbe first and then decide."

They summoned the two maids to look after Mrs. Granger, and Alex repeated his stern warning. "Do not leave her side for any reason. I want the two of you watching over her at all times. No substitutions. You do not leave except on my authority or that of my wife. No one else is to come in here unless it is Mr. Carver, the magistrate, or the doctor. *No one else.* Is that clear?"

"Aye, Your Grace," they both said in earnest.

Mrs. Crabbe was barking orders to her scullery maids and cooks when they strode in. "Your Graces," she said, *thwacking* her meat cleaver down on the table as they approached, and then wiping her hands on her apron that held traces of animal blood on it. "Are ye needing something? Maisie's about to bring a bowl of broth to Mrs. Granger."

"We need to talk to you," Alex said. "Come into my study. It won't take long, but this is quite urgent."

She nodded, not looking too happy about the request since they were taking her away from her supper preparations that were to be more elaborate than their usual dining fare. "Mind the pies, Annie. And Lucy, get the last of those chickens plucked."

She lumbered after him and Tulip, and sat awkwardly once they entered his study and he offered her a chair. Obviously, she was not used to sitting in the presence of a duke, or settling into a chair of the softest leather.

As for him, he still had trouble thinking of himself as a duke. He had been proud of his reputation as London's top investigator and sorely missed those days. "Mrs. Crabbe, tell us what you can recall about the night Elspeth Palter disappeared."

"Elspeth?" She inhaled sharply. "Yer Grace, is there a reason to resurrect the dead?"

"The dead?" He had been leaning against his desk, his hands at his sides and loosely grasping the edge of the desk, but now straightened. "Why do you refer to her as that?"

Mrs. Crabbe paled as his gaze fixed on her. "I...well...no one ever heard from her again, did they?"

"But you know what happened that night, don't you? Do not bother to deny it, for it is plainly written on your face." This was not merely a shot in the dark, for Mrs. Crabbe's first thought was to pronounce Elspeth dead while everyone else was still wondering whether she had eloped with a navy officer. "It is time for the truth to come out, Mrs. Crabbe. How many more deaths must be endured at Thornwycke because of your silence?"

She clutched her heart. "Yer Grace! I never laid a hand on anyone. Upon my mother's grave. I am a cook. I *nourish* people, not destroy them!"

"Then tell me what you know. I give you my word that you shall not be punished for anything you tell me, so long as you were not the one who killed Elspeth or assisted in her killing."

"A killing? Ye think someone murdered the poor girl? No, no." She shook her head vehemently. "No one killed her. Dear Lord, is that what everyone is thinking?" She uttered a short prayer. "Please, ye cannot tarnish poor Elspeth's reputation. She was a good girl and is meant to be in heaven. Leave it alone. Please, Yer Grace. Let her rest with the angels."

"And you think revealing the truth will have her snatched from the arms of her angels?" Tulip asked.

"Yes, Yer Grace," she replied, casting pleading eyes on Tulip. "You see...Elspeth jumped to her death."

Tulip gasped.

Alex leaned forward, eager to hear more. "How? Why?"

Tulip took hold of the woman's beefy hand and spoke to her gently. "This is not about tarnishing the poor girl's reputation, but perhaps salvaging it. You must trust us, Mrs. Crabbe. My husband is the most brilliant man alive and the most honorable. He would never do anything cruel to her memory or to you. Nor would I. But there is a real danger lurking here at Thornwycke and it is time for this evil to be brought into light."

After a moment of agonizing uncertainty, Mrs. Crabbe nodded. "That night Elspeth died...she did die, Yer Grace. I saw her body lying broken on the terrace. I was just a young cook in the household at the time and flirting with one of the footmen, Horace Crabbe. He's now my husband. But that does not matter, I suppose. It was the middle of the night and even the duke's family and their debauched guests had gone to sleep. I..."

Mrs. Crabbe began to gasp for breath.

Tulip put her arms around the woman. "Do go on," she gently urged.

"I had spent the night with Horace and needed to get back to my own bed before others woke up and noticed mine hadn't been slept in. Well, I was on my way back, and that's when I saw them...yer grandfather and Ernfield. They were standing over her body and yer grandfather was in tears and utterly distraught. *Why did she jump? Why did she jump?* This is what he kept muttering. *She agreed to become my wife*, he said."

So, it was true.

His grandfather had loved Elspeth.

Alex did not know if he was relieved or made even angrier by the revelation.

His grandfather had been in love, and yet still destroyed the lives and marriages of his own offspring.

"Well, blow me over with a feather. Took me by surprise," Mrs. Crabbe muttered. "A duke and a local girl? It was unheard of." She inhaled sharply and then groaned. "But it is the same with the pair of ye, isn't it? So maybe it was true, that I ought to have believed what I was hearing."

"Did Ernfield say anything to the duke?" Alex asked.

She nodded. "He kept saying that it was for the best, that Elspeth must have been cursed upon accepting him because this was not the natural way of things. He said that Elspeth ought to have kept to her own kind what loved her. Then he said something odd…that she should have accepted William Hester's suit and not dallied with the duke."

Tulip's eyes widened. "My uncle? Was he courting Elspeth?"

"I don't know. I thought he was in love with yer aunt, Perty. But I would not be surprised if he held a secret affection for Elspeth. Every boy in Burnham adored her. Even that cold fish, Ernfield was in love with her at one time. Oh, he'll deny it. But I saw the heat in his eyes whenever her name was mentioned or whenever she happened to cross his path. Elspeth was working at Thornwycke at the time, assisting Mrs. Dodge. Did ye know that?"

"No, I did not," Alex admitted.

"She had just started, perhaps no more than a few weeks in service before she met her untimely end."

"If she was so adored, then why ever would she jump?" Tulip asked. "And was it from the tower room?"

Mrs. Crabbe nodded. "Yes, there's where she jumped. I never saw what the duke had done up there, but I'd heard from Mrs. Dodge that he was having it decorated beautifully as a private salon for a prospective bride. Except no one knew at the time that he intended it for Elspeth, although we ought have had a clue since Elspeth was hired to assist Mrs. Dodge for this very purpose. Elspeth was as cheerful as anything the entire time, so we just assumed it was because she enjoyed her task…or maybe had a secret beau that was putting the smile on her face…and maybe putting other things elsewhere, if ye know what I mean."

Alex cleared his throat, for he did understand her meaning.

His grandfather was a rogue and would not have been shy about seducing Elspeth. That he intended to do right and marry her did not alter the fact that he was a rake and a libertine. "What did Ernfield and my grandfather do with her body?"

She broke down in tears again. "Ernfield told His Grace that he'd give her a proper burial and warned that His Grace should tell no one or else Elspeth would be damned for eternity. Please, please, let it rest. There are still many in Burnham who loved Elspeth and would be devastated if the truth came to light. It serves no purpose to resurrect the dead. Leave her in peace."

Alex dismissed Mrs. Crabbe and made certain to be gentle

about it because he saw that the woman was genuinely distressed. "Take a moment to pull yourself together," he said in a soothing manner. "You've trained your staff well, and they can carry on without you for a little while longer."

"Thank ye, Yer Grace. I'll be all right in my kitchen. Cooking gives me comfort."

He smiled kindly. "Then do as you feel best."

Tulip turned to him the moment their cook walked out. "So, poor Elspeth killed herself."

"No," Alex replied with a bitter laugh and a shake of his head. "I am more convinced than ever that she was murdered."

Tulip's eyes widened. "Murdered?"

"Yes. And you can add this one to Ernfield, as well."

She leaped to her feet. "Alex! Are you certain?"

He nodded. "I've been investigating crimes for a long time. A young lady about to become a duchess, who is given the task of decorating the very salon that will soon be hers alone, and who chirps and smiles while working, does not suddenly leap out of a tower room in despair."

"Perhaps she was masking her unhappiness."

He cast Tulip a dubious glance. "Yes, it is possible. But unlikely. In all the conversations we've had about her with others, has anyone ever suggested she was prone to swings in her temperament or her behavior?"

"No," she admitted.

He sighed. "Elspeth was a happy girl who believed she was about to marry a duke. It is as simple as that. Ernfield, whether out of jealousy because he loved her, or sheer madness in believing she was impure or a lowly commoner not fit to be a duchess, did her in. The poor girl might not have suspected a thing."

"Then why kill any of the dukes? It could not have been revenge because *he* was the killer, not your grandfather."

"I don't know, love. It could be that he simply believed them all to be impure and tainted."

"But we're not," Tulip insisted. "Ours is a true and faithful marriage."

He cast her a mirthless smile. "Yes, but he is *mad*. What do you think he sees when he looks at us?"

"A happy couple?" she remarked with wry, dark humor.

"Wishful thinking, Tulip." He took her hand and gave it a light kiss. "I am a duke. You are a commoner. Guess again."

CHAPTER 16

"WE MUST SEARCH Ernfield's quarters," Tulip suggested.

"Without doubt," Alex agreed, feeling fairly confident they might turn up some proof of Ernfield's involvement in Elspeth's death and possibly in the deaths of Alex's predecessor dukes.

Similar to Mrs. Granger's quarters, the head butler's chamber was set slightly apart from those rooms housing the footmen and butlers. "I'll do it, Tulip. I need you to keep the rest of the staff distracted. The cooks and scullery maids will all be busy in the kitchen, so I am not too concerned about them. It is the butlers and footmen whose rooms are close to Ernfield's who worry me. I'd rather they not see me prowling around Ernfield's quarters."

"And report it to Ernfield on his return?" Tulip nodded. "I understand."

"Have them work on assignments ensured to keep them occupied in the main rooms of the house. Can you do this?"

She looked determined while nodding again. "I'll have them move furniture and carpets around for tonight's party. However, I don't think we can keep any of this a secret much longer. Everyone knows Mrs. Granger was found unconscious and that it might not have been accidental. In truth, no one on our staff is as stupidly naive as I am. None of them will be satisfied if we merely tell them all is well or fabricate some story to appease their curiosity."

Alex frowned, for he did not like to see her thinking less of herself again. "You have a compassionate heart, Tulip," he said, giving her cheek a light caress. "This is in no way stupid. In fact, your compassion is a strength in you. That you are always ready to believe in the good in others does not diminish *you* in any way."

She sighed. "Well, Ernfield certainly had me fooled. It is impossible to find any good in him now."

"He had everyone fooled for decades," Alex replied. "You weren't the only one taken in by him. We all were."

"Will you be looking for anything specific when you search his chamber?"

"Evidence of poison, for one," he said with a nod. "Also, any keepsake that can be attributed to Elspeth."

"Oh, I hadn't thought of that. Would he dare hold onto anything of hers? Such as what?"

"I don't know, a locket or ring or even a hair clip she was wearing that night. Something that can be identified as hers. If a powerful, jealous rage compelled him to push her out of the tower window, then I think he would have been just as compelled to retain some token of hers."

"Jealous? You think he was in love with Elspeth?"

"Yes, so it is not inconceivable that he would hold onto her in some way."

"Ugh! How sick is that? Holding onto a keepsake belonging to the woman he loved, after he'd killed her because of that love. I wonder if they had been courting and she ended it because your grandfather began to woo her."

"Maybe. Your uncle, aunt, and Mr. Carver might be able to shed light on this. In his warped eyes, he might have imagined a courtship between them, and then considered her romantic involvement with my grandfather a vicious betrayal."

"I see."

He gave her cheek another caress because he could see that she was shaken. "I'll also be looking for those building plans to Thornwycke Hall because they did not simply walk off on their own. Carver saw them in my study just last month. If there are any secret passageways or hiding holes, I mean to find them."

This had been a priority for him from the moment they had

arrived at Thornwycke and one of several frustrations he had encountered.

He no longer doubted that Ernfield had taken those plans.

"All right. I'll be in the parlor or the dining room behaving like a flighty fribble and making our staff move furniture around."

He kissed her lightly on the lips. "I won't be long. Just make sure you stay in sight of everyone."

"I will, Alex. Don't *you* tarry too long because Ernfield might return soon."

They went their separate ways, but this left Alex unsettled because after this morning's events, he did not want to leave Tulip's side for even a moment.

A prickle ran up his spine when he walked into Ernfield's quarters.

He could feel the evil around him.

But he quickly composed himself and reverted to his experienced investigator manner while scanning the small room with an impartial eye.

Much like Mrs. Granger, Ernfield kept his quarters tidy and sparse. But there was no mistaking the aura of malevolence in here. "Yes, you are the very devil. Aren't you, Ernfield?"

Alex wasted no time in rummaging through the head butler's bureau drawers, then under the bed, and under the mattress. He felt along the mattress to listen for crinkling sounds or feel something hard buried within the straw.

Nothing.

He carefully trod across the wood floor boards, hoping to hear a tell-tale squeak that would reveal a cavity in them.

It took him a while, but then he heard it and grunted in triumph.

"Got you," he muttered, bending on one knee to carefully pry two boards apart with the tip of his knife. His heart began to pump furiously when he found a veritable treasure trove of evidence. The building plans to Thornwycke sat right atop. He dug his hand deeper into the small cavity and retrieved several vials of an unidentified substance.

At the very bottom, tucked in a small, velvet pouch, he found a gold locket in the shape of a heart. In the center of the heart was a diamond that appeared to be of the finest quality, although he was no expert.

However, even an amateur could tell the diamond was not something any working man could afford.

Was it a gift to Elspeth from his grandfather?

He removed the contents, finding a cufflink, two tie pins, and even his lost watch fob. "I wasn't losing my mind," he muttered. "You stole the bloody fob."

He placed the floor boards back as he had found them, and gave a final inspection of the room to make certain he had left it in the same condition as it was upon his entering.

He tucked the vials, the velvet pouch, and other contents in his pocket, carefully rolled up the building plans, and hastened out of Ernfield's room.

Perhaps he ought to have gone straight to Tulip, but he wanted to lock away those items in the wall safe in his study first. He also wanted to take a quick look at the building plans, especially the specifications for the duke's bedchamber.

"I knew it," he said, muttering again.

Within his own dressing area was a secret panel, no doubt locked or barricaded from the tunnel side, which explained why the panel had not budged when he'd run his hands along the walls or tugged on any protruding nobs.

In fact, he'd heard clicks when pulling down on one of those nobs but assumed that access might have been sealed off.

He had felt air and a coolness to the wall that was an inside wall and should not have been that cold unless there was a secret passageway behind it.

The building plans now spread out before him showed a tunnel behind the secret panel in his dressing room that led out into the garden. The escape access was hidden amid a grove of trees, its makeshift door hidden behind shrubbery, no doubt.

The tunnel also extended upward to the tower room.

"Of course." In medieval times, the duke's guards would have been posted up there as lookouts. The tunnel passage served as a means of escape for the duke and his soldiers back then. They could lock the tower door and gain more time escaping while the enemy pondered who was up there and what was aimed at them while they broke down the door.

In current day, that passage allowed any present duke to 'visit' whoever happened to be in that room, and remain unseen.

Alex growled softly. "I know what you did, you bloody bounder."

It would have been simple enough for Ernfield to lure Elspeth up there with a note supposedly sent from his grandfather instructing her to meet him there. Then Ernfield could have slipped in through the tunnel, struck her over the head, and tossed her out the window with no one the wiser because he would have locked the tower room door from the inside to make it appear no one but Elspeth had been in the room.

Any ruptures to her skull would have been blamed on the fall, leading everyone to conclude she was alone and had jumped of her own volition.

Alex took another moment to make note of entrance points and run his finger along the hidden tunnel and its maze-like turns to map it all out in his head. He then rolled up the plans and placed them in the safe along with the vials, pouch containing the locket, and the other trinkets including his fob.

He then strode out of his study and went to find Tulip.

To his dismay, she was not in the dining room where several footmen were busy setting the table for tonight's party. The crystal glasses and polished silverware gleamed brightly as sunlight struck the place settings.

Alex gave a nod of approval and headed for the parlor.

Tulips was not there.

His heart began to pound, for where else would she have gone? She must have been in the parlor until a few minutes ago because the furniture and carpets had been completely reconfigured and the room actually looked quite nice.

"Where is Her Grace?" he asked several footmen who had thick rags in their hands. They were on their knees on the parlor floor, busy soaking up what appeared to be ink stains.

"You just missed her, Your Grace. She ran upstairs to change out of her gown," one of them replied. "The ink spilled as we moved this writing desk and it made a mess of her gown and the flooring. But I think we got to the spill before the ink stains bled into the wood boards or the carpets."

Alex groaned lightly, blaming himself for creating this chaos.

Their dinner party was to start in about six hours, and he should have come up with a better idea than having Tulip move furniture about. "Do get on with your work. Let me not delay you."

He hastened out of the parlor and took the stairs two at a time in his eagerness to reach Tulip and tell her what he'd found.

"Tulip," he called, knocking on the door of her duchess quarters because he expected to find her in there changing out of her gown.

She would need assistance lacing the new gown, would she not?

He knocked again to give her warning he was coming in, and then turned the handle.

Locked.

"Tulip, it's me! Let me in, sweetheart."

When he heard nothing in response, he went to his chamber and hurried straight to the inner door connecting the two bedrooms. He breathed a sigh of relief upon finding it was open, for Tulip had insisted on no key and no lock between them.

But his relief was short-lived.

Tulip was not in either chamber, and there appeared to have been a struggle taken place in hers. Chairs were overturned and a vase and candlestick lay on the floor, the vase shattered.

His heart surged into his throat. "Tulip!"

He raced to his dressing area and tried the secret panel that surprisingly opened up for him this time.

Ernfield must not have been able to lock it while Tulip was no doubt kicking and punching him, and trying with all her might to fight him off.

Had he taken her up to the tower room?

He tore up the stairs and burst into that chamber through its connecting secret panel, but no one was up there.

Thank The Graces.

He thought for certain Ernfield meant to toss her out the window just as he had done with Elspeth almost two decades ago. But the window would have been open had he done that, for he could not have shut it after pushing her out or else everyone would have known it was murder and not a desolate wife leaping to her death.

A dead person cannot close the window after they've jumped.

His stomach was in a tight knot as he grabbed a candle, lit it, and then made his way down the tunnel as fast as he dared.

Where was Ernfield taking her?

The tunnel led out into the grove of trees just as indicated on the building plans. That access had also been left open, which meant Tulip was still conscious and fighting Ernfield as he'd dragged her out. The earth was dug up around the access portal which was more evidence of a struggle, but his heart tore to pieces when he noticed a thick branch with fresh blood on it.

Ernfield must have managed to knock out Tulip as soon as they had emerged from the tunnel.

Was Ernfield mad enough to take her into the salt marshes and drown her as he had just attempted to do with Mrs. Granger?

The high tide was still rolling in…or perhaps it was starting to roll out by now. He did not know and did not care.

All that mattered was finding Tulip alive.

"Oh, no. Lord, save her." He ran from the garden up to the terrace for a better view of the distant marshes. He was desperately looking for any sign of movement when a breathless Carver rushed to his side.

"Your Grace! The magistrate and his constables are here. So is the doctor, but I'm the one who told him about Mrs. Granger. Ernfield never went into town."

"Because he's here and he now has Tulip," Alex said, his heart pounding through his ears as he pointed toward the water.

The constables now joined them and all of them had eyes on the salt marshes.

"This isn't working," Alex muttered, now almost in a panic, for every second was precious and he feared they would run out of time to save Tulip. "Mr. Carver gather the workers and have them bring the boats and their rescue equipment. We're going to spread out and search every inch of those marshes. I'm certain Ernfield has taken her there."

"Blessed saints!" Carver appeared genuinely alarmed.

"Spread the word to the staff to be on the lookout for him," Alex said, continuing to bark orders in all haste. "Have the grooms search the stables and stop him from leaving. Tell them to grab him and bind him tightly, if they see him. Same for the household staff. They are to use extreme caution around him, and the house must be searched from top to bottom. Have them work in pairs for their own safety. Rescuing my wife is the priority. If they find her, they are to get her safely away, even if it means letting Ernfield escape."

"We'll track him down if he does give your staff the slip," one of the constables assured him.

Alex nodded, but he wasn't really assured because Ernfield was a madman and dangerous. "He must have taken her into the marshes. It is the only place that makes sense. But I still want every inch of Thornwycke searched."

"There!" One of the constables suddenly cried out. "I see something moving in the reeds!"

Alex tore down the terrace steps, through the garden and into the marshes in the direction the constable had pointed. The constables and others now followed him, but he wasn't looking back to know who else was with him.

Tulip was his only concern.

He spotted Ernfield dragging something toward the water that was ebbing and flowing all around him.

Tulip.

Was she still alive?

She did not appear to be struggling as Ernfield pulled her deeper into the water, but this probably meant she was unconscious.

Alex refused to believe she was dead.

She couldn't be.

Love would never be so cruel.

He withdrew his pistol, ready to take a killing shot to stop Ernfield from dragging her any further out, when the echo of a hunting rifle resounded behind him. "What the…?"

Ernfield staggered backward and blood began to spurt from his chest.

Alex ran toward Ernfield, not caring who had taken the shot or that his deranged head butler had now tumbled into the water. His only concern was to get to Tulip before she drowned, for she was face down in the water and not moving as the tidal waves crashed over her.

Was she alive?

She has to be.

He could not lose her.

Why hadn't he told her that he loved her?

The water was up to his knees as the next wave rolled in, but all he could think of was getting to Tulip and hoisting her out of these shallow waters before the tide dragged her further out where the water would be above her head.

A wave crashed over her, but he managed to grab her just as its ebbing force was about to pull her out to the sea. "Tulip!"

She remained unresponsive and he feared he was too late.

Tears stung his eyes as he lifted her into his arms. "Tulip, please. Breathe, my love."

She hadn't taken a single breath and her lips were beginning to turn purple.

No, he would not accept this.

True love had to win out.

He ran with her onto dry ground.

"Breathe, love," he repeated time and again. "Please…breathe."

He set her down as soon as they were safely on higher ground, and began to compress her ribs in the hope of forcing the water out of her lungs.

He refused to believe he was too late. "No, no, no."

But she still wasn't breathing.

Tears clouded his eyes. "Tulip, please. Live for me, my love. Don't leave me."

Someone knelt by his side.

It was the doctor.

"Let me take over, Your Grace. I–"

Tulip coughed up water just then and began to take big gulps of air into her lungs. Her throat and lungs were obviously sore, for she was breathing and coughing at the same time, as well as coughing up water and mucus and who knows what else.

The doctor smiled at him. "She's alive. She'll live. Look, her color's good. She must have been conscious enough to hold her breath as the waves washed over her."

Alex's heart was still pounding through his ears as he lifted her into his arms once again to carry her back to their bedchamber.

As he looked around, he saw the two constables dragging Ernfield's lifeless body out of the marsh waters.

Who had shot him?

He turned back toward the house where his estate manager was standing. Beside him was William Hester with a rifle in his hand and a look on his face that warned he was completely unapologetic. "I protect my family. No one harms my niece and lives to boast of it."

"Uncle William," Tulip croaked, her eyes now open as she smiled at him.

"Tulip, my sweetheart." Her uncle now burst into tears. "I knew something had to be terribly wrong when I heard Ernfield had never come for the doctor. He was always an odd fellow, but we never suspected he was capable of such lunacy. Puts everything we thought about the deaths of the dukes into doubt, doesn't it?"

"More than those deaths," Carver intoned. "But that's for His Grace to discuss with the magistrate."

William appeared confused. "More? What else has he done?"

"I think the magistrate must reopen all the deaths that occurred here at Thornwycke while Ernfield was in service," Carver replied, perhaps not yet aware that his own daughter's demise was suspicious, too. As well as the death of Edward, the poor lad who had delivered food to Martha daily from Thornwycke.

Well, it would all come out now.

Alex felt sorry for Carver, for he was about to learn that Martha's death had not been due to a natural illness.

Or did such a thing matter?

His daughter was gone and that would not change.

And what of William? Had he been in love with Elspeth as rumored? Or had that been a lie spread by Ernfield?

Tulip was cold and began to tremble in his arms. "Let me get you upstairs, love. We'll have you warm and comfortable soon. Blessed saints. Thank goodness you're alive."

"I fought him as hard as I could," she said, resting her head on his shoulder. Her voice had a pronounced croak to it, but Alex did not think he had ever heard anything sweeter. "I wasn't strong enough. I kicked him and punched him with all my might. I tried to scream but he had his hand over my mouth and held it there while dragging me through a tunnel. I–"

"Hush, love," he said while carrying her to the house. "I know about the tunnel. I found the building plans in his chamber. Let's get you out of those wet clothes, and then the doctor will have a look at you. He'll take care of you first, then we'll talk to the magistrate."

"We are at your service, Your Grace," the magistrate assured him, "however long it takes."

"Thank you, Lord Farnhum."

The magistrate and his constables, William, Carver, and the doctor all followed him to the house, the constables carrying Ernfield's body from the marshes.

Carver's workers also followed Alex, but he ordered them into the kitchen. "Have a cup of tea while we wait for the magistrate to finish with Ernfield. I think he will want to question all of us."

"Aye, Your Grace," said Dougal, who seemed to be the natural leader among these workers and often served as Carver's second in command.

The household servants clustered around Alex as soon as he strode in through the parlor, for he'd taken the terrace steps that led directly into that room, which was the shortest route to his bedchamber.

Between ink stains and now wet, muddy boot stains, the floors would need another thorough cleaning, but this was the least of his worries just now.

Tulip's breathing was still raspy, but each inhale and exhale seemed to be getting stronger and more even. What worried Alex most was the blow she had taken to her head, but the doctor would examine it and let him know if she required stitches.

He turned to the maids and footmen who were now gaping at him. "Have a bath sent up for my wife." He motioned to two of the maids. "Follow me. Her Grace needs to get out of these wet clothes."

"Oh, and I've spilled ink all over my gown," Tulip said, sounding more distressed about the garment than almost dying at the hands of a fiend. Perhaps it was easier for her to think of this than dwell on the danger she had just experienced. "Alex, I don't think this lovely muslin can be saved."

"I'll buy you a dozen just like it, sweetheart," he said, his voice tight and his heart still pounding from his own fear that he had almost lost her. "All that matters is you are safe and alive."

He would have the doctor look her over straight away to make certain the head wound was not serious. There was always the danger of a brain swell when dealing with such an injury. One might be alert and seemingly on the mend one moment, and then something in the brain ruptures and…no, not to Tulip.

He refused to entertain such a thought.

However, the doctor was also concerned with the severity of her wound and insisted on a quick, cursory examination while they were still in the parlor. "Just a precaution, Your Grace. The magistrate will require my services, too. But your wife is the priority. Let me have a look at her scalp before the maids get her out of her wet clothes and settle her comfortably in bed."

"Of course." He sank onto the settee, and insisted on keeping Tulip on his lap while the doctor looked into her eyes and began to ask her questions.

It came as a great relief to Alex when the doctor declared she would recover. "Take her upstairs and make her comfortable, Your Grace. Once she has washed up and changed into dry clothing, I'll place a few stitches to close up the wound. In truth, stitches might not even prove necessary. But we'll see. I am pleased to report that your wife is in greater danger of catching a chill than of dying from that blow on the head."

"Are you certain?" Alex dared not allow himself to feel any exhilaration yet.

"Yes," the doctor said with a smile. "My decision would have been different had her eyes not appeared focused or had her speech been slurred, which it wasn't in the least. You have leave to carry her up to her bedchamber and have the maids attend her."

Alex now let out a breath of relief and kissed Tulip's cheek. "Do you hear that, love? Thank you, Dr. Harding."

"Alex, what time is it?" Tulip asked as he carried her up the stairs with two of the maids scampering behind him.

"Coming on three o'clock, I think."

"Oh, we must get ready for our dinner party."

He laughed. "Are you serious? You are in no condition to entertain anyone. I'll have Carver send one of the grooms to advise all our guests. We'll reschedule for next week or the week after, all right?"

She sighed. "What about all the food Mrs. Crabbe has prepared?"

"I think the staff deserves a feast, don't you? We'll dine quietly in our bedchamber, and your meal will be nothing heavier than a beef broth for the next few days."

"I was so looking forward to the dishes Mrs. Crabbe prepared."

"She'll do it all over again soon, love."

Tulip once again rested her head against his shoulder as he now strode down the hall toward the duchess bedchamber. "I love you, Alex," she whispered. "I knew you would save me."

He shuddered to think how close a call it was. "Always, sweetheart. Always and forever."

He ought to have added that he loved her, but there was too much commotion swirling around them. Tulip was going to make a big thing of it when he told her, and he did not want others listening in.

He would tell her tonight when taking her in his arms because he meant to keep her securely wrapped in his embrace while she slept.

In truth, even handing her over to the maids felt like agony to him.

The maids blushed and giggled with embarrassment when he insisted on remaining in the duchess chamber to watch as Tulip was undressed and bathed.

He did not care if they thought it was improper.

He was worried that she might take a sudden turn for the worse and the maids would not understand what was happening.

For her part, Tulip must have felt the same concern.

She appeared relieved when he remained beside her, and she was not at all bashful that he watched her while she was in the tub. He would have taken over the chore of washing her, but that would have been too scandalous for these maids.

He went into his own bedchamber to quickly change into dry trousers and boots while they put Tulip in her nightgown and robe.

He returned in time to carry Tulip to his bed. "She needs watching tonight. She'll stay with me."

The maids grinned and giggled.

Tulip wrapped her arms around his neck and kissed him on the cheek.

The maids grinned and giggled some more.

"Leave us now," Alex ordered once Tulip was settled in his bed. "Send Dr. Harding up here once the magistrate has no more need of him."

He turned to Tulip when they were alone again. "You might need a few stitches, love. I'll be right here by your side. When that's done, I'll order a light broth to warm your insides. That is, if the doctor says it is all right for you to have anything just yet."

She nodded. "You are with me, that's all I need."

He took her hands in his, but his heart lurched as he felt the welts and scratches on her palms. "You almost died because of me."

"You? I do believe Ernfield was completely to blame."

Alex took a deep breath. "I should have anticipated the threat. All those deaths…"

"They were ruled accidental by some very intelligent and experienced people."

He shook his head. "I should have investigated on my own and left you in London while I found out for myself. I should not have married you until I was confident there was no danger to you. But I wanted you so badly, and I could not bear the thought of anyone else marrying you."

She laughed. "There was hardly any risk of that. I was never going to marry Caruthers, even if it meant my ruination."

"I'm sure there would have been other suitors, genuine men of good reputation. You are a gem, Tulip."

"Well, I don't know about that. But I married you and had no intention of allowing you to leave me behind."

"I should have, though. Even if you objected. But I could not bear to be apart from you once we were husband and wife. Tulip, it is long past time I told you." He raised her hands to his lips and kissed them. "I love you."

Her eyes widened and she cast him a breathtaking smile, then she hugged him fiercely. "I hoped you would come around in time."

He laughed in relief, for she seemed to be regaining her strength. "I did not need any time at all."

"Alex," she said, easing back to look at him, "I think I was already in love with you by the time you kissed me in Lady Fullerton's garden."

He arched an eyebrow. "And you think you were the first to fall in love because of this? Let me assure you, I fell in love with you the moment I set eyes on you when you bumped into me on Chipping Way."

Her eyes brightened and she laughed, obviously believing he was in jest. "Are you suggesting it was love at first sight for you?"

He nodded. "Then I spent the next few months trying to convince myself that I was wrong. But every time I saw you, I fell deeper in love. I'm sorry I did not tell you sooner. I have always loved you and always will."

She smiled at him. "No wonder I always felt safe with you. I must have sensed your affection for me, although do not give me credit for being that clever. I was so relieved when you came to my rescue that night when Lord Caruthers made such a scene."

He kissed her on her pert nose. "Once we return to London, I think I shall send Caruthers a present to thank him for bringing us together."

Tulip laughed. "Don't you dare. We do not need him coming back into our lives, especially since he will not be grateful to you. He will believe you are rubbing his nose in his loss."

Alex shrugged. "Perhaps there is a bit of that. Well, a lot of that."

"Alex! You are not mean-spirited."

"Yes, love. I can be when someone gets me angry enough, as Caruthers did that night. You're the nice one, not me. I'm only nice to you." He sighed and kissed her again. "But I shall behave myself and simply ignore the oaf when we are back in London. All right?"

She gave a slight nod. "That's better."

They said no more as the doctor arrived and set to work examining Tulip's scalp.

She winced as he gave the gash a thorough cleansing.

"Fortunately, you do not require stitches. But it was a nasty blow to the head and I've put some ointment on the wound to keep it from getting infected. Clean it with a clean cloth and some strong spirits twice a day for the next three days, brandy or whiskey ought to do the trick. Ah, I see you have a bottle of brandy right there on your fireplace mantel."

"No, not that one," Alex said, wanting to spill out its contents and smash the bottle. He did not care whether it contained poison or not, for Ernfield was dead and it no longer mattered.

But his instincts told him it was poisoned, so he would send it off to be analyzed in due course.

Might as well tie up all the loose ends.

"Well, any bottle of spirits will do to cleanse the wound," the doctor said. "Then you are to apply the ointment to that nasty gash."

"I'll attend to it," Alex assured with a nod.

"Good, good. Do this in the morning when Her Grace wakes up and each night before she retires to bed. The treatment will sting, unfortunately."

"I shall endure," Tulip said.

"You are to get plenty of bed rest," the doctor continued. "No lifting anything heavy. By the way, the same applies to Mrs. Granger. The both of you are to take it easy for the next few weeks or you'll just make yourselves worse."

After the doctor left, the magistrate requested to see Tulip.

"Blast, our bedchamber is busier than a London coaching inn," Alex muttered as the doctor traipsed out and the maids continually scampered in and out.

Tulip set aside her covers. "Let's talk to the magistrate downstairs. Carry me down to your study or the parlor. There is more to clear up about all these deaths, and lots of questions to be asked of all of us. I don't want to miss any of it."

"All right, love. But not for too long. The doctor wants you to rest."

"And I will after we have our answers. I'll be too restless, otherwise." She held out her arms to him.

He grunted and then picked her up. "Fine, but do not think you will always have your way merely by batting your big, blue eyes at me and melting my heart."

She laughed. "I love you, too. And I promise not to abuse your adoration of me."

He kissed her softly on the lips and then carried her downstairs.

The magistrate was in the parlor along with Carver and Tulip's uncle.

Alex settled Tulip on the settee and tucked cushions at her back to make her more comfortable. "I'll be right back."

He went into his study to take the items he'd found in Ernfield's room out of his safe.

"I have some things to show you," he told the men upon returning, and then realized Tulip had not known about his findings either. "Sweetheart, these will be of interest to you, too."

He held out the building plans, the vials, the velvet pouch, the two tie pins, and–

"Your fob!" Tulip cried out. "Where was it?"

"What are these things?" the magistrate asked.

"The building plans!" Carver exclaimed. "Wherever did you find *them*? I gave myself headaches trying to figure out where I had last placed them."

"Let's call these items Ernfield's loot...or perhaps better described as his sick mementos. He took a little something from his victims. That my watch fob was among these items probably meant I was to be his next victim, and he was actively in the planning stage of my demise." Alex then took the magistrate and Carver to Ernfield's chamber to show them the cavity in the floorboards. "These were all hidden in here."

"The foul fiend," Carver muttered.

They returned to the parlor where William had remained with Tulip, and Alex then explained to all what he had figured out so far. "First, let me state that Mrs. Granger and my wife's testimony against Ernfield would have been enough to have him hanged had he survived. But there's more. The locket contained in the velvet pouch connects him to Elspeth's death. The same for these building plans, for he must have known of them and studied them from as far back as her death. However, I don't think my grandfather was aware Ernfield had found those plans or knew anything of the secret passages, especially the one leading up to the tower room."

"What is the significance?" William asked.

"Ernfield knew how to get into the tower room without being seen. He lured Elspeth up there, probably with a forged note or perhaps even a verbal instruction. He then struck her over the head to knock her unconscious, and then pushed her out the window. He took care to lock the tower room door from the inside so that anyone investigating would think she must have been alone in there when she jumped."

"The foul fiend," William muttered.

Alex nodded. "After sending her to her death, he left through the secret passage."

"But no one ever found her body," Tulip remarked. "So there were never any questions raised about Elspeth dying here."

Alex nodded. "My grandfather sincerely believed she had jumped to her death and committed the sin of suicide. He must have been the one to find her, and Ernfield was lurking close by, prepared to poison my grandfather's mind with lies. He had only to look up to see the open tower window. When he later checked the tower door, he must have found it locked from the inside."

"Just as Ernfield had set it up," Tulip said in obvious dismay.

"I don't know what words were exchanged between them that night," Alex continued. "But my grandfather thought he was protecting Elspeth's memory by having Ernfield hide the body."

"Which worked out well for Ernfield since there would now be no investigation," the magistrate noted.

Alex nodded. "Exactly, but his plan would have worked no matter who found the body. The only difference being that her death would have been reported, and then determined to be a suicide."

"So, your grandfather played right into Ernfield's hands," William said. "The fiend did not even have to worry about an inquest. He got away with the murder of that sweet, lovely girl. Oh, what a vile, sick man. Elspeth was a good soul who never harmed anybody."

Alex cleared his throat. "Did *you* love her, William?"

"We all liked her, but...oh, dear heaven! That's why those stupid love rumors about me and Elspeth suddenly arose. There was so much gossip floating around. She'd run off with a navy captain. She'd run off with a married man. And then suddenly my name was mentioned. Ernfield must have been slyly telling everyone I was having an affair with her. Gad, I almost lost Perty because of his lies. Thank goodness Perty believed me."

"The disgusting wretch," Carver muttered. "He did not care who he destroyed."

Alex now turned to his estate manager with pain in his eyes. "I think Martha was also one of his victims. I'm so sorry, Mr. Carver."

He then went on to explain about Martha likely seeing Ernfield emerging from the tunnel's secret exit in the grove of trees. "Or perhaps she had seen him hiding one of his vials of poison somewhere in the house. Or seen him retrieve it. Whatever it was, she had no idea of the significance at the time, and he could not risk her figuring it out."

"So you think he used one of those vials to slowly poison her?" Carver's every word was filled with anguish and he broke down in tears. "Why did I not see this? I could have saved her."

"Everyone was fooled," Alex said, although it had to be little consolation for the grieving father. "And it was no coincidence that young Edward Wilcox died shortly afterward."

Even the magistrate's eyes began to tear up. "The innocent lad, too? All these years, we had a monster in our midst and did not know it. So many good people are now dead because of him."

Alex did not know how good his predecessor dukes were, but they certainly did not deserve to be murdered.

There was no doubt in his mind Ernfield had killed them all, and those little mementos found hidden in Ernfield's floorboards was the proof to link him to those intentional deaths.

Not that it mattered now.

The villain was dead and the danger had passed.

Carver's hands were trembling, so Alex ordered him to sit down. "I'll have one of the footmen bring in some tea for you."

"Not necessary, Your Grace. With your permission, I would like to visit my daughter's grave. I want her to know the truth and finally be at peace."

"We'll hold a memorial service for all of them who died at his hand," the magistrate said. "Do you have any idea where he might have buried Elspeth?"

Alex shook his head. "It is possible he let her body float out with the tide."

"No," Tulip said with a gasp, her eyes wide as she stared at him. "Your grandfather would not have allowed it. I think I know where she is buried."

All eyes now turned toward Tulip.

She took a deep breath. "I always thought it odd that there was no bench placed beside the willow tree when it was such a logical place for one to be. There is good shade, and it is near those splendid, fragrant roses. It is also a perfect spot to sit and read. Why do you think your grandfather never allowed anyone to place a bench there? Nor was one ever put there after he died. If we question the gardeners, I expect we'll learn that Ernfield insisted on continuing to uphold your grandfather's wishes."

"No bench," Alex muttered. "Dear heaven, of course. That is a brilliant deduction, Tulip."

The others nodded in agreement.

Alex now turned to his estate manager. "Mr. Carver, you and I will look into the matter tomorrow morning. Nothing more is to be done today. There's been enough upheaval to last us a lifetime. I also think we ought to take Mrs. Granger's wishes into consideration. She may have strong feelings about what is to be done for Elspeth."

"Oh, you are right," Tulip said, looking up at him in dismay. "She'll need to be told."

Alex raked a hand through his hair. "Yes, but it is such a difficult talk to have with her just now. Perhaps we ought to wait until tomorrow."

Tulip nodded. "I expect she will want her aunt to be properly buried with her family."

Or next to his own grandfather, Alex thought.

But he needed to consider this further before proposing any such thing.

Elspeth and his grandfather weren't married, although he was now fairly certain the old man had sincerely loved her and intended to make her his wife.

The magistrate took each of their statements, and then did the same with Mrs. Granger who had been more seriously injured than Tulip and was not strong enough to get out of bed.

It was almost eight o'clock in the evening by the time all the questioning and official duties were completed.

"Do you wish for the constables to remain on guard at Thornwycke this evening, Your Grace?" the magistrate asked Alex.

"No, Lord Farnhum. We'll be fine now." He wasn't merely

saying it to be polite, but *felt* that aura of malevolence lifting from his home. It was like the sun bursting through a thick, gray mist and spreading light all around them.

He never imagined being happy here, but perhaps he could shed the ghosts of the past now.

In truth, he would be happy anywhere, so long as Tulip was by his side.

They could make a fresh start here.

Perhaps even turn Thornwycke Hall and the Davenport farms into a proud legacy for their offspring.

William, the doctor, and the magistrate and his constables agreed to return tomorrow to discover what lay beneath the willow tree.

Carver decided to remain here overnight, for he had a spare room in the servants quarters that he often used whenever he was too tired to return home or when foul weather made travel too difficult.

"Your Grace," Carver said once the others had gone, "may I look in on Mrs. Granger?"

Alex frowned, for the woman really needed to rest after her ordeal. "Is there a reason you wish to speak to her?"

He nodded. "We both lost someone dear to us at the hands of that fiend. She might find comfort in talking to me. I truly believe I might understand her feelings better than anyone else could."

Alex glanced at Tulip, seeking her guidance because she had good instincts about such matters that had more to do with heart than logic.

She nodded.

"Very well, Mr. Carver. But do not stay too long. She was hurt and needs time to heal."

"Understood, Your Grace." He gave a nod and walked off toward the servants quarters.

Tulip smiled at Alex.

He sank onto the settee beside her. "What, love?"

"Do you not see it? I think Mr. Carver is in love with Mrs. Granger. I think those two will be married before the year is out."

Alex laughed as he gently lifted her onto his lap. "Truly? Do you think she will accept him?"

"Yes, it is quite possible that she has loved him all along. However, she must have been quite confused and wary of him because of the lies Ernfield had been feeding her. For this reason, she kept her distance, much as I did when you first came into my life. But she now knows he can be trusted. There is no longer a reason to hold back her affection."

Alex laughed again. "Seriously? But he must be a good fifteen or twenty years older than her."

"And your point? The same could be said of your grandfather and Elspeth, but that did not stop them from loving each other. Mrs. Granger is a young woman who has lost her family and obviously came here out of a need to understand what happened and possibly gain answers that might lay their souls to rest. In coming here, she felt alone and scared. Mr. Carver has been steady as a rock for her, quietly looking out for her. He is a good man who will continue to care for her and protect her."

"I will admit, I think he likes her. But how do you know her feelings?"

"The little details. Her eyes light up whenever he is near. She blushes and pats her hair whenever he approaches to speak to her."

"Ah, of course."

"You are mocking me, Alex. But I know I am right. I'm just sorry Ernfield's evil whispers kept them apart for so long. That fiend must have been worried they would start talking to each other beyond casual conversations and start putting things together."

"So he dropped poisonous hints to keep them apart. Yes, it is quite likely." He kissed her on the cheek. "Not mocking you, my love. I am chiding myself, for I was the London magistrate's top investigator. But it seems I am good with facts and not nearly as good as you when it comes to matters of the heart. I think we would have been an unbeatable team had we worked together in London."

She wrapped her arms around his neck and rested her head against his shoulder. "Perhaps this is why you were attracted to me."

"For your investigative instincts? No, love. I can assure you, my response to you was completely primal, a wolf spotting his mate. I wanted to ravish and devour you, claim you at first sight. *Mine. Mine to love and protect.* No one else was ever going to get their hands on you."

"Dear heaven, I never would have guessed." But she sighed contentedly in his arms. "I'm glad the worst is over. It is over, isn't it?"

"Yes, love."

"Are you going to read your grandfather's journal again?"

He nodded. "This time with an impartial eye, for I think anger clouded my judgment, even though I tried hard not to let it. I might have missed some obvious clues because I was filled with so much resentment for the old man. In truth, for all the Davenports. My anger is gone now. They did not deserve what Ernfield did to them."

"So, they might not have been as debauched as reputed?"

"Oh, that part was true. They were a hedonistic lot. I will not be placing any of them on a pedestal any time soon. Same goes for the three wastrels we left back in London, Harold Havers and his brothers, Neddy and Barton. I have no intention of ever inviting them here or entertaining them in London. The less we see of my family, the better."

He carried her upstairs and was just at the door to the duke's chamber when Tulip tapped him on the shoulder. "What is it, love?"

"Do you not find it odd that we haven't seen hide nor hair of the ladies who made free with the Davenport generosity?"

"Not odd at all."

"But it is odd," she insisted.

"No, love. I told you that I wrote to Carver as soon as I inherited the title and advised him I wanted them removed. I was serious about it and the tone of my letter conveyed it. I could say that I was thinking of you at the time, but you weren't even deigning to speak to me yet."

"Then why, Alex? They would have fawned over you. You could have taken any liberties and they would have adored you."

"Those *liberties* destroyed my family. My uncles and cousins were gamblers, drunks, and debauchers. My father was probably the same when it came to gambling and drinking. The only difference is that he might have loved my mother and stayed true to her. But he was too weak to challenge my grandfather. So, what good did it do them? They lived in misery, all because my father would not stand up for his love."

She kissed him. "I'm sorry I brought it up."

"It's all right." He entered the bedchamber and settled her on their bed. "Best we speak our minds, get it all out in the open, and then never bring it up again."

She regarded him earnestly. "I never will, Alex. I see how much these memories hurt you."

"But I'll heal because you are with me. Don't fret, Tulip. I am content and I know my life with you will be a happy one."

She smiled. "That is remarkably optimistic of you."

He nodded. "I have everything I ever wished for and more. And just to be clear, I did not wish to inherit the title. What I wished for was *you*. One night with Tulip, is what I wanted, and then you let me kiss you in Lady Fullerton's garden. In that moment, I knew my wish would come true."

She arched an eyebrow. "That's all you wanted? One night?"

He chuckled. "At the time, I could not even get you to talk to me. So, yes. I thought one night might be enough to have you notice me."

"I *married* you. That's a bit more than a little notice, I would say."

"Yes, but your marrying me was no assurance we would ever live under the same roof. It all happened so fast, I wasn't certain you would go through with the marriage. Or if you did, that you would want anything to do with me afterward. So, I was still making wishes about you. *Grant me one night with Tulip. Then grant me another night with Tulip. Then another. Then a lifetime.*"

"Seems all your wishes have been answered. You are well and truly stuck with me."

He chuckled. "It may be equally said that *you* are truly stuck with *me*."

"Or blessed to have you," she said with heartfelt sincerity. "You weren't the only one making wishes. After that night in Lady Fullerton's garden, I hoped for the same. *One night with Alex. Then another. Then a lifetime.*"

"You'll have it, Tulip." He kissed her gently. "Rest now, love."

He stretched out beside her and took her into his arms, holding her in his embrace until she fell asleep.

He could have slipped out of bed once she was lost in slumber, for the hour was still early. But he was exactly where he wished to be, and that was holding Tulip in his arms.

The night fell softly.

The sky turned dark and a full moon shone with silvery brightness.

Stars twinkled overhead.

Tulip's body was warm and curled against his.

He'd almost lost her today.

But by the grace of heaven, she was safe in his arms.

Yes, this was the best night ever.

And the next ten thousand nights would be even better.

EPILOGUE

Thornwycke Hall
Somerset, England
December, 1827

A LIGHT SNOW fell and the air had a wintery nip to it as Tulip eagerly awaited their guests for the yuletide feast she and Alex were hosting for their friends, neighbors, her Hester family and several members of the Farthingale family who had made the trip to Thornwycke Hall to celebrate with them.

Alex had insisted they splurge on the finest beeswax candles, a full orchestra, French champagne, Viennese desserts, and a six course meal fashioned by the incomparable Mrs. Crabbe.

It was an extravagance, but one Alex insisted they could afford.

They probably couldn't, but Tulip was not going to question him about it because Alex *needed* this celebration. It was his way of moving on from a past filled with sorrows and regrets. This night would create new memories he could ponder with joy in later years. It was also his way of restoring pride to the Davenport title.

As for her, Tulip had never felt happier because she was surrounded by loved ones. Rupert, Marigold and Leo, and Dillie and Ian were here with them to represent the Farthingale clan.

Thornwycke Hall had been decorated with boughs of holly, sprigs of ivy, and strategically placed mistletoe along the halls and over the doorways. Alex had assisted her in putting up the mistletoe and testing each out by kissing her with glorious heat under each one, much to the delight of their staff who thought it quite refreshing to have a Davenport duke who loved his wife and was faithful to her.

Tulip lost count of how many balls of mistletoe she had put up.

All in the line of duty, of course.

She loved the devouring way Alex kissed her after each one was set in its proper place. Honestly, this man was as hot as molten lava and could set fire to the place with his scorching kisses.

They now stood together by the entrance of their grand home to receive their guests as they arrived. Alex looked divine in his formal attire, the black of his coat bringing out his gorgeous, dark eyes and irresistibly masculine physique.

Tulip had sewn herself a gown of deepest blue velvet trimmed throughout with silver threads. It was a magnificent Farthingale fabric, of course.

"You look beautiful, love," Alex whispered, lightly brushing her neck with his lips. "I'd rather devour you than feast on the repast Mrs. Crabbe has prepared."

She smiled up at him. "I love you, Alex."

Her Farthingale family stood beside her on the receiving line, and she was so proud to introduce them to her Burnham friends and family. They were greeted warmly and in return had warm welcomes for the magistrate and his wife, the doctor and his wife and daughters, her Aunt Perty and Uncle William, and scads of Hester relatives who had arrived with them. There were country squires, a neighboring viscount, several baronets, and other local gentry eager to make their acquaintance.

Tulip had also invited the local shopkeepers, bankers, the local bookshop owner, and the Davenport farmers.

All were welcome and Tulip greeted everyone with gracious enthusiasm.

However, her heart was happiest upon seeing Mr. Carver and Mrs. Granger arrive. They had recently married, just as she had predicted, so their long-suffering housekeeper was now to be known as Mrs. Carver. Both had continued in their roles at Thornwycke and the house ran smoothly because of it.

Tulip nudged her husband.

"What, love?"

"They look so happy, Alex," she whispered.

He grinned. "Yes, it is obvious. I am delighted for them."

"So am I. But I wonder…" She began to scan the crowd.

"Who are you looking for now?"

"No one in particular. However, I think there could be several matches made here tonight. Love is in the air. Don't you feel it?"

"Sure," he said with a shrug and a smile.

"It is," Tulip insisted. "Do you see the way Dougal is eyeing the doctor's daughter? Oh, but she is so shy. We ought to give them a nudge."

Alex eyed the pair and laughed as Dougal started toward the girl. "I don't think he needs a nudge. If anything, he needs a leash to restrain him. I recognize that wolf look. *Mine. She is mine to love and protect. I am claiming her.* Poor fellow, he'll be married by next yuletide."

Tulip laughed. "Oh, that is wonderful. Let's see who else we–"

"How about we set aside the matchmaking for now. Dance with me, love. I'm sure everyone is eager to have the entertainment start. I've instructed the orchestra to lead off with a waltz."

"Perfect, that is an excellent way to get Dougal and the doctor's daughter together. Not to mention other young couples who might not otherwise approach each other. I hope someone asks Miss Keane, the lovely bookshop owner, to dance. Oh, look! Uncle Rupert is walking toward her."

"Marvelous. However, I was thinking quite selfishly of myself because it has been far too long since I've held you in my arms. At least three minutes." He led her onto the dance floor and drew her into his arms. "There, much better."

They twirled once around the dance floor, and then Alex motioned for everyone to join them.

Marigold was delightful and bubbly as she drew her often serious and reserved Leo out to waltz with her.

Dillie did the same with Ian who adored his wife too much to ever deny her anything.

This.

This is what she now had with Alex, this deep commitment to their union and their growing bonds of love.

As the dance floor began to fill, Alex drew her closer.

Tulip realized he was now in full, protective wolf position. "When were you going to tell me, love?" he asked, staring at her stomach.

She looked up at him and let out a soft breath. "Oh, you guessed! I was going to surprise you with the news tonight. I think I am with child. How did you know?"

He placed his cheek against hers and slowed their pace as they danced off to the side in a small circle of their own. "Sweetheart, I know every inch of your body. Does it not follow that I would notice the slightest changes? The tenderness of your breasts. The way they seemed fuller in the cup of my hands. That was the most obvious sign. I probably realized your condition before you did."

Her eyes widened. "Why did you not say anything to me?"

He cast her a wry smile. "Because it was your secret to share. I just did not expect you to take so long about it."

"It is not even three months yet." But she knew that she ought to have told him sooner. Why hadn't she? Did he feel hurt by it? "I only began to suspect a few weeks ago. I should have mentioned it then, but I was scared."

He frowned. "Scared? Why?"

"Not scared, exactly. I've heard the first three months are the most delicate and anything can happen. I was afraid to disappoint you if I turned out to be wrong...or if something had gone wrong."

"Oh, love. You could never disappoint me. Don't you think I would want to be by your side, especially if anything went wrong? I would never want you to endure the pain or sadness on your own. Tulip, I am here to love and support you."

"I know." She smiled up at him. "Truly, Alex. I know that you will always be there for me. I'm sorry I did not confide in you sooner."

He shook his head. "No apology necessary. I could have said something to you, as well. It is a bit overwhelming, isn't it?"

She laughed. "Yes! I was raised by two very loving families, the Hesters and the Farthingales. Oh, just look at them all enjoying themselves here with us. Isn't it a dream come true? But to now be about to start our own little Davenport dynasty...it is quite daunting for me."

"Same for me, but we'll figure it out together."

She thought of his unhappy upbringing and the sorrow both his parents had endured. How could he not be worried about raising their sons and daughters when his examples were the hedonistic Davenport dukes?

"My children will have you as their mother, so I am not all that worried," Alex said when she asked him about it.

He guided her in another slow twirl.

She looked up at him with bountiful love shining in her eyes. "Truly?"

"Who better than you to give them the love they deserve? Who better to raise them with their heads on straight and their hearts filled with compassion? Most of all, who better than you to show me how to be a good parent to them?"

"You were London's top investigator. I think you are smart enough to figure out how to raise a child."

"Need I remind you? Davenport, here. Look how my predecessors turned out? Look how Harold Havers and his idiot brothers, Neddy and Barton turned out?"

"True, but look how you turned out? Completely marvelous and admirable. And do not grimace, because I am being completely objective about it."

"Says the wife who looks at me with magic in her eyes. If we are to be *completely* honest about this, since this suddenly appears to be your favorite word...it is your influence that is going to matter most to our children."

"We both will matter. In loving each other and being good to each other, we will set a proper example for our wayward offspring."

"Being good to each other," he repeated with a pensive nod. "You make it easy for me, Tulip. Nothing brings me greater joy than to make you happy."

"You do the same for me. I love you so much, Alex."

The snow had stopped, leaving only the slightest dusting of powdery white on the torch-lit terrace that was empty because of the chill to the air. Alex twirled her out there, and drew her closer so that he could wrap her in his jacket. "I won't keep you out here long, my love. It's too cold."

It wasn't all that cold.

Just a bit of a nip to the air.

He kissed her with the heat of their first kiss in Lady Fullerton's garden, the one that had started it all and led to this moment.

One night.

One kiss.

And the hope for a thousand more.

"I love you, Tulip," he whispered, his lips warm against her ear.

"I love you so much, Alex." She heard laughter and animated chatter coming from inside, and the music continued to play. Everyone seemed to be in the merry spirit of their party. But what mattered most to her were these new memories created for Alex.

Happy ones.

Tulip looked forward to a lifetime of joy and irresistible kisses from him.

THE END

Dear Reader:

Thank you for reading *One Night With Tulip*! I hope you enjoyed sweet Tulip Farthingale as she found her love match with Alexander Havers, the brilliant investigator you met working for the London magistrate in *A Slight Problem With The Wedding*. Alexander now has a partner in life as well as in crime-solving. Do you think they might be up to solving more crimes in Somerset in the future?

I now have over seventy books published and am working my way up to one hundred! But the Farthingales series will always be my sentimental favorite because it was my very first and launched my career. Have you read the other books in the Farthingale series? Start with *My Fair Lily* which was my debut book, or *The Viscount's Rose* which is the romance for the eldest of the original five Farthingale sisters and should be the first to read if going by age order. You are also welcome to enjoy them in any order you like because they are each stand-alone stories meant to give you laughs, a few tears, a spicy moment or two, and ultimately leave you with a smile on your face and a warm feeling in your heart.

If you are in need of even more Farthingales, then please try my Book Of Love series where you will meet a host of Farthingale cousins, all of them sweet and innocent young ladies who cannot seem to keep out of trouble. In fact, they attract trouble wherever they turn, especially when it involves some very steamy, alpha heroes and that mysterious, red-leather bound Book of Love. Start with *The Look of Love* and enjoy Olivia and Beast as they fall in love. You might even learn some secrets of your own to finding true love.

Do you adore heroes with a dash of silver in their hair? Then I think you will enjoy my Silver Dukes series where you will meet some gorgeous forty-ish heroes who have given up on ever finding love. The betting book at White's has them as odds on favorites never to marry. But you'll love the heroines who have the brains, beauty, and sincerity to win the hearts of these heroes. Start with *Cherish and the Duke,* and be prepared for some laughs as Cherish wins the heart of her Silver Duke, Gawain, Duke of Bromleigh.

If your heart melts for wounded heroes, then I welcome you to the Moonstone Landing series where injuries of the soul as well as physical wounds are healed in the charming, Cornwall seacoast village of Moonstone Landing. Is there magic in the moonstones? You bet! They'll shimmer in the water whenever a heroine finds true love with the right hero. Start with *The Moonstone Duke* for the first of six full length books and don't miss the two novellas in this series, *Moonstone Landing* (the tender introduction to this entire series) and *Moonstone Angel.*

For all you romantasy fans, I hope you will give my Dark Gardens series a read. You'll journey to Regency England's idyllic Lake District where bluebell gardens serve as portals into the realm of the Fae and the red mountain known as Friar's Crag is the entrance to the underworld. An ancient Fae prophecy is about to unfold pitting the Fae against powerful, underworld Dragon Lords, and the mortal heroines are caught in the middle. You'll meet dragon shifters, Fae warriors, and the gentle heroines who can save them or destroy them all with the power of love. Start with *Garden of Shadows* for this series.

What's next? The Silver Duchesses series comes next and it is about the lovely, bluestocking heroines who reside on Duchess Square in London's fashionable Mayfair. They are in their late twenties/early thirties and think of themselves as spinsters who will never find love. But they are about to meet the handsome heroes who will win their hearts. First heroine is the gentle and utterly adorable Lady Berry Thane who will meet her match in rugged, tough gaming hall owner Gideon Knight. You'll sigh and swoon as their hearts collide in *A Knight On Duchess Square* (releasing in 2026).

Interested in learning more about my stories? You can subscribe to my newsletter and also connect with me on Facebook and other social media. You can find links to all on my website:

mearaplatt.com.

Please support your favorite authors by posting a review on the site where you purchased their book. Also feel free to write one on Goodreads or other reader sites that you peruse. Even a few sentences on what you thought about the book would be most helpful and appreciated. Please also consider telling your friends about any of my books and recommending them to book clubs.

Most of all, thank you for taking the time to give my books a read!

Sign up for Meara Platt's newsletter
and you'll receive a free, exclusive copy
of her Farthingale novella,
If You Kissed Me.

Visit her website
to grab your free copy:
mearaplatt.com

ALSO BY MEARA PLATT

FARTHINGALE SERIES
My Fair Lily
The Duke I'm Going To Marry
Rules For Reforming A Rake
A Midsummer's Kiss
The Viscount's Rose
Earl of Hearts
The Viscount and the Vicar's Daughter
A Duke For Adela
Marigold and the Marquess
The Make-Believe Marriage
A Slight Problem With The Wedding
One Night With Tulip
If You Wished For Me (novella)
Never Dare A Duke
Capturing The Heart Of A Cameron

SILVER DUKES SERIES
Cherish and the Duke
Moonlight and the Duke
Two Nights With The Duke
Snowfall and the Duke
Starlight and the Duke
Crash Landing on the Duke

MOONSTONE LANDING SERIES
The Moonstone Duke

The Moonstone Marquess
The Moonstone Major
The Moonstone Governess
The Moonstone Hero
The Moonstone Pirate
Moonstone Landing (novella)
Moonstone Angel (novella)

BOOK OF LOVE SERIES
The Look of Love
The Touch of Love
The Taste of Love
The Song of Love
The Scent of Love
The Kiss of Love
The Chance of Love
The Gift of Love
The Heart of Love
The Promise of Love
The Wonder of Love
The Journey of Love
The Treasure of Love
The Dance of Love
The Miracle of Love
The Hope of Love (novella)
The Dream of Love (novella)
The Remembrance of Love (novella)
All I Want For Christmas (novella)

DARK GARDENS SERIES
Garden of Shadows
Garden of Light
Garden of Dragons

Garden of Destiny

Garden of Angels

THE BRAYDENS

A Match Made In Duty

Earl of Westcliff

Fortune's Dragon

Earl of Kinross

Pearls of Fire

Aislin

Genalynn

A Rescued Heart

THE LYON'S DEN SERIES

The Lyon's Surprise

Kiss of the Lyon

Lyon in the Rough

DeWOLFE PACK ANGELS SERIES

Nobody's Angel

Kiss An Angel

Bhrodi's Angel

MISCELLANEOUS CHARMING NOVELLAS

Earl of Alnwick

Tempting Taffy

A Duke For The Taking

Once Upon A Haunted Cave

ABOUT THE AUTHOR

Meara Platt is an award winning, USA TODAY bestselling author and an Amazon UK and USA All-Star. Her favorite place in all the world is England's Lake District, which may not come as a surprise since many of her stories are set in that idyllic landscape, including her epic fantasy romance (romantasy) Dark Gardens series. Learn more about the Dark Gardens and Meara's lighthearted and humorous Regency romances in her Farthingale series, Book of Love series, and Silver Dukes series, or her warmhearted Regency romances in her Moonstone Landing series or Braydens series by visiting her website at www.mearaplatt. com.